FEEDING THE *Soul*

SOULS OF CHICAGO #1

ANNABELLA MICHAELS

Feeding the Soul
Souls of Chicago Series #1

ISBN: 978-0-9989888-0-1

annabellamichaels.blogspot.com

Cover art provided by Jay Aheer of Simply Defined Art – www.jayscoversbydesign.com

Editing provided by Pam Ebeler of Undivided Editing – www.undividedediting.com

Proofreading provided by Judy Zweifel of Judy's Proofreading – www.judysproofreading.com

Interior Design and Formatting provided by Stacey Blake of Champagne Formats – www.champagneformats.com

Copyright and Trademark Acknowledgments

The author acknowledges the copyright and trademarked status and trademark owners of the following trademarks and copyrights mentioned in this work of fiction:

University of Chicago
Ford Ranger: Ford Motor Company
Ford Shelby Mustang: Ford Motor Company
Jeep: FCA US, LLC
PFLAG Inc.
Chicago PD
Fifty Shades of Grey; E.L. James
Michelin Man – Michelin North America Inc.
Chris Young "Who I am With You": RCA Nashville
"Going to The Chapel" – The Dixie Cups
Richard Marx "Now and Forever": Capitol Records

OTHER BOOKS BY ANNABELLA MICHAELS

DEDICATION

To my husband and children,
Thank you for your unwavering love, support and belief in me.
With you in my corner I am invincible. My life would mean nothing
without the three of you.

PROLOGUE

3 years ago

Giovanni

I LOOKED OUT THE WINDSHIELD AT THE HEAVY GRAY CLOUDS. Any minute the sky was going to open up and the city would be awash with torrential rain. The weatherman had been calling for rain all day and I just prayed it would hold out for a few more minutes to give me enough time to get home. I looked at the line of traffic in front of me and knew it wasn't likely though.

I had been held up at work by Fred, one of the senior partners at Jacobs, Patterson, and Lowe, the law office where I worked. I sighed wearily when I thought of how miserable I was in my job. The partners were pompous, pretentious, money hungry sharks who only cared about the almighty dollar and not about justice or integrity. Fred had stopped me on my way out the door and told me I would need to work through the weekend *again*. I would be expected to wine and dine a potential client who was a woman well known for using men to get to their money. She was considering our law office to help finalize her divorce from husband number six, and although I was only a paralegal, I knew that the partners often wanted me to wine and dine clients "due to my good looks," their words, not mine. You would think, as lawyers, they would be a little more cautious about opening themselves up to a potential sexual harassment lawsuit, but like I said, they were pompous. I dreaded telling my wife, Juliana, that I had to work all weekend again. With each of us working full time, we barely saw each other as it was. I smiled tenderly when I thought of my beautiful, sassy wife. We had met our very first week at the University of Chicago when she sat next to me in psych 101. Juliana was there for interior design and I was getting my business degree in order to pursue my dream of one day opening my own restaurant. One look at her long blonde hair and her big, brown, doe eyes and I was a goner. It was love at first sight for both of us and we very quickly became inseparable. We found that we had many things in common and the sex between us was amazing. I dated Juliana exclusively all through college and we were married shortly after graduation. We had been happily married now for four amazing years and rarely argued.

While I had dreamed of opening my own restaurant, Juliana had begged me to get a law degree. I knew she longed for the money and prestige that would come with being married to a lawyer and after the desolate childhood she had experienced she believed that having these things would finally make her feel secure. Some people might consider her high maintenance because she always dressed like she was a member of the Kardashian family and always wanted bigger and better things in life. However, those people didn't know what a difficult home life she had grown up in. After confiding in me about how bad things had actually been for her as a little girl, I had made it my mission in life to provide her with all the things she never had before.

I wanted to start a family with her and often dreamed of seeing

Juliana pregnant with my child, but she was insistent that she didn't want any children until she was sure that we could provide a better upbringing for them than what she had with her parents. So, I began working for Jacobs, Patterson, and Lowe as an assistant paralegal and was getting ready to start law school that fall. How I was supposed to uphold the heavy workload a law degree would require, while working day and night at the law office and find quality time with Juliana I didn't know, but I would do absolutely anything for her so I continued to push myself. I just had to keep reminding myself that in a few years, I'd be done with school and would have a job at the law office, perhaps as a partner, and could devote more time to Juliana and hopefully start the family we had always talked about.

Family was everything to me. I had been raised by two loving and devoted, Italian immigrant parents. They had wanted a big Italian family, but after having me, my mother needed an emergency hysterectomy so more children weren't possible. They poured every bit of their love into me, doting on me and spoiling me terribly. I adored them and was reminded of their unconditional love as they simply held me close and told me they loved me when I admitted at age 13 that I liked girls *and* boys. At the time, I hadn't really understood what it meant to be bisexual, I just knew that while most of my friends and I talked about Madison Chesterfield's tits, they probably didn't go home and also jerk off to thoughts of how Jamie Turner looked in his football uniform. After my self-discovery, my parents quickly joined PFLAG and got me in touch with other LGBTQ teens in our area, helping me realize I wasn't alone.

I pulled into our driveway and was turning off the ignition of my ancient Ford Ranger, when the sky opened up. The sound of rain pounding on the roof of the truck cab was deafening. *So much for staying dry.* I quickly grabbed my briefcase and the flowers I had bought for Juliana and dashed towards the house, holding the briefcase over my head to try to stay as dry as possible.

I quickly ran inside, careful to remove my shoes so that I didn't get any dirt on the wall to wall white carpet Juliana had insisted on when we remodeled the house. I had warned her that it wouldn't stay white for long if we were to get pets or have children, but she had seen white carpet displayed in a magazine article about some A-list celebrity so she had to have it.

I shook the rain off of myself and removed my suit as I wandered down the hall to change into something comfortable before starting dinner. I always got home before Juliana and loved cooking, so I made our dinner nearly every night. As talented as Juliana was at interior design, it was a long standing joke between us that she had no talent in the kitchen. My sweet bride could barely butter toast.

I changed into sweatpants and a worn t-shirt with the University of Chicago emblem on it and made my way back down the hall and into the kitchen. As I sifted through the mail on the counter I glanced at the clock, noticing that it was well past time for Juliana to be home. Picking up my phone to call her, I went to the fridge to get out the ingredients for lasagna. I laid the hamburger on the counter as I heard it go to her voicemail. I hit redial but it went to voicemail again. Figuring she was delayed by the rain, I began browning the meat and heating the water to cook the noodles. Soon, I had the lasagna assembled and placed it in the oven to bake.

I picked my phone up and quickly hit redial, getting her voicemail once again. Juliana was now a full hour late. The uneasiness that chilled my body was not uncommon after the horrific way I had lost my parents in the car accident that claimed their lives. I swallowed hard and reminded myself that the chances were very slim that I would lose my wife in the same way. Taking a deep breath, I decided to call Juliana's best friend, Miles, to see if he knew where she was. They worked for the same design company so he would probably know when she had left work. I began pacing the floor as the phone rang. After four rings it too went to voicemail. Panic swept through me and I couldn't stay there any longer. I quickly turned off the oven and grabbed my keys to go look for my wife as images of her lying hurt in a ditch somewhere nearly brought me to my knees. I stopped in the hallway long enough to pull my shoes on and dug an umbrella out of the closet when suddenly there was a knock at the door. Hoping Juliana had forgotten her house key and was home safely at last, I hurried to unlock the door and swung it open.

"There you are! I was so…" I trailed off as I looked, confusedly, at the young man who stood, shivering on my front porch as rain water dripped down his hair and into his face.

"Excuse me, I'm looking for a Mr.…Giovanni Romero?" he said as he looked at his clipboard.

"That's me." I rattled my keys in my hand and stepped forward onto the porch so I could lock the door behind me. "I'm sorry, but I'm really in a hurry, so if you don't mind…" I said, trying to rush the man away.

"Oh sure, sorry, I just need your signature really quick and I'll be on my way," the young man said as a chill shook his body. I glanced up as lightening lit up the entire sky, followed by a loud rumble of thunder. If possible it was raining harder than when I first got home from work. Wanting to start looking for Juliana, I quickly signed on the required line and grabbed the envelope out of the man's hands. "Thank you, you've been served," the man said over his shoulder as he hurried down the sidewalk and jumped into his car.

It took a moment for the words to sink in, but then I shook my head. "Served?" I looked down at the envelope that had the name of a law office on it. Hurriedly, I ripped it open and scanned the pages. As the blood drained from my face, I sank to my knees, completely unaware of the icy rain that soaked through my clothes. My heart hammered in my chest and my breathing became labored. None of this made sense, there had to be a mistake. There was no way Juliana, *my* Juliana, was filing for divorce.

CHAPTER
One

Caleb

"Yes, Mom, I'll call you as soon as the interview is done," I promised for the third time.

"Oh, Caleb, I'm sorry. I don't mean to pester you; I'm just so excited you're finally back home. You know how much I want all my babies to be near me and with this job you'll be able to stay close."

"I know, Mom." I smiled when I thought of my close-knit family. My older sisters, Emma, a child psychologist, and Michelle, a preschool teacher, were each married to wonderful men and lived about ten minutes away from our parents. My older brother Landon managed up and coming musicians - including my twin brother, Carter - but lived only twenty minutes away. Carter had been living with our parents, saving money while working gigs at various clubs around the city and praying for his big break. I had no doubt he would get it someday, because he was a musical genius. Apparently, being an identical twin doesn't mean you'll share the same talents, however, because I couldn't even play the spoons if you held a gun to my head.

I was the only one who had ventured off from the nest, traveling all around Europe as an apprentice to some of the world's most famous chefs. Now after nearly four years, I was finally back home and hoping to be hired on as the head chef at Chicago's most prestigious restaurant, Romero's. Despite having been open only two years, the restaurant had a stellar reputation and often had reservations booked six months in advance. Most importantly, working there would allow me to live close to my family again. I had missed them terribly.

"With all of my babies living close, maybe they'll finally give me some grandbabies!" Mom said excitedly.

"Mom, we've talked about this; Landon, Carter, and I are still single. If you want grandbabies soon, you need to bug Emma and Michelle." I chuckled knowing she would most likely call my sisters as soon as we hung up.

"I know, but now it's legal for you each to get married so I don't understand the hold up." She sighed in exasperation. Instead of bothering me, it made me smile. Our parents had always been supportive of us. I'm sure it was a shock to have not only one gay son, but three. However, our parents never treated us any differently and wanted all the same things for our lives that they wanted for our sisters.

"Okay, Mom, let me try to get this job first, then we'll talk about the rest of my life."

"I'm holding you to that, young man!" She said with a giggle.

"I'm here, wish me luck."

"Good luck, baby, although you don't need it. You're a brilliant chef and any restaurant would be foolish not to hire you. Call me as soon as you're done. I want to hear all about it." My mom may have been more than a little biased when it came to her children, but it still made me feel special that she believed in me so much.

Sticking my phone in my suit pocket, I checked my reflection in the restaurant's front window. I was pleased with how the gray suit I had purchased in Paris fit my slim 5'7" frame. The green specks in my tie brought out the emerald green of my eyes. I quickly smoothed my hair down as the wind, the city was known for, blew a strand right back over my eyes. Taking a deep breath to settle the butterflies taking flight in my stomach, I opened the door.

Romero's, while empty at this time of day, was very warm and inviting, instantly making me feel at home. The tables were set up to allow intimate conversations and the large stone fireplace in the center of the room brought a touch of familiarity and comfort to the place. The walls were a deep red color and were adorned with pictures of small European villages, a few of which looked familiar. Seeing no one else around, I wandered slowly towards the back of the restaurant. Along the entire length of the back wall was the most beautiful mahogany bar I had ever seen. Its intricate design was expertly hand crafted and brought more warmth and elegance to the room. It was obvious that someone had put a lot of thought into the design of the restaurant and I could see why it had become so popular. Seated at the far end of the bar was a woman with long auburn hair, her head bent over the paperwork spread out before her.

"Excuse me," I said, clearing my throat nervously. "I'm looking for Ms. Summers. I have an interview scheduled with her. My name is Caleb Greene."

The beautiful woman stood up, smiling as she extended her hand towards me. "That's me! It's a pleasure to meet you. Please, call me Lauren." We shook hands and at her gesture I sat in the stool next to hers.

"Your restaurant is stunning, Lauren! It's very warm and inviting." I couldn't help but gush.

"Thank you, but it's not my restaurant. I'm the owner's assistant and the hostess here. I don't normally do the hiring, but G is away for a few days looking into new suppliers. He was quite impressed with your résumé though, as am I." Her face stretched into a cheerful smile, instantly putting me at ease.

"G?" I asked questioningly.

"Oh sorry, Giovanni Romero is the owner. You'll find that while we strive for perfection with our guests, we're very relaxed with each other. We're more like one big happy family than coworkers. G is the best boss you could ever ask for. He expects nothing but the best from us, but is fair and never asks anyone to do anything that he wouldn't do himself. He's usually either up front welcoming guests or in the kitchen working the line with the other chefs. I don't know when he finds time to get all of his office work done. The man's a workaholic, but he was made for this business," she said with a fond look in her eyes and I wondered if there was more to their relationship than just friendship.

"It sounds perfect. I hope I get a chance to be a part of that." I had worked with some brilliant, but terrifying, chefs in Europe and would love to work somewhere that was more like family than Hell's Kitchen.

"So," Lauren said draping her arm casually across the back of her stool and crossing her long legs. The woman was really quite stunning. "Tell me about yourself, Caleb." We talked for nearly a half hour about my travels throughout Europe. Lauren had been there several times and knew a few of the restaurants I had apprenticed at.

Afterward, I was shown to the kitchen where I made her my signature Zeppole, a delicious fried cookie made with ricotta cheese, which made her brown eyes roll back in her head. Finally, with a sly grin, she said, "You know this was all just a formality right? We were already blown away by your qualifications and just needed to make sure you would fit in with our little 'family' here. G already gave me the go ahead to hire you if it felt right to me. I'd like to formally extend an invitation for you to be a part of our family at Romero's," she said while bouncing on her toes.

Excitement swept through me as a broad grin stretched my face.

"I accept!" I exclaimed as she pulled me in for an exuberant hug.

"Might as well get used to it," she said as she stepped back still smiling. "You'll find that we're a touchy-feely bunch around here."

"I'm used to it, my mom hugs everyone like she's a bear mauling them." We both laughed and I felt the tension in my shoulders relax for the first time that morning. I couldn't believe my dreams were finally coming true.

We spent the next hour filling out paperwork and finalizing my very generous contract, as well as working out my schedule. I would be starting the next Monday. I found that Lauren was quite funny, and by the time I walked out the front door, my face hurt from smiling so much. I quickly called Mom who whooped and hollered her excitement through the phone, then dialed my twin and best friend, Carter.

"Hey, little brother! What's new?" Carter said, referring to the four-minute time difference between his birth and mine.

"Not much," I said, struggling to keep my voice casual. "Just wanted to let you know I got the job." I held the phone away from my ear as he screamed through the phone and I laughed out loud. Besides my mom, no one had missed me more than Carter. We had always been inseparable and my absence had been difficult for us both. He knew with this job I was home to stay.

"Congratulations! We need to celebrate, meet me at home by 7:00. This calls for dancing!" he said with another screech.

I hung up the phone, smiling broadly as I looked up at the bustling city. Suddenly the world seemed full of possibilities.

I let myself into my childhood home, taking in the familiar surroundings. The lovingly worn living room furniture, the coffee table where Carter made me crack my head open when he lunged towards me with our psycho cat; its claws open and ready. I absentmindedly rubbed the line in the back of my head where seven staples had held me together. As a result, hair no longer grew there. It was the only way my identical twin and I could be told apart. I smiled as I thought of the many pranks we had played on unsuspecting teachers and friends growing up. Of course we couldn't get away with it where our parents were concerned. Mom always said she could tell each of her babies apart, even if she was blindfolded.

"Mom?" I called out, walking into the kitchen where I smelled fresh baked cookies. On the counter I found the source of the smell. Mom's famous oatmeal chocolate chip cookies. I grabbed one and took a big bite as I went to the cabinet to get a glass for milk.

"They left about thirty minutes ago. Mom's had me replacing the flooring in the upstairs bathroom. She and Dad had to run to the home improvement store for more tiles," Carter said as he sauntered into the kitchen. "Yesss! Cookies!" He exclaimed as he grabbed five.

I eyed him as I drank the cold milk. "You better take it easy with those cookies, you're going to get fat," I teased as I glanced at him.

"Jealous?" he smirked as he ran his hand down his flat stomach.

"Maybe, if we didn't look exactly alike." We had the same lithe frame with tousled light brown hair and our mother's emerald green eyes. We both had suffered the awkward "braces" phase, but had picture perfect, white smiles now to show for it.

Carter turned his bright smile on me. "So, you got the job, huh?" Before I could answer, he grabbed me into a tight hug. "I'm so happy for you, Bubby. I don't want you to go away again." His voice shook a little with emotion as he held me and I realized just how much he had been worrying about me having to leave again to find work.

I squeezed him gently, my heart warming as I heard him use the term of endearment we had always called each other when we were little. "Me too, I'm ready to stay home. I missed all of you so much, especially you."

"Okay." He backed away from me, clearing his throat. "Enough of this sappy stuff. I need to get a shower and get ready for tonight. You've been away from American men for too long, my dear brother. Tonight, you're getting laid USA style." He grinned mischievously, wriggling his eyebrows at me as he turned and headed up the stairs to his room.

CHAPTER
Two

Giovanni

I LOOKED OUT THE WINDOW OF THE TAXI AS THE DRIVER WEAVED in and out of traffic like a stock car driver. God, I hated riding in taxis, but there was no way I was going to leave my baby in the airport parking lot for the past week. My sleek 2016 Ford Shelby Mustang had been an extravagant expense, but what else was I supposed to spend my money on? All the things I had once scrimped and saved for, like a wife and children, were no longer possibilities in my mind. Sure, it would be nice to have someone waiting for me when I came home from a long trip, children to throw their arms around my legs as I walked through the door, but that wasn't in the cards for me anymore. Juliana had killed that hope in me when she took off. Three years and I still had no idea what I had done wrong. I never even saw her during the divorce process, as she sent her lawyer in her place to inform me that I could have everything, she just wanted out. No, it was better to not get too close to anyone ever again.

Shaking off my melancholy, I handed the driver his fare as he pulled up in front of my building. I quickly grabbed my luggage out of the trunk and headed towards the front door.

"Hey, Mr. G! It's nice to have you back," the doorman said, opening the door for me with a broad grin.

I smiled quickly at him. "Hi, Avery! It's very good to be back. How's your family?"

"Oh, they're just fine. Sammy's team won their little league championship and got to have a pizza party. Jenny lost her first tooth and was thrilled when the Tooth Fairy left her a dollar." I paused a moment, taking in the look of complete adoration in his eyes. Would I have been that kind of father, excited about each and every new development in my children's lives? I would like to think so, after all that's exactly how my father had been.

"That's fantastic, Avery. It sounds like they're both very happy. Please tell Elaina I said hello and I want to see pictures of that missing tooth of Jenny's." I turned and smiled as I got on the elevator.

"You've got it, Mr. G." Avery nodded his head. "You have yourself a good night. It sure is good to have you back."

As the elevator door shut I slumped against the back wall, the smile sliding off my face. Why was I feeling so sad tonight? Usually I kept those old dreams where they belonged: dead and buried. I no longer wanted those same things, I reminded myself. Unable to live in our house after Juliana left, I had sold it and used the money to open my own restaurant. I now had the career of my dreams, a staff that were like a family to me, and the freedom to go out any night of the week and fuck as many men as I chose. While I still found women attractive, I had always leaned more towards males and since the divorce, had chosen to only be with men. I had sworn off relationships completely after my disastrous marriage to Juliana, vowing that

I would never set myself up for that kind of heart wrenching pain again.

Figuring I was feeling out of sorts because I had been away from home for a whole week, I decided that what I needed tonight was a hard, no-strings attached fuck; with a firm, male body beneath mine to get my head back on track.

Happy with my decision, I quickly entered my condo and threw my bags down haphazardly, before I headed into my bedroom. I quickly took a shower, rinsed the travel grime off of me and let the hot water wash away the last of my bad mood. After I toweled off and brushed my teeth, I went to my closet and pulled out a new pair of jeans and a simple black button down shirt. Satisfied with my reflection, I headed back out to my door and scooped my car keys up off the table. I checked one last time to make sure I had condoms and lube in my wallet, then locked the door behind me.

A feeling of pleasure raced through me as I got behind the wheel of my Mustang. "Hi there, girl, have you missed me?" I laughed as I heard Roxie's engine purr in response. "Me too, sweetheart, me too." I lovingly patted her dash, knowing I probably looked crazy if anyone saw me talking to my car, but I didn't care. Roxie was special and she deserved to be treated accordingly. I pulled out of the parking garage and turned towards one of my favorite clubs. I loved living in Chicago. I loved the atmosphere and all of the art and entertainment the city had to offer.

I pulled up in front of the club and left Roxie in the hands of the valet, tipping him generously to ensure her good treatment. I smiled at the bouncer, Gary, who quickly stood to envelop me in a bear hug. "How's it going, G? I haven't seen you in a while. Thought maybe you forgot about us," he said with longing in his eyes. Gary had never made it a secret that he was interested in me. He was a very good looking man with short, cropped hair, bright blue eyes, and visible tattoos all over his muscular arms. We had enjoyed a drink together on several occasions when he would take his break from working the front door and although he seemed like a genuinely kind man and we had a lot in common, I just didn't feel any spark. "I've been out of town for a while. It's good to be back home though," I said with a grin.

"Maybe we could have a drink later, or you could wait for me. I get off work at two," he said suggestively.

"I don't know; you guys look pretty busy tonight." I tilted my head in the direction of the line wrapping its way around the building, each person hoping to make it into the club, but only maybe half would actually succeed.

He glanced forlornly at the crowd of people. "Yeah. You're probably right, maybe next time?" he asked with hope shining in his eyes once again.

I liked Gary as a friend and didn't want to hurt his feelings, so I breathed out a thankful sigh as I was saved from having to respond when a guy who had obviously had too much to drink started shouting that he had waited in the line long enough and it was time he was let in. Rolling his eyes at me, Gary waved me into the club and turned to take care of the obnoxious patron.

I walked into the club feeling at ease with the familiar surroundings. The upscale club had a large bar across the back wall with several bartenders putting on a show as they tossed the bottles in the air and poured complicated looking cocktails, all while flirting with the customers who were quickly filling up the large tip jars. There was a spiral staircase in the corner that led to VIP rooms and a metal walkway that overlooked the large dance floor below. Loud music pulsed through me as I took in the writhing bodies on the dance floor. Some couples were grinding so seductively against each other that the only thing preventing them from actual penetration was the half clothing on their sweaty bodies. The combined smell of sweat, arousal, and possibilities made my head spin.

I breathed deeply then turned to head to the bar for a drink. I needed something to ease my lingering tension while I looked for someone who might interest me. I wasn't a manwhore by any stretch of the imagination, and often left the clubs alone when no one caught my attention. Hopefully, that night I would find someone that would ignite a spark in me.

As I sat at the bar drinking an ice cold beer, I glanced casually around the room. I felt my hopes rise as I took in the wide variety of men to choose from. Even though I was bisexual, there was something about a hard body rubbing against mine that really got me going. The way I could grip fiercely onto a man when fucking him was very freeing.

I turned in my seat to order another drink when I accidentally bumped into the person who had just sat down next to me, spilling some of his cocktail onto the bar and splashing it onto his shirt sleeve.

"Oh, I'm so sorry!" I said briskly grabbing some napkins to help clean up the mess. I dabbed at his sleeve, as I continued with my apology. "I'd be happy to buy you another drink and pay for your dry cleaning, if that helps." I quickly glanced up for the first time and I swallowed hard as I met his gaze.

He was easily the most beautiful man I had ever seen in my entire life. He was shorter than me by several inches, with light brown hair that had that sexy "just fucked" look to it, and the most amazing emerald green eyes that held me captivated. He smiled shyly at me and I noticed that he had adorable dimples. I found myself leaning forward in my seat as I was filled with the overwhelming urge to kiss those dimples.

He reached for my hand to remove the napkin that I was still using to rub his sleeve with, and the jolt of electricity I felt as his skin made contact with mine brought me out of my daze. *What the hell was that?*

"It's no problem, I'll just get some club soda to take care of the stain." I felt my cock stir in my pants at the sound of his silky, smooth voice.

"Let me get that for you, as well as another drink. It's the least I can do since this was my fault."

He smiled at me again as he nodded his head; I felt lightheaded.

As the bartender got his drink, I turned towards him again. "I know I've just made a total mess of things, literally, but would you care to dance?"

"I would love to." He smiled happily and I caught a glimpse of those kissable dimples again. I quickly got out of my seat, took his hand and felt the pleasant surge of electricity running between us once again, as I led him to the dance floor. I turned towards him, pulled him closer, and placed my hands at the small of his back. He was small, but not dainty. His body was lithe, like a runner's, and he smelled clean and delicious: like sunshine and citrus. I held him close as we swayed to the slow music and enjoyed the feel of his body next to mine. This man pushed all of my sexual buttons.

The music changed to a typical club mix with a strong, sexy beat and I quickly spun him around so his back was to my front. I rubbed my jaw against his, enjoying how my stubble grazed his smooth cheek. I felt him shiver and he reached back, placing his hands on my hips. My cock began to harden as he ground his perfect little ass against it, in time with the music. He leaned his head back against my shoulder and I moved my left hand up his firm stomach, as the fingers of my other hand entwined with his on my hip.

As desire flooded my system, I leaned down so he would be able to hear me over the music and spoke directly into his ear. "Your body feels so good against mine. I want to take you home and fuck you hard into my mattress, all night long." I finished with a quick nip of his earlobe. He shivered hard before he turned in my arms to face me.

I held my breath, waiting to see if I had scared him off with my bold statement. I was usually a bit subtler, but something about that man was making it hard for me to think clearly. He stared deep into my eyes for several long beats, as if searching for something. Apparently, satisfied with whatever he found, slowly he nodded his head. I stared, mesmerized as he licked his full lips. My cock throbbed painfully in my jeans as I pictured those full lips wrapped around my erection; him kneeling before me. *Would his hair feel as silky as it looks when I held it tightly, while I push my cock deeply into his throat?*

Leaning up to place those lips against my ear, he whispered, "Let me just go tell my brother I'm leaving."

"I'll get the car and meet you out front." I said stepping back reluctantly, as if I was afraid he would disappear once I let go. I watched him turn and get swallowed up by the crowd of dancers, and then began to make my way towards the front door. My thoughts raced through my mind. "When was the last time I was this hard, this quickly?" I had come here hoping to find a spark with someone, but instead I seemed to have found a raging inferno.

CHAPTER
Three

Caleb

I**T TOOK ME SEVERAL MINUTES TO FIND** C**ARTER IN THE THRONG** of people, but eventually I spotted him in the back corner of the dance floor. He looked completely blissed out as he danced, sandwiched between two huge guys wearing leather pants and tight black T-shirts stretched across their enormous biceps. My brother had always been the more adventurous of the two of us when it came to sex and it looked like that night was going to be an adventure for sure. Spotting me out of the corner of his eye, he leaned up onto the tip of his toes to say something in one of the men's ears. He smiled at my brother, leaned down to answer him, and then gave him a long, sensual kiss while his partner ground his hips along Carter's backside. Finally, Carter staggered towards me.

He smiled like the Cheshire cat as he grabbed me in a fierce hug.

"Dayum, those two are hotter than hell! They've been dating for five years, but they like to mix things up once in a while by inviting someone new to join them. Looks like I'm the lucky addition."

"Yeah, you have fun with all that," I gestured to the couple who were in a heated lip lock of their own. "Just be safe okay?"

"Always," he said seriously. "So, how's your night going?"

"Great actually," I said a little shyly.

Carter looked at me closely. "No way! You met someone?" His excitement was obvious as he bounced on his toes.

"You don't have to sound so shocked," I huffed, rolling my eyes. "It's not like I'm a virgin you know."

"I know and I'm sorry. It's just that I never see you hook up with anyone. I was seriously considering getting you about six cats as a homecoming gift so you would at least have some company in that apartment of yours," he joked.

"Har har." I poked him in the ribs. I knew Carter often worried that I worked too hard and didn't make enough time to meet guys, so I didn't take offense at his comment.

"Seriously though," he said looking right into my eyes, "I'm happy for you. You deserve to have some fun for a change. Life's too short for you to spend it working all the time. So where is he? I want to make sure he's going to be good to you."

"He already went to get his car." I glanced down at my watch. "Crap, I've got to go!" I quickly gave Carter a hug. "I'll call you in the morning. Love you."

"I expect all the juicy details!" Wriggling his eyebrows, he began walking backwards over to the two men he had been dancing with. "Oh, and Caleb? Use this." He tossed me a foil wrapped condom which I caught in my hand.

Feeling my face heat, with what I'm sure was the darkest blush in history, I shoved it in my pocket as I glanced around to see if anyone had witnessed my embarrassment. Carter laughed loudly then turned into the embrace of his two companions for the evening.

I hurried out the front door of the club, enjoying the cool air on my overheated body. I glanced around nervously until I saw him approaching me from the valet station. Butterflies swarmed in my belly and my mouth actually watered as I took in his exquisite form. He was much taller than me, probably around 6'3" with broad shoulders and a trim waist. He had thick, jet black hair that I couldn't wait to run my hands through. I shivered at the thought as he came to stand in front of me.

"They're bringing Roxie around now." His piercing blue eyes traveled up and down my body seductively. I felt myself growing rigid at his perusal and I saw him smirk knowingly. I could only imagine what this man could do to my body if I was this turned on from just a look.

Finally, his words caught up with me. "Who's Roxie?" I asked breathlessly.

Suddenly, I heard the low growl of an engine and turned my head in time to see the valet pulling up in the sexiest midnight blue Shelby Mustang I had ever seen. I had always loved Mustangs and dreamed of having my own one day.

"That's Roxie," he said with a wide smile, his eyes sparkling with pleasure.

I felt my knees go weak. If I thought he was sexy before, it had nothing on how absolutely breathtaking he was when he smiled. Placing his hand on the small of my back, he led me towards the car and opened my door for me. *Gorgeous and a gentleman, I could seriously get used to this.*

I sank down in the plush leather seat of his car as nerves fluttered through me at the thought of what was about to happen. I had never moved so fast with someone I had just met before. I took a deep breath and smelled a heady mixture of new car and the rich, spicy cologne I had smelled on him as he held me close on the dance floor. Somehow his scent calmed my nerves. I didn't even know his name, and yet, I felt safe with him.

I watched as he tipped the valet then crossed the front of the car and slid in smoothly.

"Are you ready?" he asked, his eyes full of lust and his voice dipping even lower.

"Yeah." My voice squeaked embarrassingly. I cleared my throat and tried again. "Yes, I'm ready. Where are we going?"

He pulled into traffic carefully before responding. "My place, if that's all right with you," he said as he laid his hand on my thigh, his fingers grazing the edge of my cock. I felt myself grow thicker in my pants and shifted just enough to relieve some of the pressure.

My voice sounded husky to my ears as I answered. "That sounds good to me." I glanced over at him and saw that he looked a bit tense, the knuckles on the steering wheel turning white as he gripped it. It made me smile to think that perhaps I was affecting him too.

"I don't normally do this, just so you know," I babbled nervously. "Go home with men I just met, I mean. Do you do this a lot? Oh God, why did I ask that? That was rude wasn't it? I didn't mean…"

"Breathe!" he chuckled as he glanced at me out of the corner of his eye. "There's no reason to be nervous. If you've changed your mind, I'll take you back to the club right away," he assured me. It crossed my mind that this was a good sign because I doubted most serial killers would give you the option to leave once they had you in their car. Oh God, why hadn't I considered the fact that he could be a serial killer *before* I got in the car with him? Maybe Carter should have given me some pepper spray instead of a condom. I was being ridiculous.

"No!" I said a little too loudly. "I haven't changed my mind. I'm just a little out of my element right now, but I'll be fine. Maybe I would feel a little better if I knew your name," I said as I took a calming breath.

"Sorry, I don't do names," he answered abruptly.

"Excuse me?" I asked, turning towards him to see if he was joking.

"I'm not trying to be rude," he explained. "But I don't exchange names or numbers. I want to be clear with you, tonight is a one-time thing. I'm not looking for anything more than one night of pleasure, but trust me, I will pleasure you, over and over again." His large hand cupped my erection.

I paused. I didn't do one night stands, like ever. I had only been with one other guy and he was my long-time high school boyfriend. While in Europe, I had been so focused on my apprenticeship and soaking up every bit of knowledge I could from the chefs I worked under, that I didn't have time for anything else. Being around this man however, was scrambling my brain, making it very hard to think straight. My eyes rolled back in my head as he applied perfect pressure, right where I needed it. I knew if I didn't see this through, I would regret it for the rest of my life. "Okay, I can handle that," I said with a small smile, praying that I was telling the truth.

I heard him breathe out what sounded like a sigh of relief. "Thank fuck," he said under his breath as he pulled into the parking garage of a sleek modern condo.

"Wow! You live here?" I asked, the awe clear in my voice.

"Yes, I've been here a few years now. It's nice to be so close to… everything." He stated as he turned off the car. The silence of the engine was deafening at first and I missed the vibration under my seat. He turned to me, the dim lighting in the garage making the car seem almost romantic. "I need to taste you." He placed his hand around the back of my neck and pulled me towards him, and my heart beat wildly as his lips touched mine. They were firm, warm, and absolutely perfect. He took control of the kiss and I felt myself melt into my seat as his tongue licked at the seam of my lips and I opened to him. Our tongues swirled around each other in a perfectly synchronized dance. I couldn't help but feel like we had done this all our lives. His kisses felt like coming home to me.

We stayed like that for several minutes until we had to separate, in order to catch our breath. His pupils were blown and he looked at me with a mixture of surprise and confusion, but he quickly opened his door and got out of the car. I discreetly adjusted my aching cock which was pressing painfully against my zipper as he came around to my side and opened my door for me, offering his hand.

"For someone who only does one night stands, you're very chivalrous," I said with a gentle smile.

"My mother would be very disappointed if I weren't," he said with a smirk.

"She sounds like she raised you well." I took his hand as I climbed out of the car.

"Yes, she did," he said and I caught a glimpse of what looked like sadness in his eyes. In a flash the look was gone. "Are you ready?" Mr. Sexy, as I had begun referring to him in my mind, smiled at me. Without waiting for a reply he led me towards a set of elevators, still holding my hand.

We got on the elevator and he started to back me up against the wall, but an older lady with a little, fluffy dog slipped in right before the doors closed. He backed away slowly and leaned against the wall opposite from me, staring directly into my eyes. His eyes, previously a bright, piercing blue were now darker, almost navy as they filled with unmistakable lust. He stared at me with intensity and I could tell he was mapping out everything he wanted to do to me, once he had me to himself again. It sent shivers down my spine and caused my dick to harden to an unbelievable level. He smirked as he glanced down at my cock, knowing how he was affecting me.

I discreetly placed my hands in front of my cock as the grandmotherly woman turned to us and smiled. "It's really blowing hard, isn't it?" she asked.

My eyes bugged out of my head and I'm sure my face was bright red as my voice squeaked. "Excuse me?"

I glanced at Mr. Sexy as he covered his mouth with the back of his fist and tried to cover his laughter with a coughing fit.

"The wind," she stated looking at us like we were crazy. "I guess they don't call it the windy city for nothing."

Letting out an unmanly giggle, I stuttered, "Yes, yes, the wind!"

She glanced back and forth between us in confusion then quickly exited the elevator as it stopped at her floor, cooing quietly to her dog about how strange some people were.

My head slumped forward in embarrassment until I felt his hand under my chin, lifting my head to look me in the eyes. "You are fucking adorable," he whispered as his lips met mine. Again, I got the feeling that I had finally come home when we kissed. He placed both of his hands on my hips as he pulled me forward against his body. I breathed in the spicy smell of his cologne and the smell that was all male, all him; his scent already becoming familiar to me.

Our kiss became heated, almost desperate as he pushed his rigid cock against my stomach. Our height difference was a huge turn on for me and I found myself wanting to climb him like a tree. Just as that thought entered my mind, the elevator stopped once again and he pulled me out by the hand and led me to his door.

CHAPTER
Four

Caleb

A S SOON AS WE ENTERED THE CONDO, MR. SEXY BACKED ME up against the door and began kissing me. His hands roamed over my back as his expert tongue swirled around mine. My knees became weak and I felt a wet spot forming, as pre-cum leaked onto my briefs. Suddenly he pulled back, making me moan at the loss of his mouth on mine. He placed both of his hands on the sides of my face as he knelt down to look directly into my eyes.

"Forget about fucking you into the mattress." I felt my heart drop into the pit of my stomach and my cock wanted to weep in frustration. "I can't wait long enough to get you into my bedroom," he said huskily as his hands moved down, gripping my ass and pulled me up the length of his body.

I knew I wasn't bulky by any stretch of the imagination, but he acted like I weighed nothing as he lifted me until I wrapped my legs around his waist. He turned, and carried me over to his couch as he nipped at my ear lobe and traced a path down the side of my neck with his tongue. My head lolled back to allow him better access. I could quickly become addicted to this incredible man and I had to remind myself that this was a one-night-only thing. I quickly brushed away the unexpected feeling of sadness that swept through me and decided that if I only had one night with my Mr. Sexy, I was going to enjoy every single moment of it.

He set me down on my feet at the end of an enormous sectional and began undressing me. His lips left mine only long enough to pull my shirt over my head, then they met again in a feverish kiss. His tongue traced a path down my exposed chest, stopping to lave my nipple. It pebbled as he nipped it with his teeth and I gave a low groan in the back of my throat. "Like that do you?"

I responded with something that sounded like "Ungnnn" as he dropped to his knees and began unbuttoning my pants. My mouth felt dry and I lost the ability to breathe, as I gazed down at this Adonis kneeling at my feet. *I must be the luckiest man on the planet to be here with him right now,* I thought to myself. All other thoughts short circuited in my head as he removed the rest of my clothing, then leaned forward into my trimmed hair and inhaled deeply. "Sunshine and oranges," it sounded like he said, but I couldn't be sure and I was too distracted to ask, as he licked the bead of pre-cum off the head of my engorged dick. "God, you taste good." Without any warning, he swallowed my cock until I felt the tip hit the back of his throat. I screamed out, instantly on the edge of control and grabbed his head, threading my fingers through his thick black mane. I felt lightening rip through my spine and settle in my balls as my orgasm grew.

Just as I was about to warn him of my impending release, he pulled off of my cock with a loud pop. I cried out in frustration at the loss, but he looked up at me with his dark, soulful eyes and whispered. "Don't worry, little one, I'll take care of you." My heart stuttered at his words.

Mr. Sexy stood up, towering over me and began taking his clothes off. I stared in awe, my mouth dropping open, completely lust-drunk as he revealed a model perfect chest. His pecs were well defined and were covered in black hair, not too thick but just the perfect amount to run my fingers through and tug on. I longed to rub my cheek against it, but my gaze continued to devour the man-buffet being revealed in front of me. My eyes traveled down over a set of abs that I previously had believed could only be airbrushed on in a magazine, then took in the V cut of his lower abs that tapered down into his jeans. He removed the rest of his clothing and my mouth watered at the sight of the happy trail that led to the most incredible, uncut cock I had ever seen, not that I had seen a lot of cocks in my limited experience. I stepped forward, wanting to feel the weight of it in my hands, but he grabbed my hips and turned me, and bent me over the arm of the couch.

"I can't wait any longer," he said gruffly as he placed a large hand between my shoulder blades, making my head tilt closer to the seat of the couch and causing my ass to lift up towards him. I held my breath as I felt his cock slide deliciously back and forth over my hole.

"So pretty," he breathed and I shivered in anticipation.

He tapped his cock against my quivering hole and I felt the sensation on that bundle of nerves rush through my entire body. I whimpered when he retreated, long enough to get a condom and packet of lube out of his pants pocket.

I glanced at him over my shoulder, eyeing his massive erection as it bobbed up and down with his movements. Something in my gaze must have alerted him and he immediately slowed down and began gently rubbing small circles on my back. "Are you all right? Have you changed your mind?"

"No, not at all it's just, umm..." I could feel my face heating up in embarrassment. I swallowed hard and answered quietly. "It's just been a while since I've been with anyone so..." I let my voice trail off.

He smiled gently at me as he leaned down kissing my spine then grabbed my hand and lifted me up. "Come with me." He began leading me down the hall and into his bedroom.

"I'm sorry if I ruined things," I whispered, looking at my feet.

"Hey," he said softly. He lifted my chin and placed a gentle kiss at the corner of my mouth. "You haven't ruined anything and I *will* be fucking you into my mattress." he said with a gleam in his eyes. "But we're going to take some time to get you ready for me first. I don't want to hurt you." I felt my heart melt at his words and I had to remind myself once again that this sexy, sweet, amazing man only wanted me for one night. I couldn't let my heart get involved.

I looked into his eyes and leaned up, pressing my lips to his. He turned us and began moving me backwards towards the bed, without stopping the kiss. When my knees hit the edge I sat down, scooting my body up towards the headboard. He placed the condom and lube on the nightstand then crawled up my body with an almost feline grace. I licked my lips as he began teasing my nipple with his tongue. My hand moved into his lush hair to hold him there, my body writhing on the bed. I moaned loudly as he sucked hard on the tight bud.

He moved down my body slowly, nipping gently at my feverish skin then dipped his tongue in my navel, swirling it around in circles. He glanced up at me questioningly when he saw the tattoo on my hipbone, but then moved lower and my body practically levitated when he licked the crease of my leg. *Who knew that was an erogenous zone for me?*

"So responsive," he purred, glancing up at me, his pupils blown wide.

He quickly grabbed the lube and squeezed some on his fingers, rubbing it until it was warm. I smiled at his consideration. "No one likes cold lube," he said with a wink.

The smile left my face and I gasped as he licked the head of my weeping cock, while simultaneously rubbing his finger along my hole. He leaned down sucking one of my balls into his warm, wet mouth as he gently pressed his finger inside my body. It had been too long since I had been with anyone and the burn made me bite my lip.

He began pumping his finger in and out of me slowly as he used his tongue to lick a line up the side of my shaft, gently grazing the head with his teeth.

"More, I need more." I moaned as I began riding his finger. He eased two fingers into my eager hole and I clenched automatically.

"Easy," he whispered, his voice sounding strained. "Let me make you feel good." I took a deep breath and willed myself to relax and just focus on the pleasure he was bringing to my body.

My eyes rolled back inside my head as he simultaneously swallowed my cock down to the root and crooked his fingers to rub against my prostate. Overwhelming pleasure shot through my body and I was soon riding his fingers wantonly.

Gently easing his fingers from my body, he quickly rose up to his knees and expertly sheathed his cock with the condom. Watching him slick his long, uncut cock made my mouth water and I longed to find out what he tasted like. I licked my lips and glanced up at his face and found him staring down at me hungrily.

"You're ready, and I seem to remember a promise to fuck you into this mattress," he said seductively. "Turn over and get on your hands and knees."

I desperately wanted to watch him as he fucked me, but I couldn't ignore the command in his voice. I had never been so turned on in my entire life. I turned around on the bed and quickly got on my hands and knees, exposing myself to him. I should have been shocked with what I was about to do; I hardly knew this man at all, but somehow I felt safe with him and knew that he would take care of me.

I felt the heat of his cock as he rubbed it against my crack, circling it around my eager hole. He was a large man and his dick was proportional to him. I closed my eyes and breathed deeply, forcing myself to relax as the head of his cock breached me. The burn was intense and I cried out.

"I'm going to go very slowly, but you need to breathe. Bear down against me, let me inside of you," he crooned. His words soothed me and I felt the head of his cock pop through the ring of muscles that had been holding him back. I gasped as his girth stretched me wider than I thought possible. He held still, allowing me to become accustomed to his size as he rubbed a soothing hand up and down my spine.

"You're doing perfect. You feel amazing around my cock: all warm, smooth, and so deliciously tight."

His words flipped a switch in me and the pain from before disappeared, leaving only pleasure behind. I began rocking slowly back and forth, grinding myself on his cock, feeling every ridge and vein and crying out in delight. He growled low in his throat and swiftly grabbed my hips with both hands as he began pounding into me.

I couldn't breathe as intense pleasure washed through me. I closed my eyes, seeing sparks behind the lids and I felt one of his hands reach forward, his fingers twisting in my hair, the other gripping my hip so hard that I was sure I'd have bruises in the morning, but I didn't care. I loved everything he was doing to me. He surged forward, his large cock going impossibly deeper and making me feel fuller than I had ever been.

He leaned forward, putting both of his hands under my arms and lifted me until I was upright on my knees, my back fitting perfectly against his magnificent chest. My skin tingled at the feel of his chest hair rubbing softly against my back. He reached for my chin, turning my face and captured my mouth in a passionate kiss, his tongue tangling with mine in an exquisite dance. He wrapped his arms around my chest as he once again took control and began expertly slamming his hips up into me.

"Oh God!" I cried out loudly as the head of his dick grazed against my prostate repeatedly. He flattened his tongue and licked the sweat from the side of my neck and reached down, taking my pulsing cock in his large hand.

"Come for me," he growled pumping my cock up and down in his tight grip. He bit down on my shoulder and a scream tore from my throat as my orgasm swept through me like a tsunami. Thick strands of cum flew out and landed on my chest in a never-ending stream. My body convulsed with the strength of my orgasm and he held me tightly against him, continuing to pump my shaft until I was completely spent.

My body slumped against his and my head rolled back onto his shoulder lazily as he continued sliding in and out of my hole. My over-sensitized body trembled as I felt his shaft glide over my anal walls and I clenched down on him involuntarily.

With a loud shout he bent forward, pushing me back down into the mattress as his orgasm overtook him. His body grew rigid over me as his muscles strained with the intensity of it. Gasping for air, he collapsed over top of me, his weight a welcome sensation against my quivering body.

"Fucking amazing!" I detected a bit of wonder in his voice. He rolled off of me and to the side, quickly ridding himself of the condom and tossed it into a waste can beside his bed, then turned me to face him. He looked at me with a mixture of bliss and concern. "Are you okay? Was I too rough with you?"

I couldn't stop the giggle that rippled up from my chest. I smiled widely at him as I answered. "That was incredible! I had no idea."

"What do you mean?" he asked in confusion. "You weren't a virgin were you?" His eyes widened in horror, making me laugh again.

"No, of course not," I assured him quickly. I looked down, twisting my fingers together in a nervous habit of mine. "I've had sex a few times before, but only with my high school boyfriend. We cared a lot about each other, but I guess you could describe our sex life as more of an educational experience. Neither one of us really knew what we were doing." I shrugged my shoulders. "Until tonight, I had only read about my prostate," I admitted shyly, my cheeks turning pink.

He looked at me with heat blazing in his eyes. "There's so much I could do to you." His deep voice brought my previously flaccid cock back to life. My breath caught as he rolled on top of me and devoured my mouth. Dear God, my Mr. Sexy could kiss. I literally felt my toes curl. I reached up, running my fingers through his hair as he slowed our kiss and whispered into my mouth. "How about a shower?" Before I could respond, I felt myself being lifted up into his strong arms and carried into the bathroom.

I woke to sunlight streaming through the window, bathing my face with its warmth. I turned my head and saw that I was alone in bed. I stretched with a loud yawn and felt the stiffness in my legs and a delicious soreness in my ass. A broad smile spread across my face as I remembered the spectacular night I had shared with Mr. Sexy. He had taken me again in the shower, then once more when we woke in the middle of the night. It was amazing how in tune he was to my body, making me soar over and over again. I never imagined that sex could be that good and I wondered idly if it was that good for everyone.

I heard noises coming from another room, so I quickly went into the bathroom to take care of business and swirled some mouthwash in my mouth. Feeling minty fresh, I wandered out of the bathroom to try to locate my clothes. Finding them folded neatly on a chair in the room, I got dressed and made my way out of the room to look for him. Turning the corner, I spotted him in the kitchen finishing up breakfast.

"There's juice in the fridge and coffee if you want any." He said without turning around and began dishing the food onto colorful plates.

"Thank you," I said as I headed to the fridge and poured myself a glass of ice cold orange juice. "Sorry I slept so long."

"That's okay." He smiled as he set a plate down in front of me.

"You were pretty worn out." I felt my face heat up at his words and heard him chuckle.

"Umm, yeah I was," I admitted shyly. I popped a piece of bacon in my mouth and groaned. "Oh, that's so good!" I looked across the table at him and my hand froze on the way back to my mouth as I caught him staring at my lips. I licked them slowly and watched as his eyes become glazed with lust.

He shook his head slightly, and his eyes cooled as he seemed to think something over in his mind. He finally spoke. "I figured I should at least feed you, before you go."

A cold chill swept through me as I heard the unmistakable dismissal in his words and I quickly laid my fork down. Clearing my throat, I pushed my chair back and stood. "I think I'm going to go ahead and leave," I said trying to keep the hurt out of my voice.

He stood and followed me to the door. Grabbing my hand before I could turn the handle, he spoke quietly, his words sounding sincere. "Look, I'm sorry, I'm not trying to be rude. I had a really great night with you, but I'm not relationship material; I'm just not looking for more than this."

Looking up into his eyes, I spoke gently. "I had a really great night too and I won't forget you. I don't think many guys would have been as patient as you when they found out how long it had been for me. For what it's worth, I think you're selling yourself short. I think you have a lot to offer someone." I leaned up on my toes and gently kissed his lips then slipped out the door.

As the elevator door closed I slumped against the wall, feeling like I had just lost something very important.

CHAPTER
Five

Giovanni

I SPENT THE REST OF MY DAY OFF DOING LAUNDRY AND OTHER mundane chores that needed to be done after having been away for a week. I was pleased with how things had turned out, the deal I had made with the new suppliers would allow us to use better ingredients in our recipes at a lower cost.

I went to bed early that night, exhausted. Climbing under the covers I pulled the extra pillow over to me and wrapped my arms around it. It had been three years since the divorce, yet I still found it difficult to sleep alone. Breathing in, I smelled the faint trace of oranges and *his* face appeared in my mind. His beautiful green eyes, his dimples that flashed at me when he smiled, his long lashes that brushed his cheeks delicately as he slept. I buried my nose in the pillow and breathed deeply. As his scent invaded my senses, I relived our night together.

I felt my cock plump up as visuals of last night ran through my head like scenes from a movie. I reached for my aching cock and began pumping my fist up and down as I remembered how his luscious lips felt against my own; the way his flawless skin tasted as I ran my tongue down his body, the silkiness of his hair as I gripped it in my hand, the erotic sounds he made as he came. My back arched off the bed and I came hard, long ropes of cum landing on my chest and one shooting all the way up to my chin. My body shook all over and my chest heaved as I tried to take in enough air.

I'd had a few one night stands over the last couple of years, but I had never thought about any of those men after they left my bed. Those were simply mutual stress relievers, just like last night was *supposed* to be. So why had I just masturbated to the memory of this guy? What was it about him that I couldn't get out of my head? Sure, he was sweet and sexy as fuck, but I had strict rules about this kind of stuff.

When I finally felt like my legs could support my weight, without causing me to face plant, I staggered into the bathroom to clean up. Looking at my reflection in the mirror I saw a sadness in my eyes that I hadn't noticed before. Shrugging it off, I turned out the light and crawled back into bed. Tossing the pillow that smelled like him across the room, I reminded myself that never again would I open my heart up to the kind of pain Juliana put me through. Relationships were not worth the risk. Besides, I sighed as I closed my eyes, I would probably never see him again.

I smiled as I pulled into my parking spot behind Romero's. Most days, I still found it hard to believe that I was able to fulfill my dream of opening my own restaurant. My mom had fostered my love of cooking at a young age, sharing beloved recipes that had been passed along through generation after generation of our family. My mom and I were always very close and some of her best advice to me had been offered over a simmering pot on the stove. My dad preferred cleanup duty and always followed behind us, wiping the counters and putting things back in the pantry. I often found him gazing adoringly at my mom as he washed the dishes and occasionally he would grab her and pull her into a dance, right there in the kitchen while she laughed at his antics. I missed my parents every single day, but cooking and seeing my customers enjoying the recipes my family had loved made me feel closer to them somehow. I only wished they were still alive to see it.

Opening a place of my own was all I had ever wanted to do with my life and I had fulfilled that dream by becoming the owner of one of Chicago's most popular Italian restaurants. Food critics wrote rave reviews about their dining experiences and we had many dedicated customers who returned for special occasions such as engagements, birthdays, and anniversaries. I whistled as I locked up Roxie and headed towards the back door of the restaurant.

The rich smell of garlic and tomatoes wafted towards me as I opened the door and the familiar sound of clanking dishes filled the air. I caught the tail end of a joke Marco, my assistant chef, was telling and everyone in the kitchen burst into laughter. At the sound of the door closing, Marco turned to me and rushed forward as he scooped me up into a giant bear hug.

Marco looked very intimidating despite his 65 years, towering over me at a whopping 6'7" and weighing roughly 290 pounds, most of which was pure muscle. In his younger days, he was well known for his street fighting skills until his dad signed him up with the Marines to help straighten him out. While serving in the military he met Maria, the love of his life and wife of 35 years. Together they had four wonderful children and were now anxiously awaiting the birth of their first grandchild. When his second child was born, he left the

Marines so he wouldn't miss out on being a father and pursued his second love: cooking.

Wanting an open, honest relationship with my staff, I had told each of them during their interviews that I was bisexual. If anyone had a problem with that, they should look for alternate employment. I still remember how nervous I was as I told this large ex-Marine and waited for his reaction, wondering if he would punch me. He simply looked at me and asked, "Okay, but did I get the job?" Marco was a unique individual who saw people for their actions instead of the color of their skin or who they loved.

After finding out about my parents' death, Marco and his wife had sort of adopted me as their own and were always trying to fix me up with the nice young men and women from their church. Marco may have looked intimidating, and I'm sure he could be if he was protecting someone he loved, but I knew he had a heart of gold and was never afraid to show affection to others. The staff all respected him and lovingly referred to him as our gentle giant.

"Man, have I missed you, Boss!" His deep baritone voice rang out over the kitchen. "It's been crazy here. You know I love to cook, but I'm not cut out for running my own kitchen," he said with a sigh. "I can't wait to get that new guy in here that Lauren hired."

"That's right, she sent me a text about that. When does he start?"

"Pretty sure it's tonight, or at least it better be or I'll be crying in my apron," he joked.

I laughed, turning to head down the hallway to my office and called over my shoulder. "Do me a favor please and send Lauren to my office when she gets here."

"You got it, Boss! Sure is good to have you back." I could hear him whistling as he started preparing the ingredients for that night's specials.

I sat down at my desk and began sifting through the pile of messages, organizing them in order of importance. After returning calls for an hour, I leaned back in my chair and sighed while taking in my surroundings. I had decorated the office myself, choosing a rich mahogany desk, two wingback chairs and a wide leather couch that took up nearly the entire length of the back wall. The walls were a pale blue color and I had hired a local artist to paint a mural of Manarola, the small town in Italy where my parents met and fell in love before moving to the United States.

Sitting on my desk, where I could see it each day, was a framed picture of my parents and me on vacation in Florida. I was three years old and my parents each held one of my hands and were swinging me up in the air to avoid a wave crashing over us. The absolute joy on their faces had only recently begun to make me smile again, instead of feeling my heart clench from the pain of my loss. My parents knew I had always wanted to open my own restaurant and were disappointed when I switched my focus to law to make Juliana happy. I hoped that I was making them proud with everything I had accomplished.

A knock at the door shook me out of my thoughts and I called out, "Come in!" A beautiful auburn head peeked in the doorway and I stood, coming around my desk with a smile.

"G!" Lauren squealed and she ran inside and gave me a fierce hug and a kiss on the lips. Leaning back, she flashed a perfect smile; her eyes dancing with happiness. "I'm so glad you're back. How did everything go?" Lauren was my assistant and one of my dearest friends. She had a keen business sense, and amazing people skills. She also had a wicked sense of humor and was stunningly beautiful. No one recognized this more than her long-time girlfriend, Gracie. Gracie was a little wisp of a woman with a pixie haircut and a gentle smile. You couldn't tell by looking at her, but she was one of the fiercest officers Chicago P.D had on its force. Lauren and Gracie had been together nearly eight years and planned on getting married someday. I just hoped their marriage ended better for them than it had for me.

We spent the next half hour discussing the deal I had struck and all the ways Romero's would benefit from it. When we were done talking business, she leaned back in her chair and plopped her feet up on my desk casually. "Okay, now tell me, how many men did you bang while you were gone? And don't leave out any details! You know how I love the details," she said waggling her perfectly arched brows at me. Even though she was only attracted to women, she still claimed that there was something about two men going at it that curled her toes in a good way.

My face flushed as an image of *him*, writhing on my bed, suddenly flashed through my mind. "There's nothing to tell, it was all business while I was gone." I knew I was bending the truth, but technically I hadn't met anyone until I came back home.

Lauren dropped her feet to the floor and leaned forward in her chair, looking at me closely through narrowed eyes. "What aren't you telling me?"

Wondering if Lauren gained her interrogation skills from Gracie, I figured it would be best to come clean, at least partially. "I met a guy and we had some fun." Seeing her eyes light up, I quickly continued, "But that's all it was and I won't be seeing him again." I raised my hand in a stop gesture. "Seriously, we didn't even exchange names."

Lauren huffed out a breath as she stood, but there was a gleam in her eyes. "I know there's more to this story and you *will* tell me everything, but I need to get out front and make sure everything is set up for dinner." I sighed in relief as she started to walk out. She turned back around, snapping her fingers. "Oh, I almost forgot, the new head chef I hired will be here in about half an hour. He makes a Zeppole that will make you want to cry and he seemed like a really sweet guy. I think he'll fit in perfectly around here. Oh, and he's cu-uuuttteee," she said in a singsong voice.

I laughed at her as I rolled my eyes. "You are so bad. You know there's no fraternizing at work."

"You've got to find love somewhere, G, and you're always here. What better place to start looking?" she asked saucily.

"I'm not looking for love, you know that. Now get to work!" She frowned at me as I shooed her towards the door. "Hey!" I stopped her suddenly. "What's his name anyway?"

"Caleb Greene." She answered with a smile.

I finished paying the bills online and shut down my computer. Standing, I stretched my back out, hearing creaks and cracks as I moved. Getting older really sucked, *not that thirty was old,* I reminded myself.

I quickly straightened up the papers on my desk before heading out of my office. I loved having my own business, but office work was my least favorite part of it. I preferred visiting with customers, getting to know the ones who came back repeatedly, and making sure everyone was enjoying their meals. Most of all, I loved helping out in the kitchen. With the delicious smells of the food cooking, Marco's jovial personality, and the hustle and bustle of everyone working together, I felt like I was back in my parents' kitchen.

I walked through the kitchen where Marco was expertly dicing vegetables and adding them to a simmering pot, the smells making my mouth water. He looked up at me and smiled as I passed through. *I'm not sure I'd ever seen Marco where he didn't have a smile on his face, I mused.*

I walked into the dining area and made my way to the hostess stand to look over the reservations for the evening. Romero's was only open at night, serving those looking for a romantic dinner or a quiet place to meet for drinks. It looked like we were going to be packed full again. *I hope the new chef works out,* I thought to myself. Carl, the previous chef, had really left us in a bind when he announced that he needed to move back to Maine immediately to take care of his elderly mother who had fallen and broken her hip. I was relieved that it hadn't taken very long to find a replacement and I trusted Lauren's judgment explicitly. If she liked the guy, then I was sure I would too.

Hearing Lauren's laughter ring out, I glanced up and saw her speaking to a man at the bar. Waving me over, she raised her voice. "G, come here. I want you to meet Caleb, our new head chef."

Just then, the man looked over his shoulder and my steps faltered, my jaw nearly hitting the ground. *Oh my God! It's HIM!* His eyes were wide and his face turned crimson as he stared up at me incredulously.

I recovered quickly, not wanting to let on that we knew each other already and extended my hand to him. "Hello, I'm Giovanni Romero, it's very nice to meet you."

"Umm, Caleb Green, it's a pleasure to meet you too," he stammered. He placed his hand in mine to shake it and a jolt of electricity travelled up my arm and made the hair on the back of my neck stand up. His green eyes met mine and I wondered if he had felt it too.

Lauren glanced back and forth between us, tilting her head to the side before looking at me questioningly. She was way too observant for my own good.

"Well, it was nice meeting you, I'm sure Lauren will help get you all set up. I have a lot to do in my office. You know, paperwork, phone calls, that kind of thing," I babbled. Lauren looked at me like she thought I'd lost my mind and right then, I'd have to agree with her. I had to get out of there.

I started back to my office when Lauren called out, "Aren't you going to have your usual talk with him since he's new?" she asked, referring to my standard admission about being bisexual.

"I don't think that will be necessary," I mumbled under my breath as I practically ran from the room. I needed to get to the privacy of my office so I could freak out properly, without an audience. Over the rushing sound of my pulse in my ears, one thought raced through my head, running on a loop: *His name is Caleb.* I squeezed my eyes shut, I was so screwed!

CHAPTER
Six

Caleb

I TRIED TO SCHOOL MY FEATURES SO I WOULDN'T GIVE ANYTHING away to Lauren, because it was obvious that Giovanni didn't want her to know that we had met already, but my heart was pounding out of my chest and my pulse raced from just the feel of his strong hand. Giovanni Romero; even his name was sexy. I was having trouble wrapping my head around the fact that the man that I had shared the single best sexual experience of my life with, my Mr. Sexy, was actually my new boss. Suddenly I realized that Lauren had been speaking to me. Shaking my head to clear my thoughts, I turned to look at her.

"I'm so sorry about that. I have no idea what's going on with G," she said, a small frown marring her beautiful face. "He's usually very outgoing, but he's been acting a little distracted since he returned from his trip. I'm sure he just has a lot on his mind and will take the time to get to know you better later."

You have no idea how well we already know each other, I thought to myself. The sudden memory of Giovanni's arms wrapped around my chest as he pounded into me from behind had my cock twitching in my pants. Needing to get myself under control, I quickly asked, "So, what's the usual talk Mr. Romero has with new employees?"

Lauren looked at the door Giovanni had disappeared through, then back to me. "I guess it would be okay for me to tell you, I mean it's not like it's a secret, everyone around here knows. It's just that Giovanni believes in being up front about who he is, that way if any-one has a problem with him, they can get over it or find another job," she said with the slight sound of a challenge in her voice.

"Up front about who he is?" My mind raced with possibilities. *Was he a hit man? A mob boss? Did he drive a white van and ask kids to help him find his lost puppy*? I shook my head; I was being ridiculous.

"G is bisexual." She stared directly into my eyes, looking for any signs of disgust or disapproval.

I smiled at her, letting out a quiet sigh of relief. "Seeing as I'm gay, I don't think that's going to be a problem."

Lauren visibly relaxed as she slid her arm into the crook of mine and smiled. "That's good to hear. Let's get you settled in the kitchen, I can't wait to taste more of your cooking. I'm still dreaming about the Zeppole you made for me, although you better not make it too often or I'll weigh as much as an elephant," she said with a laugh as we headed towards the back of the restaurant.

I was excited to become familiar with the kitchen and other staff members. I had always felt most at home when moving around a kitchen, creating food for people to enjoy.

"This is our kitchen. I don't think you had much time to look around in here before." Lauren gestured with her hand. She was right, when I was here for my interview I was so busy trying to impress her with my cooking that I hadn't taken the time to look over my new work environment. I breathed deeply as I took in my surroundings, my eyes growing wider by the minute. The room was stunning, with the most up to date devices and equipment. Absolutely anything a chef could ever dream of wanting could be found there. It was obvious that Giovanni really knew his way around a kitchen and had put a lot of thought into the design and layout to make sure it was both functional and efficient.

I felt like a kid in a candy store and my face hurt from smiling so wide. I clapped my hands together as I gushed. "This is without a doubt the most amazing kitchen I have ever seen."

Lauren laughed in delight and a big, burly man with a friendly smile walked towards us carrying a tray of vegetables. "Hi there!" His deep voice rumbled as he set the tray on the counter. He extended his hand towards me and shook mine. "I'm Marco and if God loves me at all, you're our new head chef."

Feeling very confused by his greeting, I looked to Lauren who laughed and explained. "Poor Marco has been covering all of the cooking by himself since Carl quit and Giovanni has been out of town. He's ready to have some help in here again." She rubbed Marco's back in a soothing gesture. I could tell Marco didn't mind carrying the responsibility though because his smile never faltered.

He winked at me. "I'm too old for all this. Might have to sneak in the back room and take a nap later," he said jokingly.

"You'll never be old." Lauren leaned up to kiss his cheek. "In fact, you'll probably outlive us all." She smiled fondly at him then excused herself to get to work.

"I'm Caleb by the way. It's a pleasure to meet you," I said genuinely. "So, what should I know before we get started?"

"What do you mean?" he said, looking confused. "You're the head chef so you tell *me* what to do."

"I've worked in enough restaurants to know that the best run kitchens are the ones where the staff respect each other's individual abilities and feed off of each other's strengths. They respect each other and listen to each other's opinions. I want to work *with* you, not bark orders at you. You've been here a long time and know all the ins and outs of this kitchen. So please, tell me your routine here so I can learn how I'll fit into it."

Marco looked me up and down as a slow smile spread across his face. "I think we're going to get along just fine," he said with satisfaction then proceeded to show me all around the massive kitchen.

Despite the fact that it was our first night working together, things were running surprisingly well. The popular restaurant was constantly busy, which left no room for error if we were going to get the food out to the customers in a timely manner. Fortunately, Marco was extremely adept in the kitchen and often seemed to read my mind, handing items to me before I even asked for them. He was very pleasant to work with and the time flew by as he regaled me with stories about his time in the Marines. I watched his eyes light up like a Christmas tree whenever he spoke of his wife, Maria. He obviously adored her and I found myself more than a little jealous of their relationship. I could only hope to one day find someone that would love me as much as Marco loved his wife.

It was several hours later before things slowed down. I stood at the stove, stirring a rich, creamy Alfredo sauce and laughing as Marco told me a story about the first time he was left alone to care for his newborn daughter and the disasters that ensued. When I glanced up I saw Giovanni leaning against the doorway watching me. My breath caught in my throat and I stopped stirring as I found myself unable to look away from his bright blue eyes. He turned his gaze to Marco, breaking the spell, and I sucked in a much needed breath.

"How are things going in here?" His deep baritone voice sent chills up my spine. *How could the sound of his voice feel like a caress?*

"Great, Boss! Carl was a good chef, but he couldn't hold a candle to Caleb here. Have you tried his manicotti yet? I need to take some of that home to Maria. She'll fall in love with me all over again," he said, his eyes sparkling. My heart warmed at his praise and I thanked him shyly.

"Help yourself, Marco. Maria deserves something good for putting up with your ugly mug." Giovanni smiled at Marco, obviously joking.

"You know you love me." Marco smiled affectionately, giving Giovanni a gentle noogie on the top of his head. I loved the easy going relationship they shared and was once more reminded of how lucky I was to be working here. Most of the kitchens I had worked in before were a chaotic mess of people tripping over one another and yelling at others to move faster or watch what they were doing. It was stressful and I often left at night wondering what in the hell I had gotten myself into.

Giovanni grinned at him with affection then turned to look at me as he smoothed his rumpled hair back down. The smile slid off his face and was replaced with a more serious look when he caught me grinning at him. I didn't like seeing the wall that he erected when he looked at me. "Do you have a minute?"

"Go ahead, Caleb." Marco smiled, oblivious of the sudden tension in the room. "I can handle the rest of this. Things are slowing down for the night."

Unable to come up with an excuse that would allow me to postpone this conversation, I nodded my head slightly and followed Giovanni down the hallway and into his office. Nervous butterflies swirled in my stomach as Giovanni gestured for me to sit in the chair across from his desk. I perched on the edge of it as he settled in behind his desk. He leaned back in his chair, steepling his fingers in front of his mouth and studying me warily. I sat quietly, waiting for him to speak and when he finally did, his words were not at all what

I had expected.

"I don't think this is going to work out, I'm going to have to let you go."

I could hear the sound of my pulse rushing through my ears and my eyes widened in shock. I had expected him to ask me to keep quiet about our previous encounter in front of the other staff members, I never thought I was going to lose my job over it. "Excuse me? What did you…what do…what?" I stammered out.

"Look, I have a great relationship with my staff. They're like family to me and things run smoothly around here because we all get along. There's no way I can work with you after what happened between us. Things will just get awkward and cause problems for the restaurant." His face remained blank and his eyes held no warmth.

Seeing him look completely unaffected by the conversation made my frustration rise to the surface and I felt my temper take over. "Excuse me, *Mr. Romero*," I ground out, "but I did not work my ass off for the last four years and travel all over Europe, studying under self-indulgent, pompous chefs just so your over-inflated ego could decide that one night in your bed would erase every dream I've ever had of being a head chef." I continued quickly when it looked like he would interrupt. "Was it a shock to not only see you again, but then also realize that you are now my boss? Yes! Did we have an amazing night together? Yes! Can I behave professionally despite that night? Hell yes! And what's more, I don't think you should make such a quick decision without even tasting my cooking." I finished with a firm nod of my head. With my heart beating wildly, I crossed my arms over my chest and settled back into my seat while I waited for his reaction. If he was going to get rid of me, at least I was proud of standing up for myself.

Giovanni stared at me, his piercing blue eyes a mixture of shock, admiration, and something else I couldn't name. "You have quite the temper don't you?"

"Not usually, just when I'm passionate about something."

Giovanni's eyes shuttered and darkened slightly. I blushed slightly as I replayed my words in my head.

"Fair enough. Let me taste something." My mouth went dry at the sound of his gravelly voice. I cleared my throat, willing my traitorous cock to settle down and stood to go to the kitchen. Just as I reached the door, I heard him speak, amusement ringing in his voice. "You thought our night together was amazing, huh?"

Whipping back around to him I realized what I had said during my tirade. "Well, it was for me anyway." I didn't wait for a response, but instead hurried out the door; chastising myself for telling him how amazing I thought our night had been. Giovanni probably brought men back to his place all the time and our encounter was nothing more than a blip on his radar. My shoulders slumped as I realized the men he was used to being with were probably much more experienced than I was and therefore much better in bed.

I rushed into the kitchen, my palms sweating, knowing exactly what was on the line for me. This one dish could make or break my career. I took a deep breath to calm my nerves as I gathered the ingredients for my favorite Italian stuffed chicken breasts.

Thirty minutes later I plated the food, the chicken a perfect golden brown and the ricotta cheese oozing out the sides. The smell of oregano and garlic wafted up as I carried it to Giovanni's office and knocked at the door.

"Come in," he said softly.

I entered and set the plate in front of him, acting much calmer than I really felt as I sat across from him. He looked at me briefly before cutting a bite and putting it in his mouth and I held my breath as he chewed. Normally I would've enjoyed the view of his Adam's apple sliding in his throat as he swallowed, but right now my nerves were taking up all the space in my head. He ate a few more bites and finally, after what seemed like a long time, he met my eyes again.

"This is really good," he said with a sheepish grin. "Excellent, actually. It reminds me of something my mom used to make."

I slumped in my chair with an audible sigh. "Does this mean I get to keep the job?"

He leaned back in his seat and regarded me seriously. "Do you really think we can work together?"

"Absolutely!" I assured him with a wide smile. "I'm sure we can keep things very professional and perhaps even become friends, eventually."

"Okay." He conceded. "We'll give this a try. Marco and Lauren are already big fans of yours and I think you're a very talented chef with what I've tried so far."

I leaned forward to shake his hand. "Thank you so much, Mr. Romero. You won't regret this."

He took my hand in his and I felt that now familiar ripple of electricity run up my arm. "Please, call me Giovanni or G, not Mr. Romero." He looked into my eyes with a smirk on his face.

"Goodnight, Giovanni." I liked the feel of his name on my tongue. I stood and walked to the door.

"Goodnight, Caleb," he said quietly. Just as the door was about to close behind me I heard him say, "By the way, it was for me too."

My eyebrows creased and I tilted my head. "Pardon?"

"It was amazing for me too, I just thought you should know." His voice was soft, almost shy as he kept his eyes trained on the floor.

Unable to stop the smile that broke across my face, I simply nodded. "See you tomorrow." I couldn't help the little victory dance I did in the hallway. I couldn't wait to come back to work the next day.

CHAPTER
Seven

Giovanni

I PULLED INTO MY PARKING SPOT AT ROMERO'S AND CHECKED myself in the mirror. I wasn't surprised to see the goofy grin on my face. It had been there a lot over the last week and as hard as I tried, I couldn't lie to myself about the reason why. Caleb had breathed fresh life into the entire staff at the restaurant, myself included. He seemed to have this light surrounding him and the unique ability of making everyone around him feel happier.

Caleb and Marco worked in a perfectly choreographed dance around the kitchen, laughing and talking throughout the night like old friends. Lauren and the wait staff all adored him and many of my regular customers praised the new twists to my mom's old recipes.

As for Caleb and myself, we had formed a good working relationship between us, if not a friendship yet. That was my fault though since I avoided him as much as possible, using Lauren to relay messages and spending more time in my office than the kitchen.

It wasn't that I didn't like the guy, in fact it was quite the opposite. I found myself thinking about him constantly throughout the day and often spent time watching him when he didn't know I was there. The way he moved, so self-assuredly around the kitchen with grace and precision, took my breath away; *that* was why I avoided him. Just being near him made my heart race and my palms sweat. I couldn't let any of the other staff members see how he affected me. I definitely didn't want Caleb to see how he affected me because I still had no intention of letting anything else happen between us. I would never go down the relationship route again, I repeated to myself for the hundredth time.

I entered through the back door and tried to quickly escape to my office, but was stopped by Marco who wanted to talk to me about the new supplier. I was pleased to hear that the deal I had procured was working out as well as I had planned. We spoke for a few minutes when the door to the dining room opened and a smiling Caleb sauntered in.

He smiled when he saw me there and he said a quick hello, showing off perfectly straight, white teeth. His brilliant emerald eyes shone with happiness and I suddenly felt very guilty for avoiding him. He was behaving very professionally just as he'd promised; I was the one who hid like a coward. Giving myself a mental shake, I vowed to try harder to be a friend to him. After all, his work was impeccable so it looked like he'd be with Romero's for quite a while. I was friends with the rest of my staff, there was no reason I couldn't be friends with Caleb too. For all I knew, the guy didn't even want a repeat of our night together.

"Hello," I said with a genuine smile, not avoiding his eyes this time.

His face lit up, showing those damned adorable dimples when he heard me respond to him and I could see him relax his shoulders.

Apparently my avoidance of him had been more obvious than I thought. I could kick myself for how I'd been behaving.

"Are you settling in okay?"

"Yes!" he said emphatically. "This kitchen is every chef's dream and I really enjoy everyone I work with. Thank you so much for giving me a chance."

"It's my pleasure," I said sincerely. "I've heard nothing but praise for your dishes, you're a very talented chef."

"Thank you." He ducked his head shyly at the praise and I found myself staring at him for a long moment. Marco cleared his throat and I shot my gaze over to him in surprise. *How had I forgotten he was in the room?* He was wearing a knowing smirk and winked at me as he turned to begin prepping the food for that evening. Feeling flustered, I excused myself and went to my office to get started with my day.

That night I spent more time helping out in the kitchen and found myself whistling as I once again enjoyed the part of my job I loved the most. I felt like such an idiot for having wasted the last week hiding in my office. Caleb was comfortable to be around and had an incredible sense of humor. *I would really enjoy having him as a friend.*

After we had closed the dining area for the night and the tables were cleared I went back to the kitchen to offer Marco and Caleb a hand. I caught Caleb looking at me a couple of times and it seemed like he wanted to say something but wasn't sure if he should. I wanted him to know that he could talk to me about anything, just as the rest of my staff did.

"Is everything okay?" I asked gently. Caleb's head shot up in surprise and he looked at me a bit warily. "You can say anything you want to me and I'll listen," I assured him. "My door is always open."

"Umm, okay," he said slowly, still sounding a little unsure.

I sighed. "Look, I know I've been acting strange this last week but that was my fault, not yours. You're doing an incredible job here and I really would like to be friends."

He smiled and blew out the breath he'd been holding, looking much more relaxed. "I was wondering what you do with all of the leftover food from here."

"Well, we usually just throw it away, since I like to prepare everything fresh for my customers. Why do you ask?" I tilted my head down to look into his eyes curiously.

"I volunteer at Agape House and as I'm sure you know, teenagers are *always* hungry and it's hard to keep enough food around for their appetites. So I was wondering, since you were just going to throw it away anyway, if maybe I could possibly take some of it to the center and give it to them? If you don't want to or something, it's no big deal," he rambled on nervously.

I stared at him a moment as I tried to piece together everything he'd just said. "What's Agape House?" I finally asked him.

"Agape House is sort of a safe house where LGBTQ teens can go who have been abused, kicked out of their homes, or are HIV positive. They give them a safe place to stay; offer counseling and medical care and they also help the older ones find jobs or finish school." His face became more animated as he spoke and I could tell he was very passionate about the subject. "My brother Carter volunteers his time teaching music, and my mom sews quilts for their beds. My dad helps with basic repairs around the facility, while I teach cooking and tutor some of them with their school work. I think my whole family has been involved in one way or another throughout the years."

I stood there flabbergasted. I had never met someone quite like him, someone who worked full time, yet still found time to volunteer several hours a week to help struggling teenagers. The fact that his entire family had dedicated their time to this worthwhile project was inspiring also. My respect for him grew even more. "Of course, you can take whatever is left, any time you'd like. It sounds like an awesome place."

"Thank you so much!" He said exuberantly. "The kids will love this. They don't get meals like this very often. I'll get it out of here right away."

"Wait, you're taking it tonight?" I followed his movements as he organized the food into containers.

His hands stilled as he looked at me. "I'm sorry, I got carried away." His face pinked with embarrassment.

"No, it's fine," I assured him. "I just didn't realize you were going tonight. Would you mind if I went with you? I'm curious to see this place for myself."

His shocked look would've been insulting, but he quickly covered it with a smile. "Sure, I'd love it if you came with me."

We worked together to get everything loaded in the trunk of Caleb's red VW Beetle. I had to fold my long legs into the passenger seat. It was a little cramped, but his car had more room to transport the food than mine.

In the small space of his car, I became extremely aware of his close proximity. His arm brushed mine as he turned the key and my breath caught in my throat as I felt his smooth skin slide against my own. The smell of sunshine and citrus assaulted my senses and my cock hardened as I was flooded with memories of our night together. I moaned slightly, but tried to cover it with a cough as I shifted my jacket onto my lap to try to hide my growing erection.

Caleb pulled into traffic, seemingly unaware of the torture he was inflicting on me as he headed through the city and into a rough looking area along the outskirts.

"So, what does Agape mean?" I asked, trying to distract myself from my growing problem.

Caleb glanced at me out of the corner of his eye and smiled. "It comes from ancient Greece and means 'love; the love of God for man and of man for God, as well as our love for our fellow man.'"

"Do you believe in God?" I asked him without thinking first. "I'm sorry, that's personal, you don't have to answer that," I said quickly.

"I don't mind." He laughed softly. "The answer is yes; I absolutely believe in God. I also believe in Agape love. I believe God wants us to show love and kindness to everyone, regardless of race, religion, or sexual preference and when we see someone in need, we should do anything we can to help them."

I turned in my seat, staring at his profile. He had once again taken me by surprise with his heartfelt words and his genuine kindness. He was one of those rare people who were just inherently good. I couldn't help but compare him to Juliana and for the first time I began to wonder what I had seen in her. She never saw the value in helping someone else, unless it would get her recognized in some women's club she was a part of, and she often scolded me for giving money to the homeless people who would sit outside the opera house we visited; saying that I was only supporting their drug habits and that we needed the money more than they did.

Curious about his response I asked Caleb, "Do you think giving money to the homeless supports their drug habits?"

Thinking over my question, he answered honestly. "Perhaps some of them, but I can't control what they do with the money once I give it to them. I can only control *my* actions and I know without a doubt, that God wants me to help others."

I leaned back into my seat and was quiet the rest of the drive. Lost in my own thoughts about this enigma of a man, I couldn't help but wonder how different my life might have turned out if I had met Caleb before I met Juliana.

The next day, I was sitting at my desk staring blindly at the computer screen. Thoughts of the previous night kept replaying through my mind. I was amazed at the tremendous program Agape House provided for Chicago's LGBTQ teens. I was both saddened by the atrocious things those teens had faced and thrilled that a place like

Agape House existed to provide them with the help they so desperately needed. I couldn't help the thrill that went through me at the smile I saw on Caleb's face when I signed up to begin tutoring on a weekly basis, although that wasn't the reason I did it. One night spent with Caleb and the kids at the center had awakened something in me and I realized that I had been so focused on my own pain over the divorce and my grief at the loss of my parents, that I had stopped caring about the needs of others around me. Those kids needed many things, but most of all they needed to feel like they weren't alone. Many of them had been treated so cruelly by others and had lost not only their innocence, but also their trust in humankind. I wanted to be part of a solution that would restore their faith in the world. I had been so blessed to have loving, devoted parents that I could always count on and I wanted to be someone those kids could count on too.

I smiled to myself as I remembered watching the kids as they ran up to greet Caleb when he walked in. He joked with them easily and I could tell he had developed a personal relationship with each of them. They clearly adored him and quickly devoured the food we had brought, smiling happily when we promised to bring more soon. I'm not sure I had ever seen that much food disappear that fast and there were times I feared for Caleb's safety as he reached out to place another spoonful on a plate. I suddenly understood what he had meant when he said that it was hard to keep up with the teenagers' appetites.

Lost in my thoughts, I didn't notice when Lauren entered my office and stood in front of my desk.

"G!" She shouted at me as she leaned down, right in front of my face, clapping her hands.

I jumped in my seat, startled. "What the hell?" I barked at her, my heart beating wildly.

Settling easily into the seat across from me, she looked at me curiously. "What the hell, *me*? What the hell, *you*? I've been calling your name for two minutes. Where were you?" she asked with a chuckle.

"Sorry," I said sheepishly. "I guess my mind was elsewhere."

"No kidding, care to share what has you so preoccupied?"

"Not really."

Looking at me closely, her eyes narrowed in confusion at my evasiveness then suddenly cleared as her face lit up with recognition. "Oh, I know what's going on. It's not *something* that has you so distracted, it's *someone*. Am I right? Is it the guy you hooked up with after your trip? Because you've been acting differently ever since then," she said accusingly and with way too much accuracy.

I couldn't help the nervous laugh that escaped. "Geez, Lauren, maybe you should work with Gracie, the bad guys wouldn't stand a chance against you. How is Gracie, by the way, I haven't seen her in a while?" I made a feeble attempt to distract her, but *I should have known better* I realized as she crossed her arms in front of her chest and glared at me.

"Nice try, Romero," she said drolly. "You're hiding something and you know I won't stop until you tell me, so spill it." She steepled her fingers under her chin and stared at me, unwaveringly.

"There's nothing to tell," I protested, but she quickly interrupted.

"We have been friends for years, G. I can tell when you're lying. You've been acting weird lately and I want to know why." I felt badly about the concern lacing her voice. "You know you can talk to me about anything, right? You could talk to anyone here, G, we're all family," she rambled on without stopping. "Well, everyone except Caleb. I don't know why you haven't given him a chance yet. He's a really nice guy, but you act differently around him..." she gasped suddenly as her words trailed off, her eyes growing wide as she pointed at me. "Is it...is he...did you...?"

Amazed at her unusual speechlessness, I couldn't deny her words and simply nodded my head. She squealed loudly, clapping her hands excitedly until I hushed her. I glanced at the open door, hoping no one had heard. Relieved when no one appeared, I finally admitted the truth to her. "Yes, Caleb is the man I was with when I got back from my trip. We didn't exchange names and were completely surprised when we saw each other again on his first day at work," I said in a whisper.

"I imagine so," she snickered. "So why have you been acting weird around him? Was he terrible in bed or something?"

I rolled my eyes. "No, quite the opposite actually. It was the best night of my life," I admitted quietly, my eyes glued to the desk in front of me.

Lauren leaned forward, suddenly very serious. "So that's what's wrong, huh?" She looked at me with compassion. "You know it's okay for you to feel something for someone again, right? Not everyone is going to rip your heart out like that miserable bitch," she said with a sneer. Lauren knew all about what had happened with Juliana and was never shy about showing her disgust when it came to my former wife.

"I know that, I just don't want a relationship ever again. We had fun for one night and now as it ends up, we work together. We've agreed to be friends and keep everything professional," I insisted.

"Yeah, we'll see how that goes." She laughed and I breathed a sigh of relief as we changed the subject. "So, I have something exciting to tell you," she said bouncing in her seat. "Gracie asked me to marry her!" She squealed again, thrusting her hand in my face to show off a beautiful diamond encrusted engagement ring.

I moved around my desk, wrapping her in a big hug. "I'm so happy for you, honey," I whispered in her ear. "You and Gracie are perfect together and you both deserve every bit of happiness life has to offer." Even though my marriage had crashed and burned, I still wanted good things to happen to my friends.

"Thank you, G." She sniffled and wiped a tear from her eye. "I really wanted you to be happy for us."

"Of course I am." I wore a big smile as she leaned forward, giving me a kiss on my lips and wrapped her arms around my neck in a fierce hug. I held her close as I prayed that my friends would get the happily ever after that I was denied.

CHAPTER
Eight

Caleb

"I'LL BE RIGHT BACK, MARCO, I NEED TO TALK TO GIOVANNI for a minute." I spoke over my shoulder as I washed my hands at the sink, noticing the unfamiliar frown on his face.

"No problem, I'm just going to take a quick break before the dinner rush anyway. I need to call Maria. She wasn't feeling well when I left."

"Is everything okay?" I asked.

"Yes, pretty sure it's just a cold, but I worry. I hate it when my girl's sick and I'm not there to take care of her." I smiled at how sweet the burly ex-Marine became whenever he talked about the woman he loved.

"Maria's very lucky to have you."

"Nah, I'm the lucky one," he said, nodding his head with

conviction.

"Well, tell her I said hello and I'm sending home some of my minestrone soup with you to help her feel better."

"You're one hell of a guy, Caleb, you really are. Thank you!" I watched him pull his phone out of his pocket and head for the back door, then I turned and walked down the hallway to find Giovanni.

Last night had been full of surprises. I had been hoping Giovanni would let me take leftovers to Agape House a couple of times, I didn't expect his generosity in giving them *all* of his leftovers. I was even more surprised when he volunteered to go with me, showing a genuine interest in the center. He seemed to really enjoy himself when we got there and was at ease with the teens, laughing and joking with them. It was good to see the smiles on their faces. Some of them had been through so much, that having a reason to smile was rare. Agape House was very special to my entire family and when I saw Giovanni sign up for weekly tutoring sessions, it warmed my heart.

In the short time I had known him, I'd begun to realize what a truly remarkable person Giovanni was. He was a brilliant businessman, an amazing lover, and of course a trustworthy friend. Unfortunately, I had to keep reminding myself that as much as I wished otherwise, that's all he would ever be: a friend. I wondered what had happened to him that made him reject even the thought of being in a relationship. I would give anything to be able to get closer to him, to hold him again, to feel the warmth of his body against my own.

I shook my head as I neared his office. It didn't matter what I wished. Even if by some miracle Giovanni wanted a relationship, he made it clear it wouldn't be with anyone he worked with.

I was about to knock on Giovanni's office door when I saw *them*. A mixture of shock and hurt went through me as I saw Giovanni and Lauren engaged in an intimate embrace. As painful as it was to watch, I couldn't tear my eyes away as she leaned forward, kissed his lips, and wrapped her arms around him.

I turned swiftly and headed back to the kitchen, praying they hadn't seen me. My stomach roiled with nausea and I felt tears stinging my eyes and blurring my vision. I wiped at them angrily. *Why should I care if they're together?* It's not like Giovanni was mine or had made any promises to me. In fact, he had made it very clear that our night together was a one-time only thing and he wanted to remain strictly professional at work. So then why was he with Lauren? How long had their affair been going on? Was she just another one of his flings or was she the one that would capture and hold his heart? They had been very close friends for a couple years now, so I couldn't imagine him having a cheap affair with her, only to toss her aside. When he had said that he didn't want a relationship, did he really mean that he didn't want a relationship *with me*? The questions continued to swirl through my head, making me more miserable with each passing moment.

I stepped into the kitchen and began pulling the ingredients for that evening's specials out of the pantry with shaky hands. Cooking usually helped to calm me. It was an escape for me whenever I was stressed and boy did I ever need an escape right then. I needed to get a handle on my emotions before anyone noticed and I was forced to explain why I was so upset. I didn't notice that Marco had come back in the room until he was standing right in front of me, blocking my path to the pots and pans.

"Hey, are you okay man?" he asked, tilting his head. "I've said your name, like three times or something, but you were a million miles away."

"I'm sorry, Marco, I just have a lot on my mind right now." I spoke quietly as Lauren and Giovanni entered the kitchen together, not wanting them to notice anything was wrong. My heart squeezed painfully in my chest and I quickly ducked around Marco to get the pan I needed. I must have slammed the pan down a little too hard on the stove because everyone turned to look at me, surprised by the loud noise.

"Sorry," I muttered, and began prepping the vegetables for the minestrone soup.

"Is everything okay, Caleb?" Lauren looked at me with concern. I had never felt jealousy before, but I recognized the emotion as it reared its ugly head. I felt myself wanting to scream at her that nothing would ever be okay as long as she was with the man that I wanted to be with.

"Sure, everything is just fine. Why wouldn't it be?" My words were clipped and angry sounding and I immediately felt bad as she looked at me with confusion before walking out to the dining area. I knew I shouldn't take my jealousy out on Lauren just because Giovanni wanted to be with her instead of me. She had been nothing but friendly with me since the day I met her.

I would apologize later, but right then my emotions were too close to the surface. I could feel Giovanni studying my face but I avoided eye contact, afraid I'd give my feelings away if I looked at him. How could I be this upset over a man I had known for such a short time? Why did I feel like I had lost something very important when I saw him in the arms of someone else?

My shoulders sagged in relief as Giovanni moved out of the room and I looked up to find Marco staring at me with a knowing look. "I won't ask what's going on because I'm pretty sure I have an idea already and it's obvious you're not in the mood to talk. Just remember, I'm a pretty good listener if you need it."

I gave him a watery smile and thanked him. I brushed a stray tear away with the edge of my apron. "Damn onions!" I muttered as Marco chuckled and patted me on the back.

An hour later, having become blissfully lost in my work, I had most of the food preparation complete. I looked up and gulped slightly as I found Giovanni leaning against the kitchen doorway, watching me with a look of concentration on his face as if he were working out a difficult puzzle in his mind.

"Need help with anything?" His deep voice sent an ache through me and I silently cursed myself for allowing him to affect me that way.

"Nope," I answered and quickly turned away from him, not trusting myself to say more for fear he'd hear the quiver in my voice.

I felt him brush against me and my breath caught as his warmth surrounded me. He leaned down to speak quietly in my ear. "I'd like to see you in my office, now!"

I could tell he was confused and a little pissed at my behavior and I felt like kicking myself. I had promised to act professionally around him, but instead I was acting like a jealous boyfriend when in truth I had absolutely no claim on him. Hunching my shoulders with that miserable thought, I followed him to his office and slumped down in the chair facing his desk as he took his seat.

"Care to explain what's wrong with you? You've been snapping at everyone today, and that's not like you."

"Nothing's wrong, I'm just having a bad day I guess. I know I shouldn't have snapped at Lauren. I'll apologize to her then get back to work." I started to stand, but I should have known it wouldn't be that easy.

"Sit back down, we're not done yet." The authority in his voice caused goose bumps down my arm and I sat back down, avoiding eye contact. "I understand having a bad day in general," he continued, "but you seemed fine earlier. Has someone said or done something to upset you?"

I clenched my jaw tight as I tried to figure out how to end this conversation. I just needed a little time and I would get over my crush on my boss and get my head on straight. Before I could come up with anything, he spoke quietly. "I thought perhaps after spending time together last night we were friends, but friends talk to each other. Why won't you talk to me?"

"Please, can we just forget it."

"I'm sorry, I can't do that." I glanced up and saw him running his fingers through his hair, frustration showing on his face. "Every member of the Romero's staff is like family to me, and if something is bothering one of them I want to try to help, but I can't do that if you won't tell me what the problem is."

"What if the problem is you?" I blurted.

"What do you mean?" Giovanni asked. I'm sure my face looked as shocked as his and I wished I could take back my words.

"Just forget I said anything, this is my problem not yours, but I promise not to let it interfere with my work anymore."

Giovanni stood and walked around his desk, sitting on the edge so he looked down at me. He knelt forward, taking both of my hands in his. "Please, Caleb. If I've done something to upset you, I want to know what it is so I can apologize."

The sincerity in his voice broke something in me and my words began tumbling out of my mouth before I could stop them. "I just don't get it, I know you're completely against relationships and I'm not trying to push that, but why did you say we couldn't be anything more than friends since we work together, if you're just going to be with someone else at work?" I rushed on, barely stopping to take a breath. "I mean, if you really want to be my friend, I think you could start by being honest with me. If you're not attracted to me, or you didn't enjoy our night together, just tell me the truth instead of blaming it on work; since that's obviously not a factor here."

"What the hell?" he sputtered as his face turned red. "I don't even know where to start with all of this. I don't have a clue what you're talking about. What person am I supposedly with at work?" he demanded.

I threw my shoulders back as I stood to face him, trying to look taller than I actually was. If he was going to continue lying to me then there was no hope of us being friends. "I saw you in here with Lauren. You were kissing and holding each other. I know it's none of my business if you two are together, but I don't like being lied to. Especially from someone claiming to be my friend," I hissed, using my fingers as quotations when I said the word friend. I looked up at

Giovanni, who still towered over me and was surprised at the amusement I saw dancing in his eyes. I had expected him to look angry or guilty at having been caught in a lie, instead he moved passed me and left the room.

I stood there a moment, not sure if I should stay there or leave. Did I even still have a job after yelling at my boss about his personal life? I covered my face with my hands and groaned, frustrated with myself for fucking up this once in a lifetime job because I couldn't keep my mouth shut. Just as I was about to walk out, Giovanni returned to his office holding Lauren's hand. Seeing them like that cut through me like a knife. I no longer wanted to hear what he had to say but braced myself regardless.

"Lauren, would you share the good news with Caleb please?" I glanced back and forth between them, nervously. Lauren's face lit up as she lifted her hand to show me a giant rock on her ring finger. I felt the blood drain from my face and I swallowed hard, trying not to throw up. How long had they been dating? Oh God, were they together the night Giovanni and I slept together? I was horrified by the thought of being part of his deception and wondered how he could be so cruel as to throw it in my face this way. Not to mention that Lauren was a wonderful woman and didn't deserve to be cheated on. I looked to Giovanni for answers and was shocked to see him grinning like the Cheshire cat. Anger surged through me at his callousness, but before I could say anything Giovanni spoke up.

"Tell him who you're marrying, honey." Childishly, I wanted to cover my ears while chanting lalalala loudly enough to drown out the hurtful words I knew were coming.

"I don't need to hear this," I mumbled, but was interrupted by Lauren who was staring dreamily at her ring.

"My girlfriend, Gracie," she gushed. "We've been together eight years. She kept saying she just wasn't ready to get married so I had no idea she was planning on asking. Oh, Caleb, I can't wait for you to meet her."

"Gracie? You're engaged to marry your girlfriend?" I asked weakly. I wasn't sure I had heard her correctly over the sound of my blood rushing through my ears.

"Well, I guess technically she's my fiancée now." Unaware of my humiliation, Lauren excused herself to go tell the rest of the staff. Giovanni shut the door behind her then turned to face me, trying to gain control of his mirth. He lost control as the laughter he'd fought so hard to hold in burst free. I felt heat flash through my face. I had never been so embarrassed in my life and he was thoroughly enjoying it.

"Go ahead, laugh it up." I stood facing him with my arms folded across my chest and a frown on my face.

His laughter quieted but his eyes danced with mirth. "I'm sorry, I couldn't resist and you sort of deserved it."

I glared at him for several seconds before giving him a small grin, seeing the humor in the situation. I felt overwhelming relief that he wasn't marrying Lauren and that I hadn't been *the other woman* so to speak. "So what about the kiss?"

"I was just congratulating her, I swear. Lauren and I have never been anything more than friends."

"I'm so embarrassed. You must think I'm such a fool. I'm sorry I jumped to conclusions."

"Don't be, it was really adorable watching you get all jealous." His smile faded as he grew serious. "Caleb, I was telling you the truth when I said I don't do relationships. I won't put myself through that again."

"Who hurt you?" I whispered. I couldn't resist the need to touch him so I reached forward, taking his hand in mine and smiled to myself when he let me.

Giovanni stared at me for several moments. Just when I thought he wouldn't answer, he began to speak. "Her name is Juliana and she was my wife." Wanting him to keep talking, I hid my surprise and gently squeezed his hand. "We met in college; she was getting her degree in interior design and I was a business major, having always dreamed of opening my own restaurant." He paused, smiling a bit as he glanced around his office, but his smile drifted away as he continued. "We were young and head over heels in love, so I asked her to marry me as soon as we graduated. I thought we were very happy and we began talking about having children. I wanted to be a father more than anything," he admitted, his eyes clouding over. "We had four wonderful years together and then suddenly she didn't come home after work one night. I was worried something had happened to her and was getting ready to go search for her, but instead a man knocked at my door and served me with divorce papers. To this day, I still have no idea what I did wrong, but it was bad enough that she didn't even try to get anything from the divorce. Her lawyer handled everything and I haven't seen her since the night before she left me. I guess she couldn't wait to get away from me." His voice sounded hoarse and his face was masked with pain.

Unable to hold back, I wrapped my arms around his waist and hugged him to me tightly. He stiffened at first, but then placed his hands gently on my hips. I looked up into his blue eyes that were marred with sadness and vulnerability. I placed my hands on either side of his face as I whispered. "It was her. *She* was the problem, not you. I don't know why she left, but I can tell you this, she was a damn fool," I insisted vehemently. "You are the most incredible man I have ever met in my life. You are brilliant, kind, and sexy as hell. Anyone would be lucky to be loved by you." I leaned up and brushed my lips against his.

I moaned as he began kissing me back. The kiss which started out gentle, soon had my body feeling like it was on fire. I felt his warm tongue glide against my lips and I opened my mouth to welcome him in. My head swam as I breathed in the intoxicating mixture of spicy cologne and Giovanni's own personal scent. I was quickly becoming addicted to that scent.

His hands that had been on my hips moved around, cupping my

ass and kneading the taut globes. I sucked on his tongue as he began maneuvering our bodies backward until I brushed up against his desk. He leaned over me, causing me to sit down on the edge of the desk and tilt backwards. I looked up to see his blue eyes clouded with lust and I felt a surge of electricity run through my body, thrilled with the knowledge that I was the one causing him to look like that.

"Yesss," I hissed as he began grinding our now achingly hard cocks against each other, pushing against me with just the right amount of pressure. He licked down the side of my neck and I began wrapping my legs around his waist, when there was a knock at the door. Giovanni buried his head in the crook of my neck and growled in aggravation then quickly helped me stand and we stepped away from one another and began straightening our tousled clothes.

We were both out of breath, but Giovanni managed to sound normal as he called out "Yes?"

Marco popped his head in the door and I looked at Giovanni, alarmed that we had gotten so carried away that we hadn't even realized the door was unlocked, taking the chance that anyone could have walked in on us. Marco had turned a disturbing shade of green and was sweating profusely. He explained that he was suddenly feeling very ill and needed to go home. He must've been coming down with whatever his wife had. I was sorry he was sick, but thankful that he was preoccupied enough that he didn't seem to suspect what we had been up to before the interruption.

"That's fine, Marco," Giovanni eyed him with concern. "Go home and rest, we've got everything under control here. I'll call and check on you and Maria tomorrow."

"Are you sure, Boss? We have that big dinner party coming in tonight and there's still a lot to do. Caleb can't do it all on his own." Worry was written all over Marco's miserable face.

"He won't be on his own," Giovanni glanced at me. "I'll help him tonight."

CHAPTER
Nine

Giovanni

AFTER FINALLY CONVINCING MARCO THAT CALEB AND I would be fine running the kitchen without him, he went home. I turned to look at Caleb as I raked my eyes up and down his body, taking in his hair that I had made messy with my fingers and his flushed cheeks, gliding over his lips that were still red and plump from kissing me, down his firm chest and his trim waist, and finally landing on his cock which I knew from our first night together, felt heavy and perfect in my hand.

I knew I was breaking my own rules by starting something up with him again, but I'd be damned if I could stop. I had spent the last week telling myself not to touch him, but he was quickly becoming like a drug to me. Every day I spent near him, the more I wanted him. Just breathing in his clean, citrusy scent got me hard as a rock. I felt my cock twitch and glanced up to his face. His bright, green eyes were staring right at me and he smirked at my blatant perusal of his body. I simply shrugged my shoulders, knowing I had been caught red handed.

I cleared my throat. "Okay, we have a lot to do tonight so we better get started."

"Un uh, I don't think so," Caleb said shaking his head slowly as he walked towards me.

"Excuse me?"

Caleb leaned up towards me and I bent down so he could whisper in my ear. "In here, *I'm* the boss," he said huskily, his warm breath tickling my ear. A shiver raced down my spine at his words and when he backed away with a smile wide enough to show his dimples, I nearly dropped to my knees right there in the kitchen. *What in the hell is this man doing to me? And why am I so powerless to stop it?* At a loss for words, I simply nodded my head.

The next few hours sped by as we prepared hundreds of dishes that were quickly snatched up and taken to waiting customers. We worked surprisingly well together, often anticipating each other's thoughts before they could be voiced. Several times throughout the night we'd catch each other staring and find ourselves unable to look away until one of the wait staff came in to pick up an order.

Caleb was a lot of fun to be around and I found myself laughing more in this one night than I had in the last four years as he regaled me with stories of some of the more temperamental chefs he had studied under while in Europe and the Mediterranean.

"I've always wanted to travel abroad," I admitted as I wiped down the counters.

"Why haven't you?"

"I've been too busy getting this place up and running and just haven't found the time yet."

"Well, your restaurant is obviously a huge success; you should take some time to enjoy it. If you could go anywhere, where would you want to go to the most?"

"I've always dreamed of visiting Italy, in particular, Manarola. It's the little village where my parents met and fell in love. They always told me such wonderful stories about it that I really want to see it for myself someday. It's the reason I had the mural painted in my office. Just looking at Manarola makes me feel closer to them."

Caleb tilted his head as he looked at me. "How long have they been gone?" he asked with gentle understanding.

"Five years," I answered softly. "They were going out to dinner and were hit by a teenage driver who'd only had her license for a week. She ran a stop sign and they died instantly."

"I'm so sorry Giovanni. I can only imagine how painful that was for you." His face was full of compassion. He was quite easily the sweetest man I had ever met and it drew me to him even more.

"I guess there are worse things that could happen than dying beside the person you love most in the world. It's comforting to know that they're still together." I turned to the sink to wash my hands and took a moment to collect myself as tears threatened to spill over.

We were suddenly interrupted by the rest of the staff as they headed home for the night. "Goodnight, Lauren, and congratulations on your engagement," Caleb said kindly.

"Thank you so much." She beamed at him then turned to kiss me on the cheek and wrapped me in a quick hug. I glanced over her shoulder to see Caleb giving me a mock glare so I winked at him.

I made sure the door shut behind Lauren then turned and found Caleb bent at the waist, reorganizing the trays on the lower shelf. His perfect ass wiggled alluringly as he struggled to move the heavy stack. He had kept me teetering on the edge all night, most of the time without even realizing it. Watching his tight little body moving fluidly around the kitchen as he worked had me fantasizing about his body writhing against my own. Naked. The small taste I'd had of him in my office had left me longing for more. As if I was being pulled by an invisible thread I moved forward, unable to stop myself.

I grabbed his hips and pulled him towards me roughly, my cock lining up with the crack of his delectable ass. He stood up and leaned his back against my chest and he let out a breathy laugh. "Well, that didn't take long."

I spun him around to face me and knelt down to look directly in his eyes. "Oh, so that was on purpose then?"

"Yup!" He stated unapologetically, his eyes holding mine in a challenge.

I quickly yanked him towards me, crushing our bodies together. "Be careful what you wish for, little one," I growled at him.

I backed him up against the refrigerator and covered his mouth with mine, ending any sassy response he might have had. He ran his fingers through my hair, pulling just enough to make my cock impossibly harder as he swept his tongue against mine. I moaned loudly as he reached down to cup my swollen cock, slowly rubbing me through the thin material of my pants.

Our lips parted as we each gasped for air and he looked up at me, the green of his eyes barely visible around his blown pupils. "Please, Giovanni."

Hearing him beg broke my last bit of self-control. "Hold on," I hissed. Cupping his ass, I lifted him effortlessly and he wrapped his legs around my waist. I walked him out of the kitchen and down the hallway to my office.

"I'm really starting to like how you manhandle me." His words made us both chuckle.

"Then you're going to love what happens next," I teased, wiggling my eyebrows at him.

"Trust me, I remember," he answered cheekily. I let him down gently, his perfect body sliding deliciously against mine until his feet touched the floor. I took his mouth in a devouring kiss as we began undressing.

I quickly removed the last of my clothes and watched as Caleb's shirt hit the floor. Suddenly, he stopped moving and just stared at me, biting his lower lip as he took in every inch of my body. When he looked back up at me, his eyes half lidded and full of lust, I knew I had never felt more desired in my entire life; it was a powerful feeling. He smiled slowly, revealing his dimples and I leaned forward to tease one then the other with the tip of my tongue. Caleb looked at me with surprise. "I've been dying to taste those," I whispered.

I took his hand and led him over to my couch, where I slowly sat down so he was standing in front of me. I looked up at him and my breath caught in my throat, stunned by his beauty. His tousled brown hair had fallen over one eye, his flawless complexion was pinked up from excitement, and his lips were plumped full and just slightly wet from our ferocious kisses. Caleb was always a sexy man, but Caleb aroused and hungry for me was a fucking work of art. I wondered if he had any idea the effect he had on me.

I ran my hands up his chest, memorizing the smooth ridges and planes of his body. He gasped loudly as I leaned forward to suck one of his nipples into my mouth. He grasped my head, his fingers fanning through my hair and yanked hard as I grazed my teeth gently over the taut nub. My hands smoothed over his back and down to the globes of his ass. Pulling him towards me, I nuzzled my face against the bulge in his pants, slowly rubbing back and forth against him and breathing in the perfect scent that was all Caleb.

I moved my hands to the front of his pants and allowed a finger to dip down inside the waistband, teasing him and causing him to thrust forward, bumping my chin with his covered cock. I grasped the button of his pants and then glanced up at him questioningly. He nodded his consent and I slowly undid his pants and lowered his zipper. I reached my hands in and pulled out his leaking cock. He had a long, cut cock with a perfect mushroom shaped head that made my mouth water. Caleb moaned, throwing his head back on his shoulders as I licked the pre-cum off the tip of his cock. The deliciously salty flavor of him burst on my tongue and I became ravenous. I hungrily lapped at him and began stroking his dick, trying to coax more cum out of him. Wanting to drink him down, I swallowed his cock all the way, taking him deeply inside my throat and swallowing around him, making him cry out in pleasure. His trimmed hairs tickled my nose and I held him in the back of my throat as I breathed him in.

I sucked his swollen cock for several minutes until he cried out. "Stop! Too close." He pushed at my shoulders until I released his cock, with a wet pop. I leaned back against the couch and stroked my aching cock as he shimmied out of the rest of his clothes and then slowly lowered himself onto the couch, straddling my lap. His fingers swatted my hand away and I threw my head on the back of the couch, closing my eyes as he grasped my cock in his firm hand and began stroking it, adding a twist each time he reached the tip.

I forced my eyes open, not wanting to miss the view as he lined our cocks up and began stroking them together. He swiped his hand across the tips of our cocks, combining our pre-cum and using it to lubricate our shafts as he jacked us off. Caleb tilted his head down to capture my mouth in a searing kiss, never slowing his strokes.

I reached a finger up between our mouths, letting our combined tongues wet it then reached behind him, spreading his ass so I could circle my slick finger against his puckered hole. He ground against me, bucking wildly, as I tapped at his hole then gently slid my finger into his tight body.

Caleb quit stroking us as he leaned forward, his forehead against my own. I could feel his warm breath fanning my face as I added a second finger, twisting it every so often and scissoring them to open him up. He lifted his head and his eyes were wild with lust, pupils completely blown and he gasped. "More, I need more, Giovanni, please!"

Hearing him say my name with such wanton abandon had me

instantly on the edge of release. I clamped my jaw tight and held him still. "I need to get a condom." I glanced at my desk then let out a frustrated groan. "Fuck!"

"What's wrong?" Caleb asked in confusion as he slid off of me.

"I just remembered, I have no condoms here. I've never done anything like this at work so I've never bothered to keep any here. I'm so fucking sorry," I said with a long sigh.

His shoulders slumped in disappointment, but then his face lit up in a bright smile. He reached down to his pants, pulling out his wallet and triumphantly holding up a foil packet. He saw the questioning look on my face and quickly explained. "My brother Carter gave me this when I told him I was going home with you the night we met at the club, but then we ended up using yours, so it's just been sitting in my wallet ever since."

"Remind me to send Carter a thank you note…or a gift basket… or a fucking car!" I said, swallowing his laughter with another kiss. I stood, dragging him with me to my desk and wrapped my arms around him, kissing him deeply. "Are you sure about this?" I asked, looking into his eyes for any hesitation.

"I'm absolutely positive about this." I saw some unnamed emotion pass through his eyes and his words seemed to hold a double meaning.

Not wanting to examine it too closely, I turned him around to face the desk. I leaned away from him so I could see my fingers glide gently down his spine, following the dip in his back and cupping the spectacular globes of his ass. He wriggled his ass in my hands, pushing it against me as I kneaded his firm cheeks. "Eager are you, baby?" I said huskily; he moaned in answer.

Leaving a hand on his ass, I opened a desk drawer and rummaged through, quickly finding a small bottle of lotion. Caleb glanced over his shoulder and his eyes widened.

"Looks like you *do* get busy at work," he winked at me teasingly.

"My hands get dry from washing them all the time, smartass." I smacked his ass, making him jump as he chuckled. Caleb bent over the desk, placing his head into his folded arms and pushed his ass out towards me in invitation.

I slicked my fingers with lotion, warming them with my breath before I slid two of them into his tight hole. After a few twists he relaxed his grip on my fingers and I was able to slowly add a third. Caleb was soon grinding against me, clearly ready for more. He let out a disappointed moan as I removed my fingers and I chuckled. "Don't worry, sweetheart, I'm just getting started." The endearment slipping out before I could stop it.

I picked up the foil packet and quickly tore it open with my teeth. I spit the corner of the packet onto the floor as I slid the condom down my thick shaft. I squeezed more lotion into my hand and glanced down to slick up my cock.

"What the ever loving fuck?" I yelled in dismay.

Caleb whipped around in surprise. "What's wrong?"

We looked at each other, then down at my cock, then back at each other before howling with laughter. Thanks to Caleb's brother, my cock was now sheathed in a neon yellow condom picturing a smiley face with a cartoon bubble that read, "Let's get it on!" It was several moments before we were able to quit laughing and Caleb stood before me, wiping tears from his eyes.

"It's a testament to you that we can see all of the picture and words," he said with a giggle.

I chuckled with him then kissed him gently. Our laughter soon died as it was replaced with the fire igniting between us once again. Turning him around, I swiftly applied a liberal amount of lotion to my cock. Pushing down between his shoulders until his head rested on my desk, I began sliding into his waiting hole, holding still until I felt him relax beneath me.

I slid back out and chuckled to myself as I saw the smiley face looking up at me. *I couldn't remember ever having so much fun during sex.* "What is it about you?" I whispered so quietly he couldn't hear.

I pushed forward, groaning loudly as I felt his heat envelop my cock. His walls were smooth and silky, gripping me tightly as I pushed all the way in until my hips were nestled against his ass. I held there for a minute, reveling in the feel of his body surrounding my shaft and wishing I could stay there forever.

"Giovanni," he gasped, "I need you to move!" He began rocking his ass against me and I grasped his hips with my fingers as I began to thrust into him, deeply. I bent my knees, changing the angle of my thrusts, searching until he screamed my name as I hit his gland perfectly. Caleb panted loudly as his fingers scrambled to find purchase on the desktop. He let out a low cry as he met my thrusts with his own.

He stood up and his bare back slid against my chest deliciously as our sweat mingled. I reached up, lightly placing my fingers around his throat and nipped at the soft lobe of his ear. "You are fucking perfect," I whispered in his ear.

Caleb reached his hand back and gripped my hair as he turned his chin, claiming my mouth in a passionate kiss. Pushing against me gently, he walked us backwards until I was forced to sit in my desk chair. He lowered his body with mine, my cock still lodged deeply inside of him.

My head swirled as he began grinding his body up and down on my cock in a reverse cowboy. My hands had a mind of their own; wanting to touch him everywhere, all at once. I slid them over his smooth back, his rippling abs, then let them flow up to tweak his nipples between my fingers. Caleb sat forward, bracing his hands on my knees as he began rocking wildly. My breathing became shallow as I reached down, spreading his cheeks so I could watch my cock sliding in and out of his snug hole. I clenched my jaw trying to hold off my fast approaching orgasm.

I wouldn't last much longer so I gripped the arms of my chair and began thrusting my hips up into him as he grabbed his cock and began pumping, lost in ecstasy. I kept thrusting until he cried out, throwing his head back in abandon. Feeling his tight hole strangling my cock as he came, pushed me over the edge as my orgasm ripped through me with shocking strength.

I collapsed into my chair as I struggled to catch my breath and reached around his chest, feeling his heart racing against my palm. I slid a finger through the cum splashed on his chest and brought it to my mouth, licking it clean. He turned his head to look at me and smiled, looking completely sated. My heart did a little flip as our gazes held and I realized, I genuinely *liked* this man. I felt lighter somehow when I was with him and I'd be lying to myself if I said I didn't want more of him.

"That was amazing," he said, his breathing still slightly ragged. He grazed my jaw with his lips then carefully lifted himself off my lap and began gathering his clothes from various places around my office. I removed the condom, tied it up, and threw it in the trash can under my desk. I glanced his way and we shared a chuckle at his brother's joke.

"I would have killed Carter if his twisted sense of humor had stopped this, you know."

"I don't think even the threat of an impending tornado could have stopped us tonight."

Caleb smiled and walked towards me as I zipped my pants. "So, I was thinking…"

"That's never good," I teased.

He stood tall so he could wrap his arms around my neck and trailed his tongue along my throat. My cock stirred and I wondered how in the hell it had the energy to do that after the mind blowing orgasm it just went through. *This man was going to be the death of me, but what a sweet way to go.*

"We've had sex twice now," Caleb continued, pulling me back to the conversation.

"Amazing sex," I interrupted, using his words. My hands once again rested on his trim waist.

Caleb smirked at me. "Exactly. We've had *amazing* sex twice now and we still manage to work together with no problems. So, it stands to reason that if we're able to keep things professional while working and we are both enjoying the already established amazing sex, then there's no reason we shouldn't continue." He tilted his head up to mine, looking cautiously hopeful.

I stared at him thoughtfully for a moment. With my previous sexual encounters, I had been satisfied with just one night of sex, not giving the men a second thought afterwards. With Caleb, however, I found myself craving him more with each touch. That alone should have been enough to scare me off, but I heard the words leaving my mouth before I even had the chance to think things through. "As long as we're both aware that this is for enjoyment only and we remain *just* friends, then I say yes."

Caleb's eyes dimmed slightly, but he quickly nodded. "Okay." He sealed his lips to mine in a lingering kiss.

"You really should add persuasive reasoning to the skills set listed on your résumé." I pinched his ass.

"I just might have to do that," he laughed as we grabbed our keys to head home.

CHAPTER
Ten

Caleb

I HAD THE NEXT TWO DAYS OFF WORK SO I CAUGHT UP ON SOME much needed laundry. I found myself missing Giovanni and wishing I was at work instead. I decided to kill some time by giving my apartment a good cleaning.

I had tried to make the small space homier by painting the walls bright colors and hanging pictures of my family; using cute throw pillows and blankets on the furniture, but nothing could hide the water stains on the ceiling or the cold wind which swept through the ancient windows. I sighed as I scrubbed the olive green stove that should have died in the late 70's, but somehow kept hanging on. Perhaps now that I was earning a hefty salary at Romero's, I would be able to set enough aside for the deposit on a nicer place.

I had just finished scouring my bathroom when there was a

knock on the door. I looked through the peephole and smiled widely, unlocking the door to allow Carter to come in.

Carter's smile reflected my own as he went to hug me. "Hold that thought." I held my hands up to block him. "I just finished scrubbing my toilet and need to wash my hands like you wouldn't believe."

He chuckled as he followed me to wait outside the bathroom door as I scrubbed my hands. When I stepped back out we hugged each other tightly. We were both very affectionate, having been raised in a loving home by parents who never hesitated to show us how much they cared.

"God, I've missed you." I studied his tired face. "Where have you been all week?"

"The band had a couple gigs in Cincinnati. They have some great clubs there and the crowds seemed to like us."

"Of course they did." I smiled at him, loving how modest he always was. The truth was Carter was a musical prodigy. When we were only two years old, he was beating out songs on the drums that had been a Christmas gift for Landon. At four years old he climbed up on our grandparent's piano bench and began playing chopsticks. By six he had mastered the guitar, playing full songs after hearing them only once on the radio. As we got older his once sweet, melodic voice had become deeper and a bit gravely, which had all the girls in school swooning when his band performed at our senior prom; unfortunately for them Carter was one hundred percent gay. "I'm sure they loved you. It won't be long before you get a recording contract, I just know it."

"You really think so?" His eyes lit up at the prospect.

"I'm positive," I answered honestly. Carter and his band had worked so hard to get to the point they were at and I really hoped they would get rewarded for it.

"Thanks, that means an awful lot coming from you. So what's up with you? How's the new job?" Carter settled on my couch, tucking his legs up under him.

I plopped down on the couch next to Carter, pulling my legs up in the same fashion without thinking. We often mirrored each other's gestures and finished each other's sentences without realizing it, until someone would point it out. Mom always shrugged and told people it was a twin thing. "The job is everything I was hoping for and more. I really love working at Romero's. Everyone gets along great; they treat each other like family. Oh, and let me just tell you," I gushed, using my hands as I talked, the way I often did when I was excited. "I couldn't have designed a better kitchen in my dreams. It has every imaginable fixture and gadget a chef could hope for."

Carter smiled widely at my enthusiasm. "What about your boss, is he scary like that chef on TV that's always screaming at people and making them cry?" he asked wrinkling his nose.

"No, Giovanni's nothing like that at all." I felt a fluttering in my stomach as I said his name.

Carter tilted his head to the side as he studied me closely. My brother had always been very perceptive. "What aren't you telling me?"

I stared at him for several moments considering my options, but I knew that I could never get away with lying to my twin. Besides, Carter was my best friend and I honestly wanted to share what was happening, so I began telling him all about Giovanni.

"So you didn't know he was your boss?" Carter asked incredulously.

"Nope," I said making my word pop. "We didn't exchange names that night."

He stared at me, his mouth hanging open. "I can't believe you finally did it."

"Did what? You know I've had sex before, it's not like I was a virgin." I heard the defensiveness in my voice.

"You might as well have been," he mumbled under his breath. Seeing my glare, he hastily added, "Oh, come on, what you and Andrew did in high school barely counts."

"At least we cared about each other. When was the last time you slept with someone who you didn't meet by sticking your dick through a hole in a wall first?"

"Once! I tried a glory hole once! I never would have guessed that a podiatrist could suck dick so well." I laughed as his eyes took on a far away, dreamy look. "Look, all I meant was, you've only been with one other person in your entire life and you were in a committed relationship with him. I just want you to enjoy all that life has to offer. There is a huge buffet of men out there just waiting to hook up with you."

"I'm not looking for random hook ups though. You know that's not who I am."

"Well, you hooked up with your boss, right?"

"Yeah," I admitted quietly.

"Oh man, you're falling for him aren't you?" He accused.

I could have denied it, but it would have been pointless. Carter had always known me better than any other person on the planet. We could read each other's minds most of the time and had even had our own *twin-speak* as children. "He's an amazing man," I answered simply.

He studied me for a long moment before saying anything. "Well, it sounds like I need to get to know him then, don't I?"

I smiled at him, a wave of tenderness for my twin washing over me. Even though we had very differing views on sex and relationships, I never doubted that Carter would support my feelings and do whatever he could to help me find my happiness. "I would love for you to meet him, but it's not like that, for him anyway." I could hear the disappointment in my own voice.

"What do you mean?" I saw the concern shining in his eyes.

"He shares your feelings about relationships, meaning he doesn't want one. I don't think he's a sexual deviant like you though." He smacked me lightly and I smirked at him. "He was married once and his wife hurt him pretty badly. I don't think he's allowed himself to get close to anyone since."

"Well, if anyone can get him to take a chance again it's you. You're the best man I know."

"Thanks, that means a lot to me," I said sincerely. "We agreed that we want to keep spending time together, but just have fun, no commitments."

"Please promise me you'll be safe, not just with your body, but also your heart. I don't want to see you get hurt."

"I will, I promise…" I trailed off as his words sunk in. I narrowed my eyes at him in a glare.

"What the hell is that for?" he yelped as I pinched the soft skin under his arm, hard.

"*That* is for almost putting a possible end to the most incredible sexual experience of my life!" I yelled.

"What are you talking about?" Carter rubbed at the red mark I had left on his skin.

"The smiley face condom? It was so embarrassing. Where the hell do you even find shit like that?"

He began laughing so hard he nearly fell off the couch. I swatted lightly at his head as he clutched his stomach trying to catch his breath. "Sorry man, I just wanted you to be safe," he said when he could finally speak. "I noticed you said I *almost* put an end to it. So, can I assume things ended well?"

"Hell yes it did!" I said slapping his raised hand in a high five. We looked at each other and then began laughing. "This doesn't mean you're off the hook though, I *will* get even with you, eventually," I said in all seriousness.

"Bring it on, little brother. I don't think you could ever do anything to embarrass me though. There's not much I haven't done, sexually."

"I don't want to hear about your sex life," I said emphatically, covering my ears.

Carter just laughed. "Come on, let me tell you about the

threesome I had with those guys you saw that night at the club," he pleaded.

"I'm serious dude, don't make me hurt you." I pointed my finger at him threateningly.

"They were hot! I'm telling you, at one point they had me between them, do you know what a spit roast is?"

"Stop!" I yelled as I threw my hand over his mouth and tackled him, both of us falling to the floor in a laughing heap. I got him in a headlock and was getting ready to administer an impressive noogie when there was a knock at my door. "Hey, son!" Dad said as he brushed passed me into my apartment. Rick Greene was a larger than life kind of a man. Standing tall at 6'2", with broad shoulders, thick salt and pepper hair, and laugh lines that crinkled around his hazel eyes. His exuberant personality drew people to him. My dad was the kindest, most loving father I could ever hope for. The unconditional love he showed each of his kids and the complete adoration he had for our mom helped hold our family together throughout the years. It was easy to understand why all of his kids idolized him.

"Hey, Dad, what are you doing here?" I asked as I shut the door behind him.

"What, you don't want to see your old man?" he said, feigning hurt.

"You know I do and you're not old."

"That right there is why you're my favorite," he joked as he hugged me.

"Hey! I heard that," Carter said as he hugged our dad. We laughed, knowing that Dad had said the same thing to each of his kids at one point or another.

"Hold that thought," Dad said as there was another knock at the door. Carter and I looked at each other questioningly and I moved to the door. I opened it, surprised to see my older brother Landon, holding four pizzas. Behind him was my sister Michelle's husband, Jason, and my sister Emma's husband, Mark, each holding chips and a case of beer.

"Are we having a party I didn't know about?" I looked around in confusion.

"The women all went out together tonight so we decided we should have a guy's poker night, so here we are," Jason explained.

"Besides, it's been so long since we've all been together. We needed to celebrate the fact that you're finally back home, where you belong," Landon added, throwing his arm around my shoulder. "I missed you, squirt."

I wrapped my arm around his waist as I glanced up at his handsome face. He looked the most like our dad, while Carter and I favored our mom. "I missed you too, all of you." I smiled as I looked around at my family. As much as I had enjoyed travelling, nothing could compare to being surrounded by the people you loved most in the world. *It's so good to be home.*

"Okay, let's play some poker." Carter began rubbing his hands together. "I need to win some money tonight."

"What else is new?" Mark teased, elbowing him in the ribs lightly.

Two hours later, Carter looked up from his cards, a smug smile on his face. "Full house, kids." He gloated as he fanned his cards out on the table. "Hey, don't worry about the money. We're family," he continued sweetly. "That means I'll accept personal checks."

We all moaned as I went to the fridge to get another round of drinks. "So, what are the ladies doing tonight?" I sat back down, passing beers out to everyone.

Mark and Jason chuckled as Dad told us that they went to dinner and a movie. "They went to see that new movie about the millionaire that likes to tie that girl up and spank her."

Landon sputtered around a mouthful of beer. "Isn't that the one that's like porn for women?"

"Yeah, they all say it's a love story, but it has all kinds of bondage and kinky shit in it," Mark said rolling his eyes.

"Hey now, don't knock the bondage and kinky shit," Carter snickered as Landon cocked his brow at him.

"Well, your mom's read all the books and believe me, it has spiced things up for us in the bedroom. Not that we needed any help there." You could have heard a pin drop as we all looked up at Dad in horror. He just smiled at each of us, as if he hadn't just dropped a bomb in the room. "If she got that worked up from just reading the books, then I can't wait to see what she's like after seeing it on the big screen."

"No, just no!"

"I think my ears are bleeding!"

"I will never be able to look at Mom again!"

We all shouted at once as we jumped up from the table, having unanimously decided that poker night was over.

Dad laughed loudly as he followed the guys out the door, quite pleased with himself. "Goodnight, son, it's great to have you home again." He pulled me in for a hug. "I love you very much and I'm proud of you."

Glowing under his praise, I hugged him back. "I love you too, Dad." I watched them as they made their way out to their cars.

"Dad, please stop!" I heard Landon shriek as Dad apparently said something else inappropriate and I shut the door, chuckling to myself. My family was crazy, but I loved them.

After cleaning up the kitchen and taking a quick shower, I climbed in between my sheets, tired from a busy day. I picked up my tablet to read for a bit before going to sleep. I couldn't wait to dive into the next installment in a series by my favorite gay romance author. The sex scenes were always hot and that Gram character really cracked me up with all the crazy things she did and said.

I had just settled in when my phone dinged, letting me know there was a text. Reaching for it, I felt a thrill go through me as I saw Giovanni's name on the display.

You awake?

Yes. My heart beat wildly as I sent a text back.

Everyone missed you at work tonight.

I beamed as I read his text. *Who's everyone?* I texted back coyly then held my breath as I waited several minutes for him to respond.

Me, he finally sent.

I'll admit, I let out a very unmanly squeal before answering, *I missed you too. I thought about you all day.*

I'll see you soon. Sweet dreams, Caleb.

They will be now. I tacked on a winky face emoji.

I lay there for a while longer, thinking of how crazy I was about the man that I was falling in love with. Finally, as I drifted off to sleep, with a smile on my face, I prayed that he'd be there to catch me as I fell.

CHAPTER
Eleven

Giovanni

I SMILED AS I READ OVER THE TEXTS BETWEEN CALEB AND ME FOR about the hundredth time that day. I had no idea how someone that I hadn't even known for very long could hold such power over me, but as I worked yesterday in Caleb's absence, I found myself replaying our time together on a loop through my mind. Especially in my office where we'd shared an incredible night of passion.

I tried to keep busy by placing purchase orders, going over the budget with Lauren, and paying bills, but Caleb was always in the back of my mind. *I wonder if Caleb would be willing to work every day we were open so I wouldn't have to experience this torture any more.* I turned my phone off again and wandered out of my office, hoping to find a distraction.

I spent the next hour helping Marco get everything ready in the kitchen, then went to see if I could be of any assistance to Lauren in the dining area. As I walked in, I saw her standing near the front door speaking to someone.

"We're not open yet, but if you'll wait here for just a minute I'll see if he's available." Seeing me walk in she smiled. "There you are. I was just coming to find you. There's a gentleman here who says he's a friend of yours." *HE'S HOT!* She mouthed to me, gesturing over her shoulder.

Curious, I stepped forward so I could see who it was. I took in the short cropped hair, the broad shoulders, and the trim waist as the man stood ramrod straight in the foyer. He turned as he heard me approach and I stood frozen in place, my jaw hitting the floor in shock. "Micah?" I whispered.

"G!" He smiled broadly and stepped forward to grab me up in a tight hug. "God, it's good to see you, man."

I stepped back, taking his face between my hands so I could get a good look at him. "You look good," I exclaimed.

"You haven't changed a bit."

We stood there smiling at each other until we were interrupted by Lauren. "I take it you two know each other?"

I stepped back from him and turned to make introductions. "Micah, this is Lauren Jacobs, a dear friend of mine and my right hand girl here at work. Lauren, this is Micah Hamilton, my best friend since we were seven years old and my brother in every way that counts." Micah's eyes softened at my words.

"It's a pleasure to meet you, ma'am," Micah said as he extended his hand to shake Lauren's.

"You too, I can't wait to talk to you some more and hopefully hear some humiliating stories about G as a kid," she winked playfully at me as she walked over to answer the phone as it began ringing.

"Let's go into my office so we can talk." I led him back through the restaurant. After making introductions once again between Micah and Marco, we finally entered my office and I shut the door to give us some privacy.

"This place is beautiful," Micah said proudly as he sat down. "I am so happy for you that you finally got to open your own restaurant and you're obviously very successful." There were very few people whose opinion mattered to me more than Micah's, so his words filled my heart with pride.

"Thanks, it's been a lot of work, but I love it as much as I'd always hoped I would." I smiled at him, still feeling shocked that he was really here. "How are you? How long are you here for this time?"

After high school, I went to college while Micah had enlisted with the Navy, quickly moving through the ranks and becoming an elite Navy SEAL. His visits, though always short and infrequent, were spent catching up with each other as much as possible. We spoke on the phone often, but it had been three years since he'd been able to come for a visit. As a matter of fact, the last time he was home was right after Juliana left me. He helped me pick up the broken pieces of my life and figure out what to do with my future. I couldn't have made it through that dark time in my life without him. I had missed him terribly.

Micah leaned back in his chair, clasping his hands across his flat stomach as he gave me a small smile. "Actually, I'm home to stay. I've retired from the SEALs." At my shocked look, he held up his hand to fend off any questions. "It was time for me to get out and no I don't want to talk about it, but when I'm ready you'll be the first one I tell," he said solemnly.

I didn't miss the pain in his eyes, but nodded my head in silent agreement. I knew from experience that pushing him would only make him shut down, so I would wait for him to approach me when he was ready to open up. "So, what happens now? Where are you staying? What will you do for work?"

"I found an apartment in the city and I've decided to start my own private security firm."

"I can't tell you how excited I am to have you home again. I've missed you so much." Emotion caused my voice to shake.

Micah smiled at me warmly. "I've missed you too, G. Now tell me how you've been."

"I'm good. This place takes up most of my time, but I'm happy."

"Have you ever heard anything from Juliana?" he asked, watching me closely.

"Not a word." I knew my tone was clipped, but I really hated thinking about her- not because it still hurt- but because thinking about her was a waste of my time and tended to piss me off.

"You know, once I get my private security firm up and running, I can search for her if you want. Maybe finally get some answers for you, get you some closure." Micah had spent many nights talking me through my bouts of depression and feelings of self-doubt after Juliana left me, so I knew he was only trying to do what was best for me, what he thought I wanted.

My eyes moved around my office as I considered his offer seriously for a few minutes before settling on the couch where I had held Caleb, feasting on his exquisite body just two short nights ago. I felt my body warm with thoughts of him. "No, thank you. I wouldn't want to see her even if you were able to track her down." My answer surprised me when I realized I truly meant it. Just a couple of weeks ago I would have jumped on any opportunity to find her and get the answers I had so desperately craved for the last three years. I would be a fool not to recognize what had caused the sudden change in me. Once again, I was bewildered and more than a little frightened by the impact Caleb was having on my life.

Micah cocked his head to the side and narrowed his eyes at me. "Well, I'll be damned! Somebody finally chipped away at your wall. Who is this angel I need to personally thank?" A broad grin flashed across his face and I could see more than a hint of relief in his eyes. I felt more than a little guilty as I realized how worried Micah had been about me.

I chuckled slightly. "Don't get carried away now, I'm not getting into a relationship ever again. I'm just having a bit of fun with someone, but we've agreed to keep things casual."

"You need to learn to trust again, G, someone just might surprise you someday. Not every relationship ends like yours and Juliana's. Although I'm glad to hear you've at least moved on from random hook ups to casually seeing the same person. Now come on, I want details."

I smirked at him. Micah was like a dog with a bone when he went after something and I knew there was no way he'd ever let the subject drop. I knew I might as well tell him enough to placate his curiosity. "His name is Caleb and he's my head chef." Micah whipped his head toward the door so fast it was comical. I held up my hands to stop him from jumping up out of his chair. "He's not here tonight, so settle down," I chuckled.

"Damn! Guess I'll just have to come back tomorrow. I need to check out this workplace romance." He teased me before turning serious. "Seriously though, if he makes you happy, then I'm happy."

"It's just fun, nothing serious," I insisted again, but Micah just smiled a knowing smile at me. It was obvious he didn't believe my protests and I was starting to have doubts myself.

Deciding it would be best to change the subject, I took Micah into the kitchen so I could feed him one of our signature dishes. His eyes teared up a bit as he tasted my mom's lasagna for the first time in probably five years. "Man, this takes me back to sitting in your mom's kitchen. Mama Romero always made the best lasagna. She'd be real proud of you, G, real proud." His words were like a balm to my soul and we smiled at each other as we cleaned our plates.

"So, you want to get out of here and go get a drink somewhere?" Micah asked me.

I was just about to tell him I couldn't leave the restaurant when I heard Lauren speak up behind me. "Yes! Please take him. He's been doing nothing around here but getting under foot and moping for the last two days since you know who has been gone."

I spun around in my chair to shush her when Marco spoke up. "Seriously, Boss, get out of here. Caleb will be back tomorrow and you can be happy again." I stared at him incredulously making him laugh loudly. "I may be older, Boss, but I know what a man who's crazy about someone looks like, I see it in my mirror every morning, and it's pretty obvious when that started happening. Right about the time our adorable new chef started working here." Marco stood back, folding his arms across his chest with a smug look on his face, as if daring me to deny his accusations. I couldn't.

"I think you just got told," Micah mock whispered.

I reached over and swatted at the back of his head. "I plead the fifth, but I'm out of here. I'll see you brats tomorrow."

"Yay! We won!" Lauren gloated as she hurriedly escaped to the dining area. I hung my head, shaking it back and forth in resignation while Micah and Marco laughed.

After running to my place so I could shower and change, we headed out. I decided to take Micah to my favorite club, if he was moving to the area he would need to know the best places to pick up men.

Having been best friends since we were children, it had been very scary for me to admit to Micah that I found guys attractive. We were fifteen and my parents had known for several years that I was bisexual, but it took me a long time to work up the nerve to tell Micah. He meant the world to me and I had heard too many guys at school saying nasty things about gay people, calling them fags and other terrible slurs. It would've broken my heart if Micah called me those things or looked at me with disgust. Eventually, my parents convinced me to be honest with him, saying that I couldn't be true to myself if I was withholding something so important from my best friend.

My heart raced as I waited for him to come over to my house

after school. We went outside and began tossing a baseball back and forth, while I tried to fight back the urge to vomit. Micah finally stopped, holding on to the ball. "So, why are you acting so weird?"

"I like girls," I said, my face heated with what else I needed to say and I forced myself to spit the rest out. "And guys," I stood there shaking, waiting to see what he would do.

Micah grinned widely at me. "Thank God! Me too," he exclaimed simply, as he resumed our game of toss. "Except the girl part, they're kind of gross." I'm not sure I had ever felt so relieved in my life. My parents later admitted that they had suspected Micah was gay and wanted us to be honest with each other, so we could support one another. That day solidified our friendship and strengthened the bond that still existed between us.

I smiled at the memory as I pulled Roxie up to the club's valet service. "What's that smile about?" Micah asked.

"Just glad you're home," I said simply. Micah clasped his hand on my shoulder as we entered the club.

We made our way to the bar as the heavy bass reverberated through my chest. We each ordered a cold beer and I noticed the way the bartender eyed Micah up and down, like a starving man. While we had always been more like brothers than friends, and had never seen each other in a romantic way, I could admit that Micah was a stunning man. At 6'0" he always had been, with his stormy gray eyes, golden skin, and dark hair cut short in a military fashion. I chuckled at how many heads turned his way when we sat down at the bar.

We were on our second beers when the man next to Micah began flirting with him. I swiveled my stool around to check out the sea of people on the dance floor. Sweaty bodies filled the dance floor, bumping and grinding against each other to the beat of the pulsating music. I scanned the crowd until my eyes landed on an extremely tight, sexy body that seemed very familiar. I tried to convince myself it wasn't really Caleb, but then the beefy guy he was grinding up on spun him around, giving me a perfect view of his face.

"Dude, I've been talking to you for two minutes and you haven't heard a word I said, what are you staring at?" Micah asked, snapping his fingers in front of my face.

"Caleb's here," I said trying to calm my racing heart. *What was he doing here with someone else?* I knew we never said we were exclusive and I was the one who had insisted on keeping things casual between us, but I never expected to see him out with someone else two days after I fucked him on my desk.

"He is? Where?" Micah asked excitedly, craning his neck to look all around.

"Over there, grinding on the Michelin Man." I sneered in their direction as I contemplated my ability to rip the man's arms off with my bare hands.

"Wow, he's hot!" Micah said approvingly. "Who's he with?"

"Fuck if I know," I growled, clenching my teeth.

I glared at them, unable to look away as Caleb swayed his body against the larger man then reached back to wrap his hands around the back of the man's head. A fierce wave of jealousy rushed through me as I remembered what it felt like to have that body grinding against me, not all that long ago, in this same damn club.

When Mr. Big and Beefy reached down and began cupping Caleb's cock and Caleb tilted his head back, offering his lips up to him, I saw red. I was across the room and dragging Caleb out of his arms before I even realized I was moving out of my seat.

"What the hell?" the large man snarled, moving towards me. Micah got in front of him, spreading his hands on the man's massive chest and said something that must have placated him because he turned and headed to the bar.

I stood there staring at a wide eyed Caleb as I tried to get my emotions under control. I had never felt jealousy like that before and it confused me. It was my rule to not have a relationship, so why was every cell in my body screaming, "MINE!"

"What the hell is your problem?" Caleb yelled, as he looked at me like I had suddenly grown two heads.

"My problem? What the fuck are you doing grinding up on some guy when you had my cock buried in your ass just two days ago?" I yelled back, my anger surging again. I took a deep breath and was about to suggest we go outside so we could talk when he got the strangest look of recognition on his face and an amused giggle escaped his lips. *Was he insane? How could he think this was funny?*

I stared at him in confusion until I felt a tap on my shoulder. "Everything okay here boys?"

I spun around at the sound of the familiar voice and stood looking at... "Caleb?" I screeched. My head spun as I helplessly looked back and forth between the two men in confusion.

Taking pity on me, Caleb, who had apparently just walked up behind me and witnessed the entire embarrassing scene, placed his hand on my back. "This is my twin brother, Carter."

"You must be Giovanni. I've heard a lot about you." Carter was still laughing.

"Your twin; Carter is your twin," I repeated stupidly. I felt my face heat up with mortification. That's it; I was going to have to move. Sell my restaurant and move far, far away, where no one knew me.

"People mistake us for each other all the time, it's no big deal and I really am happy to meet you," Carter said kindly, grabbing my hand to shake it.

I felt numb as Micah reached around me to introduce himself to Caleb and Carter. He shook their hands, then leaned into my ear and whispered, "Smooth, G, real smooth." Micah winked at me before he led Carter to the bar, explaining that he had offered to buy his date a drink while we worked things out and would take Carter to him.

I released a long breath and then turned back around to face Caleb, an apology on my tongue. Instead of the hostile look I had expected, I was surprised to see a happy smile on his face. Crooking his finger at me so I would lean down, Caleb whispered in my ear. "I think you care a little more than you let on."

I think you're right, I almost responded. "Come home with me?" I asked instead. Caleb nodded and I took his hand, leading him out of the club.

CHAPTER
Twelve

Caleb

MY HEART WAS RACING IN ANTICIPATION OF SPENDING THE night with Giovanni as I climbed into his Mustang. I watched him as he walked around the front of the car and slid into the driver's seat. The engine roared as he started the sleek car. "Hello again, Roxie," I said, rubbing my hand across the dash sweetly, making Giovanni chuckle.

I turned my head towards him and felt my cock plump in my jeans as I drank in his beautiful features, visible only by the lights of the dash. My eyes traveled down his profile, from his long lashes that curled at the ends, his straight Roman nose, his strong jaw, and the long column of his throat that I planned to spend time trailing with my tongue. I couldn't wait to be naked together, to feel his hot flesh gliding against my own.

He turned his face towards me and held my gaze before he turned back to watch the road. He swallowed nervously. "Caleb, about tonight…"

"Tonight was fucking hot!" I interrupted. He looked at me in surprise and I laughed. "What, you expected me to be pissed off?"

He glanced at me quickly. "Actually, yes. My behavior was embarrassing, uncalled for and I hope you'll accept my apology. I don't know what came over me."

"I thought it was fucking hot watching you go all caveman when you thought someone else was touching me." I swiveled my body in my seat, leaning over the console and cupping his denim covered cock with my hand. I heard his breath catch as I slowly rubbed my fingers up and down his quickly growing shaft. I smiled at the effect I was having on him and leaned up to place my lips next to his ear, whispering seductively. "There's one thing I've regretted about our time together."

"What…What's that?" he stuttered and his knuckles turned white as he tightened his grip on the steering wheel.

"That I haven't gotten to taste you…here," I said, squeezing his dick with the perfect amount of pressure. He moaned loudly as he accelerated the car, which sped through the streets, taking us to our destination. "Do you have any idea how many times I've jacked off to the memories of you bending me over and fucking me? Of the taste of your lips on mine?"

He let out a deep growl as he removed one hand from the wheel and covered my hand with his own, pushing it against his cock as he pumped his hips up trying to get more friction. "You're not the only one," he rasped. "I've enjoyed reliving the feel of your cock sliding down my throat and the taste of your balls on my tongue. I nearly rubbed the skin right off of my dick remembering the feel of your tight hole grabbing onto my cock like it never wanted to let go."

I groaned, dropping my forehead to his shoulder. "You win," I conceded, trying hard not to come in my pants from his words alone.

"Tonight, we both win." He turned the car into his parking garage and whipped into the first available spot, barely turning off the ignition before he was out of the car and around to my side. He opened my door and reached for my hand, smoothly pulling me out of my seat. "Let's go, little one." I smiled at the now familiar endearment, wondering if he even realized he used it on me.

He grabbed me as soon as the elevator doors shut, pulling me into his arms and devouring my mouth. My lungs burned with the need for oxygen, but I didn't care; my need for him was stronger. I pulled his shirt up out of his jeans and began running my hands all over his smooth flesh. My body was greedy for his. I wanted to touch him, smell him, *taste* him everywhere, all at once. The elevator shuttered to a stop on his floor and we raced to his condo, desperate for each other.

His lips were on mine again as he kicked the door shut behind us and quickly pulled my shirt over my head then turned us until my back was against the wall. He locked his fingers with mine and raised them so my arms were high above my head, then he lifted his head to look directly in my eyes. "The things I'm going to do to you…" He trailed off, his eyes heavy with lust.

My body shook as his hands slowly glided down my raised arms, along the sides of my neck, smoothing over my chest, and landing on the waist of my pants. He gripped the front of my jeans and yanked my hips forward roughly. I couldn't breathe as I stared up at him in a lust filled daze. He popped the snap on my jeans and teased his finger along the waistband of my underwear. I whimpered as he slowly unzipped my pants and dipped his hand inside my boxer briefs, gripping my shaft tightly in his fist, before he began gliding his hand up and down. My eyes rolled up into my head as he rubbed his thumb over the weeping head of my cock and my legs turned to jelly as he removed his hand and stuck his thumb in his mouth, moaning as the taste of my essence coated his tongue.

He stepped back, his eyes never leaving mine as he swiped his shirt over his head and let it drop to the floor, then unbuckled his belt and slid it from his jeans. His jeans followed his belt to the floor and my mouth watered as he hooked his thumbs onto the elastic of his tight black boxer briefs and slid them down his legs. I quickly followed suit with my own jeans and briefs until I stood nude before him, my cock achingly hard and straining up against my stomach.

He leaned forward and took my mouth in yet another scorching kiss. My hands moved up, snaking their way around his neck and pulling him closer to me. A deep groan escaped his lips and he cupped my ass, swiftly lifting me up against him until I was forced to wrap my legs around his waist. I gasped and then laughed. "I love it when you do that, Gio." His eyes flashed at the nickname and he quickly moved us to the couch where he sat down, my legs straddled on either side of him.

I licked at his mouth before I captured his lower lip between my teeth and tugged on it, lightly. His tongue trailed down my throat and I kissed the top of his head, my fingers fanning through his thick hair. I sat up on my knees to align our cocks and began rocking back and forth, rutting up against him and mixing our pre-cum as he captured my nipple between his lips and sucked hard, making me cry out from the pleasure I was feeling. His mouth moved to lavish attention on my other nipple, while he reached around and rubbed his finger up and down my crack. His finger quickly found my eager hole and he tapped at the sensitive nerves there, awakening them.

I was quickly edging closer toward the point of no return, so I pushed against his shoulders until he released my nipple. He looked at me with desperation and tension, his voice wavered. "What is it?"

"I'm not missing out on this again. I need to taste you, Gio."

He nodded in consent and I hastily slithered off his lap and onto the floor. I sat back on my heels and stared at his magnificent cock, with its ring of foreskin surrounding the engorged head. "Caleb!" He rasped and my head shot up to look him in the eyes. "Touch me," he pleaded.

I licked my lips and reached my hand out to run a finger down the length of his steel hard shaft. His hips jutted up at the contact and he breathed out through his clenched teeth. I ran the tip of my finger around his foreskin, spreading his pre-cum all around the thick head. His fingers gripped the cushion of the couch as I leaned forward, swiping my tongue across the head of his cock. The flavor of this incredible man swirled on my taste buds and I swore I had never tasted anything better. His spicy, masculine scent filled my senses, making me dizzy. I pulled his foreskin between my teeth and gently tugged on it, then licked around it in a soothing nature.

Giovanni's breathing had become labored and I looked up to see his chest heaving, a fine sheen of sweat covered his firm pecs and glistened along his rippling abs. My gaze scrolled over the deep cut v of muscles that I longed to lick. I reached up and grabbed his hands, placing them on the top of my head. He looked down at me with glassy eyes, noting my silent invitation, then he gripped my hair and lined my mouth up with the head of his cock. I opened up, loving the way his girth stretched my lips wide around him. He bucked his hips up gently while pushing down on my head and I felt his silky cock slide along my tongue until it hit the back of my throat. He held me there for several seconds and I swallowed around him, causing him to lose control, his hips bucked up wildly towards my waiting mouth.

I took it all and relished the feel of him possessing me. I sucked his cock for several minutes, hollowing my cheeks on my upward strokes. "Stop!" He gasped breathlessly.

I leaned back on my heels, licking my lips and looking up at him coyly through my lashes. "Not good?" I asked innocently.

He reached down, grasped me beneath my armpits and lifted me up his body as he stood. I wrapped my legs around him and he swatted my ass, hard. My eyes widened in surprise as he said, "That's for being mouthy." His eyes sparkled with amusement.

"I thought you liked my mouth," I answered saucily.

"I liked it a little too much, that's why I needed to stop you. Now it's my turn to show you what my mouth can do."

My heart beat wildly at the promise in his words. He carried me into his kitchen and laid me down on the island. The marble top was cool, but felt incredible on my overheated skin. I looked up at him, thrilling at the hungry look on his face as his eyes devoured my naked body, spread out before him like a buffet. "Tell me about your tattoo." His fingers trailed over the ink on my left hip. It was a small red heart with the time 2:38 a.m. written in the middle in black ink.

"It's the time I was born. Carter has a matching one that says 2:34 a.m."

He bent down and placed a gentle kiss over my tattoo and my heart swelled in my chest. His hands ran over the tops of my legs gently before working their way down to my inner thighs and pulling them apart roughly so I was laid out, spread eagle.

I suddenly felt very vulnerable as his eyes raked over my naked body. "You are so beautiful," he whispered as if he sensed my nervousness. He reached up and slid his index finger inside my mouth. I eagerly closed my lips around it, swirling my tongue around his digit. He pulled it out slowly and let it slide over my lip and over my throat, leaving a wet line down my torso and ending at my happy trail. My head fell back against the marble as I let my eyes slide shut.

They popped open a moment later when I felt something warm and wet glide over my hole. "Gio!" I gasped. I tilted my head up to look at him, only to find him kneeling with his head between my legs. I stared in disbelief as he looked at me, widened his tongue and swiped it along my hole, not letting up that time. My eyes rolled up in my head at the overwhelming sensations that flooded my body. I had heard of rimming, but never had it done to me before. I knew I should feel embarrassed at the highly intimate act, but I couldn't bring myself to feel anything except pure bliss. Giovanni teased my hole with his expert mouth as he nibbled and sucked at it, spearing me with his tongue, until I was out of my mind with pleasure.

"Please, please, please," I begged unashamedly. Giovanni stood and quickly opened the cabinet behind him, rummaging around until he found a bottle of olive oil. The drawer below produced a condom and he smiled at me in triumph. He quickly sheathed his thick cock with the condom and slicked himself up with oil. I panted as he greased my hole and worked a finger in gently. He looked down as he worked both of his slick index fingers into my hole in a sawing motion and my back jackknifed off the counter when his finger pressed against my prostate.

"Fuck me now." I gasped as he slid his cock all the way in with one smooth motion. I welcomed the burn that came along with him filling me. He held still, allowing my body to adjust to his invasion, trembling at the restraint he forced upon himself so he wouldn't cause me pain.

"More!" The word barely left my mouth before he gripped my hips and slid my ass to the very edge of the counter. He entered me again and began pumping his cock into me, grazing my prostate with each stroke. My body slid across the smooth surface of the marble with each powerful thrust. I hooked my legs around him, pulling him in and he pounded into me relentlessly, his hands gripping my thighs so hard I would probably have bruises, but I didn't feel the pain. My sole focus was on the delicious sensation of having his body joined with mine.

As my need began to build, I reached down and tugged on my cock at a fast pace. Fire raced down my spine and my balls drew up tight as I shot thick strands of cum all over my chest. I lay there gasping for air as Giovanni pumped in and out of me several times before going completely rigid. He threw his head back and screamed out, "Caleb!" as I felt his hot cum fill the condom inside me. He was the most breathtakingly beautiful thing I had ever seen.

He pulled out gently, leaned over me, and began lapping at my stomach and chest, cleaning the cum from my body. My chest squeezed almost painfully and moisture filled my eyes as I realized I was completely, one hundred percent, in love with Giovanni Romero.

I woke slowly the next morning, my mind not wanting to leave the beautiful dream I was having. My eyes fluttered open and I smiled as I saw Giovanni sleeping soundly. It hadn't all been just a dream; I really had spent the night with the man I loved. His arms were wrapped securely around me and his legs were entwined with mine. I breathed deeply, enjoying the spicy, manly scent I had come to associate with Giovanni. I leaned forward and nuzzled my face gently against the crisp hairs on his chest, enjoying how they tickled my cheek.

I felt him stir and looked up to see him gazing down at me. "Morning," he said with a lazy smile.

"Good morning." I kissed his chest then worked my way up his throat and finally landed on his full lips. "I'm sorry, I didn't mean to wake you." I kissed him gently.

"I don't mind." He nipped gently at my lower lip. "At all." He rolled our bodies until he was lying over me, the weight of him a comforting blanket to my body. He licked at my lips, willing me to open to him. I did and his silky tongue swept in to mate with mine, dipping in and out much like his cock did to my body last night. I felt my body heat up at the memory and I reached down between our bodies grasping both of our cocks in my fist.

I captured his gasp in my mouth at the feel of our shafts, slick with our juices, gliding against each other. He thrust his hips up, fucking my fist and I felt the thick veins of his cock as it rubbed against my own, heightening my pleasure. I sucked his tongue like a cock and he began thrusting his hips frantically. I felt my orgasm rush through me just as he stiffened above me, straining, and we both came hard all over my chest.

He dropped down over me, not caring about the mess of our combined seed between us. Gasping for air, I combed my fingers through his hair holding him close to me. I would never grow tired of this man. Once his breathing had evened out he lifted himself gently, but I quickly pulled him back down. "Just another minute," I pleaded.

"I don't want to hurt you," he whispered, lowering himself to rest his weight on his forearms that caged me in on either side of my head.

"You won't." We laid there, gazing into each other's eyes and I reached up to place my hands on either side of his perfect face. Unable to contain my feelings any more I whispered, "I am so in love with you." His eyes grew wary and I felt him tense above me, so I held on tighter not letting him escape. "I know you've been hurt and I know you're not ready to say it to me," I continued calmly, surely. "But after last night, I know you care and that's enough for now. I just had to tell you, I love you with my whole heart, Gio."

His body relaxed slightly, but he was still cautious as he looked into my eyes, searching. "Why do you call me Gio?" he finally asked.

Sensing his need to change the subject, I smiled at him shyly. "Everyone calls you Giovanni or G. I wanted something that was just mine, something that would help me stand apart."

"You already stand apart," he whispered softly then began kissing me deeply. He may not be ready to open his heart to me yet, but his words gave me hope that someday he would.

He lifted off of me and chuckled at my pouting face. "First one to the shower gets a blow job." He laughed loudly as I quickly jumped from the bed and nearly face-planted when my feet became tangled in the sheets. I could still hear him chuckling as I rushed into his en suite bathroom to turn on the faucet in his giant walk-in shower.

After a long hot shower, where Giovanni proved he was a man of his word and I proved to be a gracious winner by returning the favor, he went to the kitchen to make breakfast for us. I took my time wandering around his condo, trying to learn everything I could about this man. The first time I had been here was such a whirlwind; I didn't get a chance to really look at anything.

His place was modern and sleek with pale gray walls throughout and bold, masculine furniture. It was clean and organized, but not in an OCD kind of way, just a neat and tidy, cared for kind of way. He obviously had no qualms with spending money on his personal surroundings, if the 90" LED TV taking up an entire wall in his living room, or the astonishing view of the city from his floor to ceiling windows, was anything to go by. Not to mention the state of the art, fully equipped kitchen he was cooking in. I felt myself blush as my gaze landed on the marble topped island counter and I remembered the way he had spread me out on it and played my body like a finely tuned instrument.

"Uh-hem." Giovanni cleared his throat causing me to jump and my face to flush furiously at being caught. He wore a sexy smirk on his face as he sauntered over to me and rubbed his lips back and forth against mine. "It's so fucking sexy when you blush," he said, his breath ghosting across my lips. A shudder ran down my spine at his nearness and he chuckled, knowing the effect he had on me.

He made his way back into the kitchen to finish breakfast and I wandered over to the enormous stone fireplace to look at the framed pictures he had displayed on the mantle. There was a picture of an older couple, gazing at each other lovingly and I knew immediately they must be Giovanni's parents because he looked exactly like his father, but had the same piercing blue eyes as his mother. The next picture was of Giovanni, Lauren, and Marco standing in front of Romero's as they cut a giant ribbon on what I assumed was opening day. The last picture was of Giovanni and Micah: the man I had met last night. They were young, probably sixteen or seventeen years old and appeared to be camping as they were sitting side by side with marshmallows hanging on the ends of the sticks they held. They were smiling and Giovanni had his arm thrown around Micah's shoulder as Micah laid his head on Giovanni's shoulder.

He called me to breakfast and I shuffled to the table and spread my napkin across my lap. "Thank you, this looks amazing." I cut into the omelet he had made and my stomach growled loudly at the sight of the cheese, peppers, and mushrooms inside.

He chuckled at me. "Eat up, we've both worked up quite an appetite," he said pointedly, making me blush again. "I don't think I'll ever get tired of that," he murmured.

"So, how was everything at work while I was gone?" I asked as we ate.

Gio stared at his plate, suddenly very interested in the food there. "It was fine," he answered gruffly and I wondered at the change in his attitude. When he glanced up and saw the confusion on my face, he simply shrugged his shoulders. "It was a long two days, all right?" He started eating again, avoiding my gaze. A wide smile spread across my face as the meaning behind his words sank in.

"I missed you too." I responded easily and went back to eating, but not before witnessing the smile playing on his lips.

When we were finished eating, I offered to wash the dishes since he had cooked, but he insisted on standing beside me as he dried the dishes and put them back in their proper places. We worked quietly together until he caught my gaze once again returning to the pictures on the mantel. "What's wrong?"

We had both proven our jealous tendencies already so I decided a direct approach would be best this time. "I noticed the picture of you and Micah on the mantle and I met him at the club last night... with you."

"What do you want to know?" Giovanni asked quietly.

I felt a small moment of panic; did I really want the answer to this question? "Exactly how close are you two?"

Giovanni leaned back against the counter and pulled me to stand between his legs, placing his hands on my hips. He looked at me through his thick lashes and smiled sweetly. "Micah and I met when we were seven years old. We became inseparable and stayed that way all through school. We supported each other when we discovered that he was gay and I was bisexual and my parents adored him. He had a rough childhood and when his dad learned that Micah was gay, well, let's just say he took it very badly. So Micah moved in with me and my parents for the last two years of school, becoming more of a brother than just a friend to me. After school, I went off to college and Micah enlisted and became a Navy SEAL. I haven't seen him in three years, but he showed up at Romero's yesterday to let me know that he has retired from the military and is moving back home. We went out to celebrate and that's why we were at the club together. Micah is the best friend I've ever had and I can't imagine my life without him." He leaned towards me to brush his lips against mine and I sank against him in relief.

"So, you never experimented together?" I teased him.

He smiled against my lips and slid his hands down to cup my ass and pull me closer, brushing our erections together deliciously. "Not once. We've never seen each other that way, but I'd be more than happy to experiment with *you*." He sealed his mouth over mine in a heated kiss.

We made out for several minutes until I pulled back and looked at him. "I have another question…"

He sighed. "You have nothing to worry about, I promise." He trailed kisses down the side of my neck.

I laughed as he hit a ticklish spot. "I believe you, this is about something else. I wanted to ask if you would spend Easter with me and my family." I rushed on, afraid of his refusal. "We spend the whole weekend at my parents' cabin in Tennessee and all of my aunts, uncles, and cousins as well as my grandparents, come as a sort of family reunion and there's games and tons of food and…"

He placed his hand behind my neck and pulled me forward, silencing me with a kiss. "I would love to spend Easter with you, thank you for asking me." He answered simply.

I squealed and threw my arms around his neck, peppering his face with kisses. "I'm so excited, thank you." I kissed him one more time. "I better get going so I can get changed before I'm late for work.

My boss can be a real tyrant," I said laughingly, ducking out the front door as he reached for me.

"Maybe he should punish you when you misbehave," he growled in my ear when he caught up to me at the elevator.

"In that case, I'll make sure I'm *very* naughty." He chuckled and kissed me the entire time we rode the elevator down to his car.

CHAPTER
Thirteen

Giovanni

"THANKS AGAIN, LAUREN, I REALLY APPRECIATE YOU handling everything at work so we could get away. Especially this close to the wedding, I know you're crazy busy." I turned out of my parking garage and headed to pick up Caleb at his apartment.

"That's okay, you'll more than make up for it when I'm gone on my honeymoon," she said teasingly.

"Definitely. Call me if there's a problem."

"Will do, G. Don't worry about anything here. Have fun meeting the parents." I growled at her laughter and disconnected the call. She had teased me mercilessly about this being a "meet the folks" week-end and I guess in a way it was, but I assured her over and over that what Caleb and I had wasn't anything serious. The problem was that while I had tried to convince her of that, I was having more and more trouble convincing myself.

Being a logical thinker, I listed the facts in my head as I drove. 1) I liked spending time with Caleb. When I was around him, I laughed more and felt more at peace than I had in ages. I couldn't wait to go in to work to see his smiling face and I dreaded his days off because they tended to drag by slowly. 2) The sex between us was hands down the best sex of my entire life. 3) I no longer wanted to go to clubs in search of anyone else. As a matter of fact, I didn't even get the slightest bit aroused by men that I would have found sexy before I met Caleb. 4) The thought of him being with anyone else made me want to actually hurt someone. 5) I honestly cared about him and his happiness.

When he told me he loved me, my first instinct had been to run, I didn't want to experience the kind of pain I had felt when Juliana left me ever again. I had guarded my heart for years, never getting too close to anyone, never leaving myself vulnerable. Yet, somehow this man had found a way in and he seemed to have set up camp in my heart. As he always did, he picked up on my nervousness and assured me that he was okay with me not saying the words back to him, even though I knew he deserved better. I cared about him more with each passing day and I had finally begun to trust him, but I just wasn't quite ready to take the plunge into another relationship yet. Huh, that was the first time I had ever thought that sentence to myself with the word *yet* at the end. I was shocked to discover that I wasn't completely closed off to the idea any more. Apparently, I was changing.

I pulled up to the curb just as the reason for that change stepped out the front door of his apartment and walked towards me, his suitcase dragging behind him. A smile lit both of our faces as I jumped out of the car and grabbed his suitcase out of his hand and placed it next to mine in the trunk of my car before climbing into the driver's seat.

Instead of pulling away from the curb, I turned to him and pulled him close, kissing him slowly and thoroughly, soaking in his clean, citrusy smell. My heart rejoiced at having him near. *Why did I always feel most at home when I was in his arms?*

"Are you ready to go?"

"The real question is, are *you* ready?" He laughed. "My family can be a bit much to take when they're all together."

"I'm sure they're not that bad." I assured him as I pulled away from the curb.

"Okay, let me put this in perspective, the last time I saw my dad he was telling me about how reading *Fifty Shades of Grey* really amped things up between he and my mom in the bedroom."

I glanced over at him, trying to tell if he was really serious or not and began laughing when I saw him shudder repulsively at the memory. "That's classic. By the way, I love how you wait until we're in the car, on our way to meet them, before telling me that so there's no way I can back out."

"Would you have backed out if I had told you earlier?" He arched his brow at me.

"Not a chance." He smiled at me and I reached over to take his hand, threading my fingers through his. He sighed contentedly and settled in for the long drive.

Several hours later, we turned onto a long winding driveway that led to a beautiful, three story log cabin with a huge deck on it and large windows that allowed a panoramic view of the breathtaking landscape that surrounded the house. New spring flowers were just beginning to pop up from the well-tended garden at the front of the house, welcoming its visitors with a rainbow of colors.

We stepped out of the car and I quickly removed my jacket, breathing in the clean mountain air. It was a beautiful spring day and much warmer in Tennessee than Chicago. I opened the trunk and grabbed both of our suitcases as we heard a shriek and a woman I assumed was Caleb's mom began running out of the house to greet us.

He let out a tiny yelp, followed by a laugh as she grabbed him in a fierce hug. He wrapped his arms around her, returning the hug and kissing her cheek. "Hey, Mom, I've missed you so much."

"Oh, baby, I've missed you too. I'm so happy you could come." She looked at him with complete adoration and I felt my heart give a little squeeze in my chest as memories of my mama looking at me the exact same way floated to the surface.

"Mom, I want you to meet someone. This is Giovanni Romero, he's my friend and my boss at the restaurant."

I extended my hand to her. "It's a pleasure to meet you, ma'am. Thank you so much for having me here this weekend."

"We don't stand on formality here, sweetie, you can call me Kathy or Mom since everyone else around here does, it's the only way you'll get me to answer. We are thrilled to have you, the more the merrier I always say." She swatted my hand away and wrapped her arms around me in a sweet hug. I hugged her back gently, feeling instantly comfortable around her and glanced over the top of her head to see Caleb smiling, his emerald eyes sparkling in the sunlight.

"Come on in the house, everyone else is already here."

"Everyone?" I must have looked as nervous as I felt because Kathy quickly reassured me that it was just the immediate family. All of the extended family wouldn't arrive until Sunday morning.

We walked into the cabin and I looked around at the vaulted ceilings and living room that held several love seats and comfortable chairs, along with an enormous stone fireplace. Music and laughter drifted up from somewhere and Kathy led us down a flight of steps into a basement. We walked through a cozy home theater before entering a hallway which opened up into a large game room complete with pool and air hockey tables, poker tables, and the kind of old school, stand up arcade games I hadn't seen in years.

"Squirt's here!" someone shouted and we were immediately surrounded by Caleb's family who all talked over one another as they took turns kissing and hugging him affectionately. Finally, Caleb stepped over to me so he could make introductions.

"Everyone, I'd like you to meet my friend Giovanni Romero. Gio, this is my dad Rick, my sister Michelle and her husband, Jason, my other sister Emma and her husband, Mark, my older brother Landon, and of course, Carter." I shook hands with each of them as we were introduced until I got to Carter and froze as I felt my face flush with embarrassment.

"We've already had the pleasure of meeting," he said waggling his eyebrows at me deviously.

"Carter," Caleb growled out a warning, but Carter just laughed as he quickly explained what had happened at the club that night.

"I'm really sorry about that..." I started but was interrupted by Caleb's mom who scolded Carter for embarrassing me. She wrapped her arm around my waist and steered me over to a chair and sat me down. Caleb sat down next to me and everyone else settled around us.

"Everyone has always mixed the two of them up, even their closest friends and family." Caleb's sister Emma told me sweetly.

"They liked to take advantage of it in school," Landon interjected with a wry smile. "I don't know how many classes they switched on test days."

"Hey, he was better at math than me, it just made sense," Carter jumped in.

"And there was no way I would have passed music composition without him," Caleb agreed.

"There's only one way to tell them apart," Caleb's dad spoke up. "The scar on the back of Caleb's head, where he split it open and had to have seven staples put in to close it back up."

I turned to look at Caleb and reached over, rubbing the back of his head. I frowned as I felt the raised scar along his scalp. I felt my stomach roll at the thought of him being in pain. He looked at me with a soft smile and I realized what I had been doing and quickly removed my hand folding it into my lap. I looked up to find Kathy studying me thoughtfully before she gave me a small wink.

The doorbell rang, announcing the pizza delivery and everyone scrambled out of their seats to go eat. Caleb and I stood as Carter walked over to us. "Hey, sorry about giving you a hard time earlier."

"It's fine, I knew you were just teasing and I can take it," I said with a smile.

"I'm glad you're here, seeing you two together makes me feel like smiling," he said the last word in a singsong voice.

I chuckled and Caleb groaned, his face turning a bright shade of red as Carter referred to the smiley face condom he had given Caleb. "That's right," I drawled, "I have *you* to thank for that don't I?" I smiled widely as Carter and I shared a fist bump.

"Why do I get the feeling that it would be best to keep you two apart?" Caleb asked as he took my hand and dragged me to get some food. I could hear Carter's laughter following us up the stairs.

After dinner, we all settled in the living room where Caleb's dad started a fire to ward off the chill of the cool spring evening. It was warm and cozy as we all snuggled into the comfortable love seats. Caleb sat next to me and reached for my hand that was laying in my lap, threading our fingers together. I glanced around to see what reactions there might be from his family, but it seemed no one had noticed except for Caleb's sister Michelle who smiled at me. Caleb had told me that his family was very supportive of him and his two brothers, who were also gay, but I had seen many people who reacted differently when actually faced with public displays of affection between two people of the same gender. That didn't seem like it was going to be an issue with Caleb's family and I relaxed some of the tension in my shoulders that I hadn't even realized I'd been holding in.

I watched Caleb's family interact with each other as they told countless tales about their childhood and teased each other in ways only the people who had known you throughout your entire life could. I laughed when they told the story about how a thirteen-year-old Caleb threw up all over their guide when they went white water rafting. "I couldn't help it," he groaned at the memory. "I don't do well with bumping up and down like that."

As his family moved on to tell an equally embarrassing story about Emma, I leaned over to whisper in Caleb's ear. "You must have outgrown it, because you do just fine with bumping up and down on my cock." He turned a lovely shade of red as a tremor went down his body and I had to fight the urge to grab him by the hand and drag him off to the nearest bed. I glanced over to find Carter watching us with a wide grin on his face. I'd have to learn to be a lot subtler, the guy clearly missed nothing and loved to use it to tease his siblings mercilessly.

I yawned unexpectedly and apologized as I checked my watch, surprised to see that we had been talking for a couple of hours. I felt so at ease around Caleb's family and had enjoyed hearing their stories so much, that the time had just flown by. However, after the long drive and sitting by the cozy fire, I found myself suddenly exhausted.

"Oh, you must be so tired after your long drive. Let's all get to bed. We have a lot to do tomorrow if we want to be ready for the rest of the family to get here on Sunday." Kathy stood and patted my arm.

Everyone helped straighten up, refolding the throw blankets and placing them on the backs of the couches and discarding their plastic cups as Landon snuffed out the last bit of the smoldering fire. Rick checked to make sure the doors were all locked and I went to the front hallway to retrieve the luggage we had left there when we arrived. Caleb tried to take his bag from me and I was rewarded with his dimples as he smiled at me when I insisted on carrying his.

He led us up to the second story where there were six bedrooms and three bathrooms. We continued on to the third story which contained five more bedrooms and two bathrooms. The shock must have shown on my face because Caleb chuckled. "My grandfather was a genius when it came to investing his money, especially when it came to both oil and railroad companies. He became extremely wealthy and when he died, everything was divided between my mother and her two sisters." He shrugged his shoulder easily as he led us into what I assumed would be our bedroom. It was decorated in the same rustic, cedar furniture that had been used throughout the cabin, giving the place a rich, woodsy smell.

We quickly put our clothes away to try to prevent any further wrinkling and I slid our empty luggage into the closet. I went into the bathroom where I quickly washed my face and brushed my teeth. While Caleb took his turn in the bathroom, I took off my clothes, leaving only my boxer briefs on. I folded my clothes neatly and placed them on a chair by the window. I stood, looking out the large picture window at the expansive backyard and the woods beyond, with what appeared to be a narrow stream running along the property. The moon was full, casting a beautiful, ethereal glow on everything it touched.

I breathed deeply as my thoughts swirled in my head. I couldn't remember the last time I had felt so at peace, not just because of the beautiful surroundings or Caleb's loving family, but because of Caleb himself. Caleb Greene was easily the finest man I had ever met. He was funny, kind, smart, talented, and fucking sexy as hell. Perhaps Lauren and Micah were right and it was time to open my heart up again. It was obvious that Caleb had been raised by two loving, committed parents who had shown their children what a good marriage looked like, much like my own parents. It was very different from Juliana's parents who had spent many years fighting and cheating on each other before ending their marriage with a bitter divorce. Maybe Caleb, unlike Juliana, would know how to stay and work through relationship problems rather than bailing at the first sign of trouble. I was beginning to believe that if there was ever another person that I could trust my heart with, it would be Caleb, but there was still a part of me that was afraid to take that step; afraid of getting hurt again.

Feeling cold from standing in nothing but my boxer briefs, I scrambled to the bed and slid in between the sheets. I was just beginning to warm up and my eyes were getting very heavy when Caleb came back in the room and began taking his clothes off, folding them neatly before setting them aside. I forced my eyes open so I could enjoy the sight of his beautiful body and flawless skin as it was exposed to me.

He grinned shyly when he caught me staring and he hurried to turn off the light and climbed into the bed, making me jump when his ice cold toes grazed my leg. "Sorry, baby," he said curling up against me to gain warmth and my stomach fluttered at the endearment.

"Thank you for bringing me here. Your family is amazing." I turned on my side facing him and captured his lips with my own.

What started out as a quick kiss, soon turned very heated and Caleb rolled me onto my back as our tongues dueled with each other. I dropped my head back on the pillow with a sigh as he slid down my body, leaving warm, wet kisses along the way. He nipped at my hip bones and licked a path along the muscles above my groin. I needed to feel his mouth on me so I slid my fingers into his hair, gently guiding his head down lower. The little tease chuckled and I felt his hot breath ghost across my cock, through the thin layer of fabric covering my groin.

He looked up at me, the moonlight shining through the window making his features clearly visible and I was suddenly held captive by his beautiful green eyes. We stared at each other for what seemed like a long time and I saw such a mixture of love and trust and happiness in his gaze, that I had to close my eyes against the unexpected surge of emotions that crashed over me. I wanted to tell him how I felt about him; how important he had become in my life.

Caleb lowered his head and began tonguing my shaft through the fabric of my boxer briefs, leaving it wet and incredibly hot and forcing all coherent thoughts aside. I lifted my hips, allowing him to slide the underwear down over my legs and toss them carelessly over his shoulder. He leaned back down and nuzzled his cheek against my cock then buried his nose into my groin, breathing deeply. He licked at the tender skin where my hip met my groin before sucking on it, hard. I knew what the gesture meant, he was marking me as *his*. I found myself wanting to do the same, to claim him as my own, but I couldn't make myself do it yet.

I groaned loudly as he took my cock into his mouth and he reached up to cover my mouth with his hand so I wouldn't wake everyone in the house. I nodded to let him know I understood and he removed his hand as he picked up the pace on my cock, sucking hard on the tip before he swiftly took me the rest of the way down his throat. I reached down and placed one hand on the back of his head while the other slid under his neck to feel the smooth skin of his throat. I could feel the movement against my hand as his throat worked its way down my cock and I saw stars when he swallowed hard around me.

Caleb moaned around my cock and I glanced down to see him up on his knees, his hand working his own cock at a furious pace. It was the hottest thing I think I had ever seen and I couldn't hold back my orgasm any longer. As my body jackknifed up off the bed, I clenched my teeth to ward of the scream that threatened to burst from my chest and came hard in my lover's mouth. My hand, still against his throat, felt him swallow over and over as he took my huge load. He pressed his mouth against my hip as he followed me, his seed spilling into his hand.

When his orgasm had subsided, he finished licking every inch of my sensitive cock until it was clean. Standing up, he leaned over the bed to kiss my lips, his tongue swept in my mouth and I could taste the slightly bitter taste of my cum that lingered there. He stood back up and started to retreat, but I grabbed his hand before he could escape and pulled it towards me, sucking his fingers slowly, each in turn, before licking at his palm to clean the remaining cum off of it. Caleb's cum tasted so good, as sweet as the man himself; much like the man, after one taste, I found myself addicted. His eyes were half-lidded and had turned a dark, hunter green with his arousal. I finally released him to go to the bathroom and clean up, chuckling to myself as he stumbled to the door on shaky legs.

I was already half asleep by the time he climbed back into bed and snuggled up against me, kissing my shoulder tenderly. "Night, sweetheart," I murmured sleepily and drifted off with a smile on my face as I heard his words.

"Goodnight, Gio. I love you."

The next day was a whirlwind of activity as everyone was assigned jobs to help get things ready for the arrival of the rest of Caleb's family, or as they lovingly referred to it, *the invasion*. Emma, Michelle, and their husbands went outside to set up the games while Rick and his three sons made sure all of the extra bedrooms were set up with clean towels and fresh sheets. I helped Kathy in the kitchen, preparing the Easter feast that the entire family would enjoy the next day. I was surprised that Caleb hadn't been assigned to cook with us, but I suspected that Kathy had some things on her mind that she would like to discuss with me privately.

I was placing pineapple rings on top of a ham as Kathy stood on the other side of the island counter, slicing potatoes for scalloped potatoes. I caught her glancing at me a few times with questions in her eyes. "Is there something on your mind, Kathy?"

She looked a bit embarrassed. "I'm sorry, Giovanni, its none of my business."

"You can ask me anything you want and I'll do my best to answer."

"It's just that, well, Caleb mentioned that you were divorced…"

"Yes, for a little over three years now." Before I knew it, I had told her the entire story. She came over and placed her hands over mine with a look of concern in her eyes.

"You poor boy." She placed her hand lovingly on my cheek. "I'm so sorry you were hurt, dear, but…"

"What?" I prodded.

"I can tell you are a fine young man with ambition and integrity. It's easy to see why Caleb is so crazy about you, but you have to understand that I'm a mother and I worry about my baby getting his heart broken." She held her hand up to stop me from saying anything before she continued. "I know you've been hurt, badly. It's also very clear to me how much you care about my son. Please promise me that you'll be careful with him. Caleb has never been one to do things halfway, that's why I know that when he falls in love, he'll hand over his heart and never look back. So, please be careful with him, because I know he'll be careful with you."

"Believe me, the last thing I ever want to do is hurt Caleb. I care about him very much," I assured her quietly.

"Thank you, Giovanni." She hugged me tightly and kissed my check. I found myself liking Kathy Greene even more as I saw what a protective, loving mother she was. She reminded me so much of my own mother, especially as we moved around the kitchen, cooking together.

We had just finished up and Kathy was explaining to me how much she was looking forward to having grandbabies when Caleb walked into the kitchen. "Mom!" He groaned. "Please, leave Gio alone."

"I don't know what you're talking about," she said, feigning innocence as she wiped down the counters.

We chuckled as Caleb took my hand. "Come with me, we have twelve dozen eggs to color."

CHAPTER
Fourteen

Caleb

I GROANED LOUDLY AS GIOVANNI SLID HIS LONG, THICK COCK into my greedy hole. I grasped the edge of the table as he pegged my prostate expertly and I bit down on a cloth napkin as a scream built in my throat from the pure ecstasy he was bringing to my body. The table rocked back and forth with his hard thrusts and a water glass toppled off the side, smashing as it hit the hardwood floor. I could feel my orgasm building as he continued to stretch me wide with his large shaft. "Oh God, Oh God, Oh God!" I chanted as fire raced through my spine. I heard clapping and looked around to see all of the customers had quit eating and were now giving us a standing ovation.

I jolted awake with a loud gasp. My heart raced as my eyes darted around the still dark room, trying to get my bearings. I took a deep breath as it all came back to me: I was in my room at the cabin, my head laid on Giovanni's warm chest and my leg was thrown over his body possessively. I had been dreaming that he was fucking me in the middle of Romero's' very full dining room. *WTF? Where had that even come from?* I had never been an exhibitionist, that was more Carter's style than my own. I guess Giovanni had woken up my primal side more than I realized.

I lay there, listening to his heartbeat and his even breathing. My rock hard cock twitched as it begged for me to finish what my dream had started. I tilted my head as I listened for the sounds of anyone moving around in the house. Hearing nothing but silence, I slid my body slowly until I was over him, straddling his narrow hips. His eyes fluttered open and he grinned up at me with a sleepy smile.

"Morning," he whispered, his voice raspy with sleep.

"Morning, baby, this is your wake up call." I smiled at him seductively as I rocked my hips back and forth. We both gasped as his morning erection slid up and down my crease while my cock began seeking friction against his body, leaving a wet trail of pre-cum across his rippled abs.

I leaned down to kiss his welcoming lips and he wrapped his arms around me as he held me close. "Someone woke up happy," he murmured against my lips. "Did you have sweet dreams?" I felt myself blush furiously and he tilted his head back against the pillow as he eyed me curiously. "You did, didn't you? Care to share with the class?" he teased.

"No!" I said a little too forcefully and buried my head in the crook of his neck to hide my embarrassment.

He pushed me back gently until he could see my face, his look serious. "I'll let this go because I can tell you're uncomfortable, but, Caleb, I want you to know there is absolutely nothing you could ever say to me that would make me think less of you. No fantasy I wouldn't happily try to fulfill."

Unbelievably turned on by his words, I simply nodded my head.

"We should probably take a shower soon before everyone wakes up and uses all the hot water." I glanced out the window as the first few rays of sunlight started to peek over the mountains in the distance, bathing the earth in beautiful pinks and oranges.

"Okay, but with this many people in the house the hot water won't last long. It would probably be best if we showered together to conserve water." He looked at me innocently before capturing my mouth with his in a lingering kiss.

I leaned back to look him in the eyes with mock seriousness and laid my hand flat against my chest. "It is so amazing how selfless you are, putting my family's hot water needs before your own like that. Simply amazing," I finished, shaking my head back and forth.

"What can I say, I'm a nice guy," he smirked at me.

"You, sir, are a prince among men," I said with a laugh as we scrambled out of bed and grabbed fresh clothes and a toiletry bag.

We sneaked quietly down the hall, so as not to wake anyone and locked the bathroom door behind us. After we brushed our teeth, I turned the shower on and placed my hand under the running water as it heated up. Giovanni came up behind me and wrapped his arms around me, pulling my back against his firm chest. I sighed contentedly and leaned my head back against his shoulder. He cupped my jaw and turned my head so that he could claim my mouth. His fingertips skimmed over my chest and landed on my nipples. I gasped loudly when he pinched both of my nipples between his strong fingers and my knees turned to jelly. I turned in his arms and smiled wickedly as I wrapped my fingers around his thick cock, using it to tug him gently until he followed me into the shower.

My eyes followed the hot water as it flowed down his broad chest and it made my mouth water. This man, *my man*, was exquisite. Giovanni poured soap into one hand then wrapped one strong arm around my waist as his other snaked between us until he gripped both of our cocks in his large, soapy hand.

I looked up at him, his eyes had turned a dark blue with his arousal, his lips were swollen from our kisses, and a sexy stubble lined his jaw. "This is going to be quick and rough, but you have to stay quiet, are you ready?" I almost came from his words alone, but then he tightened his grip and began jacking our cocks together.

He held me tight and I was captured in his unwavering gaze as he began moving his hand at a punishing pace, twisting his wrist when he reached the tips of our dicks. Other than the running water, the only sounds in the room were the erotic squishing of the soap as it squeezed through his fist and our ragged gasps as we held our mouths open, breathing each other in and out. I watched a kaleidoscope of emotions flicker through his eyes and I hoped he could read all the love I held for him in mine.

I reached up and held onto his thick biceps, steadying myself as my legs shook beneath me, threatening to make me fall. I felt my orgasm as it quickly approached and could tell he was nearing the end by the sounds of his labored breathing and his pupils, which had blown wide in his gaze.

His hand slipped from my waist and searched for something behind me. It must have been soap because his slicked finger slid down my crease and found my puckered hole, thrusting inside. My eyes widened in surprise, but I was soon overwhelmed as he found my prostate and rubbed it repeatedly with his fingertip.

"Gio," I gasped and he closed his mouth over mine, swallowing my cries as my orgasm threatened to crush me under its ferocity. His orgasm hit on the heels of mine and I drank his moans in. When he was finished, he leaned back against the tiled wall, taking me with him. We held each other as our heart rates began to slow and our breathing evened out.

I nuzzled my nose along his chest, the light hairs there tickled my face. I kissed his neck and then reached for the soap on the shelf behind me. I held his gaze as I lathered the soap in my hands and began to gently wash his body. I used my hands to care for him, to show him what he meant to me, and I could see the understanding and the wonder in his eyes. When I was finished, he washed my body with the same tenderness I had shown him and I was thankful that the water hid the tears in my eyes. I loved this man so much that my heart ached.

As we toweled ourselves dry we looked at each other, smiling. "That was amazing," I whispered, stepping forward to kiss his lips.

"You were amazing." He swatted my ass as he turned to walk out.

We opened the door quietly, but found Landon, Emma, Michelle, and Carter each leaning against the hallway wall grinning widely at us. I turned as red as a tomato and Giovanni covered his face with his hands as they simultaneously began laughing and applauding us. My embarrassment increased as I saw my parents step into the hallway. They looked at each of us as my siblings tried to get their laughter under control.

"What did we miss?" Dad asked in amusement.

"Oh, nothing much," Emma said between fits of laughter.

"Just Caleb sneaking out of the bathroom," Michelle clutched her stomach as tears streamed down her face.

"With his boyfriend," Landon finished, starting off another round of laughter among the four of them.

I should have been more concerned about Giovanni's reaction to Landon's use of the word *boyfriend,* but I had more important things on my mind, such as wishing the ground would open up and swallow me.

My parents started laughing and Dad threw his arm around Mom. "What's the big deal?"

"You kids think your dad and I haven't 'conserved water' many times throughout the years?" Mom waggled her eyebrows at us as she used her fingers to make quotations around the words *conserved water.*

"As a matter of fact…." Dad continued, but his words were drowned out by the sounds of the other six adults in the hallway screaming and slamming doors as we escaped to our rooms.

We had all just finished a simple breakfast of toast and coffee when the doorbell rang. Dad answered it to a chorus of excited voices, as the rest of my family swarmed into the house. Michelle snickered at Giovanni's wide eyed expression. "The invasion has begun."

After all of the hugging and introductions were over, we headed out to the backyard to start the egg hunt for the excited children. I had twelve little cousins who all rushed to gather up a basket off of the picnic table so they could begin searching for eggs. My cousin Cindy's youngest, a tiny blonde haired girl named Mia reached up, standing on her little tiptoes as she tried to grab a basket. She scurried around the table, climbing up on the bench, but just as she was about to reach the basket, she slipped and started to fall.

Before anyone else could react, Giovanni lunged forward and scooped the girl up into his arms, keeping her from falling. He set her on her feet in the grass and handed her the basket. I watched as he knelt down and whispered something to her. Her face lit up with a smile and she grabbed his hand, pulling him out to the yard with her.

A half hour later the eggs had all been found and the children gathered together and counted their bounty to see who had found the most eggs. Giovanni helped Mia count her eggs and then stood and walked over to me with a smile on his face.

"Not too bad, fifteen eggs," he boasted proudly.

"Maybe next year I'll get you your own basket," I teased.

"Yesss!!!" He pumped his fist in the air.

I laughed and he stared down at me with a strange look on his face. "What?" I asked, feeling suddenly self-conscious.

"Those damned dimples," he growled and just that quickly, I wanted to drag him back to our room and lick every single inch of him.

He chuckled when he saw the effect his words had on me. I didn't want to pop a boner in front of my entire family so I tried to get control of myself by thinking of Pierre, a chef I had studied under in France who was a genius in the kitchen, but had never mastered personal hygiene.

Luckily, it worked and my erection soon dwindled in the nick of time because my Aunt Sheila walked up to us at that moment. I had always adored her and was happy to get to introduce her to Giovanni. Aunt Sheila was a loud, boisterous woman with a great sense of humor. She often had no filter and said whatever came to mind without thinking first, but she was never vicious or cruel.

"Caleb, sweetheart, I barely got to meet this handsome man in all the craziness earlier, I came over because I want to get to know him." She winked at Gio as she looped her arm through his.

"Aunt Sheila, this is Giovanni Romero, he owns the restaurant where I'm the head chef."

"Honey, you did good. He's hot!" She side-whispered, loud enough for everyone within three feet to hear and made me blush wildly.

Giovanni chuckled next to me. "Thank you, ma'am, it's a pleasure to meet you."

"Enough with that ma'am stuff, it makes me feel old," she grumbled jokingly. She crossed her arms over her rather large bosom and studied him through narrowed eyes. "Well, I can tell you're smart because you hired my Caleb and you're obviously handsome, but are you a good man?"

"He's the best man I've ever met, Aunt Sheila." I answered sincerely before Giovanni could respond. "He's kind and fair with his staff, treating them like family and he donates the leftover food from the restaurant to a local club for LGBTQ teens. You should see how sweet he was with the kids there and with Mia a little bit ago." I stopped when I realized I was gushing and saw Giovanni with his mouth hanging open, a look of awe on his face. *Did he not know that's how I saw him? That I was completely head over heels for him?*

"That's good to know, Caleb," Aunt Sheila looked at me with a knowing smirk. "It was nice to meet you; I hope we see more of you." Giovanni just nodded, his eyes never leaving mine.

As she walked away I pulled him towards me and slid my arms around his waist. "What are you thinking?"

He stared at me a moment more before clearing his throat. "I just didn't realize…"

"That I really love you?" I whispered.

"People use those words all the time."

"I've never said those words to another man and I take them seriously," I said indignantly.

"I care about you, Caleb, a lot, but that's all I can give you right now," he whispered. I could see the apology in his eyes.

My heart expanded as he opened himself up to me more than he ever had. "That's enough for now. Just promise me you'll let me love you." I raised my hand to cradle his face and he leaned down to kiss me sweetly, our eyes stayed open the whole time. I saw a mixture of tenderness, hope, and fear in his eyes and I swore to myself that I would continue to chip away at his walls until I could climb inside.

The moment was interrupted when we heard Aunt Sheila as she spoke loudly to someone. "Man, I bet they heat that kitchen up in more ways than one." Embarrassed, I hid my face in Giovanni's chest and could feel his laughter rumble through his chest.

"Your family is awesome."

We paired into teams of two to begin the Easter Olympics. It was a tradition I had looked forward to each year where the adults competed against each other in a series of games that were all egg related. The kids got to be the judges and they relished the esteemed position, but they usually found it hard to remain serious once the adults started acting like fools. The winners received a special Easter basket, which usually contained candy and baked goods that my mom had made and the title of reigning champions until the next year. Last year's reigning champions were Carter and Landon who were paired up again this year.

When it was my turn to choose a teammate, I chose Giovanni, of course, and we moved to the side to formulate a strategy.

"All right, soldier," I said, clasping my hands behind my back and pacing back and forth, imitating a military commander and making Giovanni laugh. "This is the situation; you see those two boneheads?" I pointed over to Carter and Landon. "They took something from me last year, something of great value, and I'm determined to get it back. You get what I'm saying?"

"What was it, sir?" Giovanni asked, trying to keep a straight face.

"My pride, son, my pride. Do you know what it does to a man to lose his pride? It ain't pretty. Now hear this, we're gonna go in there and give it all we've got and we will take back my pride, you hear me? Failure is not an option."

"Sir, yes, sir," Giovanni said with a salute. I laughed and grabbed him for a kiss. "God, you're fun," he whispered against my lips and I could feel his smile against my own.

I pinched his butt as I backed away with a wink. "I thought you already knew that," I said flirtatiously.

Just then my Uncle Jim gave out a loud whistle with his fingers in his mouth. "Okay everyone, we're going to start with an egg balance relay. Everyone line up, facing your partner and place a spoon in your mouth. One of you will carry an egg on the spoon and walk carefully over to your partner where you will transfer the egg to your partner's spoon. You will then run back to your starting point and wait for your partner to return the egg to you. If at any point you drop the egg, your team is out. Sound simple enough?"

There were murmurs throughout the group until Uncle Jim

whistled again to regain our attention. "In case any of you thought this would be easy, I forgot to mention one thing that's different this year. At the start of the relay you will lean down, placing your forehead against the baseball bat provided and spin around five times before placing the egg on your spoon." He smiled at all of us with obvious amusement. Everyone groaned and the children laughed in glee at what they knew would be fun to watch.

"Your family's a little cutthroat with their games, aren't they?" Giovanni murmured with a smirk.

I nodded my head and chuckled. "You haven't seen anything yet and I'm pretty sure my brothers cheated their way to a win last year." He raised his eyebrows in surprise.

We decided I would go first since I had the most experience. As the countdown began, I assumed the position, head bent over the baseball bat. When my fourteen-year-old cousin, Tommy, blew his whistle, all of the starters began spinning around our baseball bats. I counted five turns around the bat and then stood, wobbling on my legs as I reached into my pocket, retrieving the egg and spoon. I placed the spoon between my teeth and carefully lay the egg on it. I looked for Giovanni, but he appeared to be spinning in the distance in front of me. He laughed at me as I stumbled towards him, struggling to keep my balance and not drop the egg.

As I moved forward, I was suddenly bumped from behind by Carter who laughed mischievously and warbled a half-hearted apology from around the spoon clamped between his teeth. I was able to keep the egg from falling from my spoon and glared at my brother's attempt at cheating. I turned and concentrated on reaching Giovanni quickly.

When I reached him, he squatted down so we were the same height. I tilted my head slowly, easing the egg from my spoon to his. "Good luck, baby, kick those cheaters' asses." I winked at him before racing back to my starting position which would serve as the finish line.

I reached the end and turned to cheer my man on as he quickly made his way towards me. Landon was right on his heels, but Giovanni reached me about ten seconds before Landon reached Carter, gracefully dropping the egg back onto my spoon. The kids all cheered wildly as Tommy ran over and raised both of our hands as he declared me and Giovanni the winners of that round.

Gio did a little victory dance to everyone's amusement and I smiled at seeing him so carefree and happy. *Was this what he had been like before he had suffered so much loss in his life? Was this the real Giovanni?* I felt myself falling for him even more and I wanted to see him just as happy all the time.

Carter and Landon came over and in mock anger, pointed two fingers towards their eyes and then at us in an "I'm watching you" gesture. We simply laughed and I told them to bring it on.

We lined up for the next game as Uncle Jim explained how it would work. "In this challenge you will make your way through an obstacle course, one partner at a time. You will follow the course on your knees, pushing the egg with only your nose. Your hands will be tied behind your back to prevent cheating." He looked pointedly at Landon and Carter who gazed up innocently while everyone snickered. "Once your partner reaches the end and touches the post you may start your half of the obstacle. The team to reach the post first, wins."

Giovanni offered to go first this time and I helped tie his hands behind his back before he dropped to his knees. I placed an egg on the ground in front of him and at the sound of the whistle, he started hurriedly maneuvering through the obstacles.

"Seeing him all bent over with his hands tied behind his back reminds me of that threesome I had," Carter whispered in my ear.

"Still don't want to know," I said laughingly as I shoved him away from me. He cackled as he went over to get his hands tied for his turn.

My cousin Megan tied my hands for me and I dropped to my

knees behind my egg. I took a moment to enjoy the view of Giovanni's perfect jean-clad ass swaying in the air as he bent over his egg. My mind wandered as I remembered the feel of that smooth, luscious ass flexing in my hands as he thrust into me.

I was jolted out of my fantasy as I heard my name being called. "Come on, Caleb, get your head in the game!" I whipped my head up to see that Giovanni had finished the course and was standing at the post waiting for me. Carter had already begun pushing his egg and I scurried to catch up. Luckily, he got hung up in a hole in the ground and I was able to regain the lead. I placed my hand on the post at almost the same time as Carter and we looked to the judges for a ruling. The kids gathered in a huddle, discussing the outcome before declaring me and Gio the unanimous winners. Giovanni picked me up and swung me around before kissing me thoroughly. I was out of breath by the time he set me back down on my feet. Everyone laughed as I swayed on my feet.

The final challenge was an egg toss where partners stood facing each other and tossed an egg back and forth, taking one step back away from each other with each turn. Giovanni leaned down whispering in my ear. I looked up, catching the mischievous gleam in his eye and smiled widely at him. "I like the way you think, baby."

Everyone lined up as they faced their partners and at the whistle, began to carefully toss their eggs back and forth. Giovanni winked at me then we turned and threw our eggs at Landon and Carter who looked shocked as the yolk dripped from their hair and down their faces. Giovanni and I grabbed our stomachs, laughing hysterically.

Tommy huddled with the other judges before announcing their ruling. "After winning two out of three challenges and creating one heck of a sneak attack, that was really awesome," he added excitedly, "we have decided that Caleb and Giovanni are this year's Reigning Champions of the Easter Olympics."

My family cheered as Landon and Carter shook our hands begrudgingly and I laughed as Giovanni swept me into a huge hug, peppering my face with kisses. "We make a pretty good team, don't we?" I asked.

"Yeah, I'm starting to see that," he murmured. Before we could say anything else, Mom and Aunt Sheila called us all to dinner.

There was plenty of talking and laughter as my family visited with each other and enjoyed the delectable feast my mom and Giovanni had prepared. After several compliments on his culinary skills, he invited everyone to visit Romero's whenever they'd like, for free, stating that if they liked his cooking, they'd be amazed when they tasted mine. I blushed at his praise, but was warmed by his words.

Giovanni was in the middle of a conversation with my brother-in-law Jason, when Mia came over and carefully climbed up on his lap. Giovanni looked up at me in surprise, but then smiled down at the little girl when she handed him a cookie that she had brought over for him. He bent down taking a bite of the offered cookie then he spoke quietly to her as she nodded her head at him seriously. I felt someone squeeze my hand and turned to look at my mom who had caught me staring. She smiled at me gently before turning to speak to my aunt.

After dinner, everyone helped clean up and then Giovanni and I gathered our things to make the trip back to the city since we had to work the next day. We were passed around as everyone took turns hugging us goodbye.

"We put your victory basket in your car," Landon and Carter told Giovanni as they shook hands.

"Thanks for being such good sports," he answered with a chuckle.

"No problem, we don't get mad about stuff like that," Carter assured him.

We finally sank into the seats of the Mustang and sat there for a minute, breathing in the peace and quiet after a whirlwind weekend. Gio leaned back in his seat and turned his head to the side so he could look at me. "Thank you for inviting me here this weekend," he whispered with a gentle smile on his face. "I had forgotten what it was like to be around a mother and father who cared so much."

I swallowed hard as my heart ached for his loss. "They were thrilled to meet you and I was happy to have you here. I'm so glad you came with me." I leaned over the armrest and kissed him sweetly. "I think I may have some competition though," I teased.

"What are you talking about?" Roxie roared to life as he started her up.

"Mia seemed pretty sweet on you, what were you two whispering about all day anyway?"

He barked out a laugh. "I saw that the older kids were going to find all the eggs before she could, so I told her I was close friends with the Easter Bunny and he had told me where he hid the eggs. After that, I was her new best friend, she even shared her cookie with me," he said smugly.

I reached across to weave my fingers with his. "Well, I suppose that's okay, as long as she's the only one you're sharing cookies with."

"Believe me, sweetheart, your cookies are the only cookies I want." He let his voice dip low with meaning.

"Damn right," I answered haughtily then we both started laughing. "Seriously though," I said when we had stopped laughing. "You're very good with kids. Did you ever think about becoming a father?"

He stiffened slightly in his seat before responding. "I always wanted children. I really thought Juliana and I would have kids but, you know…"

"I'm sorry, I didn't mean to bring up anything painful," I said quietly.

"It's okay, you can always ask me anything. It's just a dream I gave up a long time ago."

I squeezed his hand in mine. I wished he would realize that all of his dreams didn't have to die just because he had married someone who clearly didn't deserve his love and devotion. I kept my thoughts to myself however, not wanting to start an argument after our wonderful weekend together.

Several hours later we pulled into the city and he looked over at me. "I'm not ready to let you go yet, will you stay with me tonight?"

"I'd love to," I answered simply, smiling up at him. I didn't ever want to let him go.

As we pulled into his parking garage and wearily climbed out of the car, I heard him start laughing from where he was retrieving our bags from the trunk. He popped his head up to look at me. "Um, Caleb, unless your mom is a very dirty baker we've been pranked by your brothers."

"What do you mean?" I asked as I walked around the car to look inside the trunk. I stared wide eyed at the victory basket my brothers had so graciously put in the car. However, instead of finding the usual sweet treats my mom baked for the basket, it was full of condoms, flavored lubes, and a rather large, black butt plug which, frankly, scared me to death. One look at Giovanni's face had me laughing with him. "Guess we better put some of this to use, huh?"

"Race you upstairs," he said, neither one of us felt very tired anymore.

CHAPTER
Fifteen

Giovanni

THE NEXT MORNING, I WOKE FEELING LIKE I HADN'T IN A LONG time: peaceful, content, happy. I smiled as I remembered the fun I'd had over the weekend. I couldn't remember the last time I had laughed so much or felt so comfortable around people I had just met. It was clear that Caleb's family were very loving and kind people. It was no wonder that Caleb had turned out to be the amazing man he was.

I looked over at him and was surprised to see his eyes open, staring at me with a gentle smile curling his lips. I smiled back. "Good morning, sweetheart."

His smile widened as he crawled over my body. "I love when you call me that," he whispered against my lips.

I tilted my head up to push my lips more firmly against his and his tongue swept inside my mouth, doing a teasing dance with mine. "I think we have enough time for breakfast before we have to get to work. What are you hungry for?"

A naughty look came over his face as he pushed his groin against mine. I groaned loudly and my fingers kneaded the firm globes of his ass, pulling him even closer to me. "I'll grab something at work, I'd rather do this instead."

He reached over and opened the drawer of my night stand, pulled a condom and lube out, and laid them on the bed before kissing me feverishly. Our cocks ground against each other, ratcheting up our need until we were both frenzied and gasping for air. He leaned up on his knees and with shaky fingers, reached for the lube. He poured some on my fingers and then blew a hot breath on them to warm them. "Get me ready."

The command in his voice surprised me, I'd never heard him sound like that and I found myself wanting him to take control, *needing* him to take control. I reached under him as I stared into his eyes and grazed his hole with my fingers. His eyes rolled back in his head as I began to circle my fingers around his sensitive entrance, dipping the tip of one finger in and pulling it back out quickly. He let out a frustrated growl the third time I did this. "Stop teasing and fuck me with your fingers. I want to feel you stretch me," he demanded in a deep voice that had me nearly coming right then. I clamped my jaw to try to hold back my orgasm and slid two fingers in and out of his greedy hole, twisting and scissoring them as I coaxed his body into opening up for me. I added a third and he let out a long, low moan as he began to ride my fingers in earnest. His eyes glazed over and I swore I had never seen anything hotter in my life.

"I need to fuck you, now." He slid down my body, grabbed the condom, and easily ripped it open. He leaned down and used his tongue to swipe a bead of moisture from the slit in my cock and moaned happily at the taste, then he sat up and expertly slid the condom down the length of my shaft. I fought for control as he slicked my cock with the lube and then lifted himself over my body, hovering above me for a moment before lowering himself onto my throbbing cock.

We both groaned in pure ecstasy as I filled him completely and he gripped my cock with his tight, warm walls. He lowered himself until he was fully seated, his ass resting on my groin and he sat still for a moment, allowing his body to adjust to the invasion. He gazed down at me with a look of complete adoration and trust and I knew in that moment that this man owned me, body and soul. Somehow he had broken through all of my defenses and found me. I loved him completely and it scared the shit out of me. He must have seen something in my eyes because a brilliant smile spread across his face and he bent down to kiss me slowly, sweetly: a promise.

He reached for my hands and threaded our fingers together. Using my hands to support himself, he began to ride up and down my cock, circling his hips seductively on the way down each time. I looked down at where we were joined and stared in awe as his body stretched around my cock and he pulled me into his seductive heat over and over. I felt a familiar tingling in my spine and knew I wouldn't last much longer. I looked up to see Caleb as he rode my cock with his head thrown back in complete abandon and my tenuous hold on my control snapped.

I threw my head back into the pillow as I bucked up off the bed, thrusting my cock into him deeply, until my orgasm ripped through me. My body clenched tight and a scream tore from my throat as I filled the condom. I continued thrusting into him, pegging his prostate until he went rigid over me, shouting my name as his cum spurted out of his long cock, coating both of our chests.

Caleb collapsed over me and wrapped his arms around my neck as he struggled to breathe. I pulled him in close and slid my arms around his still shaking body. We held each other for a long time, his body still convulsing around me and my cock still twitching inside him, as the aftershocks of my orgasm subsided.

"I love you more than you'll ever know," I heard him whisper against my neck. I lifted his face, holding his jaw gently in my hand and stared into his eyes, finding nothing but truth. I wanted to say those words back to him, the words I never thought I'd ever say to anyone again, but old fears crept in before the words could form on my tongue. Instead, I kissed him slowly, deeply, hoping my kiss could convey my true feelings to him. "We should get ready for work." He gave me an understanding smile as he rolled off of me to go shower and a new fear built in my chest; *how much longer would he wait for me?*

After showering and stopping at a drive-thru restaurant for a bagel and coffee, I dropped Caleb off at his apartment so he could change into clean clothes and unpack his luggage while I went on to work. When I arrived at the restaurant, Marco was already preparing the kitchen for the day. "Hey, Boss, have a nice Easter?"

"I did, how about you?"

A huge grin spread across his face and he bounced on his heels a bit as he told me, "Amy had the baby, a little boy named Anthony Marco, they named him after me."

"Congratulations, Grandpa!" I smiled at his exuberance.

He stopped and stared at me, his eyes filling with tears. "I'm a grandpa," he whispered in awe as if he was just realizing it for the first time. He nodded his head a few times as another smile took over his face. I had never seen him look so proud.

He folded his body around mine in a big bear hug just as the back door opened and Caleb walked in, arching an eyebrow teasingly at finding me in the arms of another man. I slapped Marco on the back a few times and he released me, turning to swoop a surprised Caleb into his arms. Caleb laughed and hugged him back. "I'm a grandpa, Caleb!"

"Oh, Marco, that's wonderful! I want to hear all about it and you better have pictures."

Marco began describing the big event to Caleb and pulled out his wallet to show off the requested pictures. Lauren walked into the kitchen looking stunning in a pale blue wrap around dress, her smile brightening when she saw me. "G, we missed you around here. Did you have a nice trip?" She kissed my cheek.

"We did," I said with a warm smile as I glanced over, catching Caleb looking at me as he nodded his head at Marco's words. Our gazes held for a minute until I heard Lauren laughing next to me.

"You are such a goner, aren't you?"

I looked at her innocently. "I don't know what you're talking about."

"Oh, come on, it's obvious you're crazy about the guy." She arched a brow, daring me to deny it. I wasn't sure what to say so I just nodded. She hugged me quickly and whispered in my ear, "It's about time, G, you deserve to be happy again." She left to get things ready in the dining area and I headed to my office.

A few hours later, I had finally finished catching up from my days off so I shut down my computer and went out to check on what else needed done for the evening. A thrill went through me when I stepped out of my office and ran into Caleb walking towards me in the quiet hallway. "I was just coming to find you." He looked very serious.

"What's wrong?"

He continued walking, causing me to back up until I hit the wall behind me. "It's been at least three hours since I got to taste your mouth and that is three hours too long." He leaned up, licking at my lips until I opened up to him.

My chuckle turned into a groan as he reached between us and pressed his palm against my groin. A spike of lust surged through me and I turned him quickly until his back was against the wall, making him gasp in surprise. I sucked at his bottom lip, drinking in the taste of him, then trailed my tongue down his jaw. He tilted his head giving me access to his neck. I licked and nibbled my way down to where his neck met his shoulder and sucked hard at the tender flesh, leaving my mark behind. He groaned and I caught him as his legs gave out.

"I love how responsive you are." I licked the soft spot behind his ear. He trembled in my arms and gave a happy sigh as he laid his head against my chest. We stood there for several minutes, content just to hold each other, each of us lost in our own thoughts.

"I better get back to work," he grumbled.

I chuckled at his disappointed expression. "We'll have more time tonight. Come home with me again?"

Seeming happy with my request, he kissed me quickly and pinched my ass. "I'll be looking forward to it, Mr. Romero." With a seductive grin he turned and walked down the hallway, shaking his ass at me before going back into the kitchen. I groaned and reached down to adjust my hard cock in my pants; the next few hours were going to drag by until I could be alone with him again.

I spent the next half hour dragging bottles of alcohol out of the cellar in the basement and restocking the bar with Derek, my bartender. "Thanks, G, I think we're all set now," he said as I placed the last bottle of tequila on the shelf and he wiped down the gleaming counter top.

"Okay then, let me know if you need anything." I clapped him lightly on the shoulder and made my way around the bar to see what else needed attended to.

Soon, the dining area was full of customers and I wandered from table to table, introducing myself and making sure everyone was enjoying their dinner. I spent awhile visiting with Carl and Edna Mitchell, an elderly couple that dined with us frequently and whom I had gotten to know quite well. It warmed my heart to see them eating the manicotti and eggplant parmesan that my mom used to make, but now contained Caleb's own unique twists to them. The changes he had made gave the dishes a fuller, more robust flavor and I knew my mom would have approved. Caleb was a gifted chef and I was very proud of him.

I smiled as I thought to myself how lucky I was, in more ways than one, that he had chosen my restaurant to work in. I shuddered at the thought that he could have very easily chosen any of the other fine restaurants in Chicago and I might not have met him. In the short time I had known Caleb, I found myself looking forward to seeing him every day. He had very quickly become the most important person in my life. Maybe it was time for me to tell him that, I thought nervously. I knew in my heart that I could trust Caleb. He was a good man deep down to his core and he would never hurt me like Juliana had. Now, I just needed to get my brain on board.

As if my thoughts conjured her into existence, I walked around the corner and stopped in my tracks. I blinked a few times to clear my vision, not sure that I was seeing correctly, but I was. Sitting at a small table at the back of the room, near the bar, was my ex-wife. I stood in shock, my feet frozen to the floor, taking in her appearance. Her long blonde hair had been cut into a sleek modern style that framed her jaw, making her seem older and more sophisticated. Her face had a few lines that hadn't been there before, which gave her a serious, almost harsh appearance. She was sitting at the table alone, looking over the menu. Before I could even think about what I was doing, I was walking over to her table.

She glanced up from the menu and did an almost comical double take. Her eyes connected with mine and widened. I could hear her gasp as her hand flew to her throat. Still in shock, I stopped when I reached her table and just stared at her for several long minutes.

It felt like I was numb as I looked into her eyes, questioningly. "Juliana?" I managed breathlessly.

"Giovanni." Her voice wavered as she stood to face me. "I didn't know…I should have realized…so you finally did it." As she stammered, her eyes kept darting over my shoulder and she began wringing her hands nervously. My eyes caught the glint of a diamond on her left ring finger. "You finally opened your own restaurant, I should have realized when I saw the name."

"Where have you been?" I asked stupidly. I had a million questions running through my brain, but that was the only one that made it passed my trembling lips.

She opened her mouth to speak, but was interrupted when a man rushed over and leaned down to kiss her cheek. "Sorry I'm late, darling." I felt like I had been sucker punched as he turned my way and I came face to face with Juliana's best friend, Miles. His face turned white and his mouth opened and closed like a fish. The three of us just stood there staring at each other for several minutes, each caught off guard and struggling to come up with words.

At some point Caleb had stepped into the room and after seeing what was taking place, came over to stand near me. I barely noticed as he laid his hand on my back in a silent show of support. My brain was too busy trying to connect all the dots to notice anything else.

I turned my head quickly to glare at Juliana. "How long have you two been together?" I demanded.

"Let's just calm down, Giovanni." Her eyes darted to Miles, looking very worried.

"How. Long?" I asked again with more force, not caring that other customers were staring.

"Four years," she whispered, looking at the floor.

I wouldn't have thought she could hurt me any more than she already had, so I was surprised when pain shot through me at her admission. We had only been divorced for three years, so they had obviously started their affair while we were still married. An entire year and I had never known it was going on. I had believed her all those nights she had said she just needed time with her *best friend*, never imagining that Miles had become much more to her than that.

"So that's why you left me?" My voice became steadier as anger and betrayal flooded my veins. "You were having an affair and that's why you left me? For *HIM*?" I pointed to Miles whose eyes were bugging out of his head. "So, I guess that's why you never answered my call that night, isn't it, Miles? You already knew right where *my wife* was, didn't you?" I sneered at him in disgust.

Feeling brave, Miles straightened himself and stood in front of me, a snide smirk etched across his weasely face. "That's right. Juliana was with me, right where she wanted to be. With a man who could give her all the things you couldn't."

I stood there with my blood boiling and my hands in tight fists at my sides. I wasn't usually a violent man, but in that moment, I wanted nothing more than to beat Miles' ass. However, a very small part of me remembered that we were in a full restaurant, *my* restaurant, and I needed to retain control of myself.

Caleb suddenly pushed his body between ours, poking his finger into Miles' chest. "Look here, you miserable excuse for a man, Giovanni is the most incredible man anyone could ask for and if she was too *stupid* to notice," he said as he wrinkled his nose up in Juliana's direction, "then she never deserved him in the first place."

Juliana let out a snort and we all turned our heads her way, wondering what she could possibly find funny right now. "I should have known you'd swing the other way once I left; you never could stop all of your queer tendencies." I was surprised by the viciousness in her voice. As I looked at the sneer on her face, I hardly recognized the woman I had married all those years ago. "But really, Giovanni, sleeping with the kitchen help is low, even for you. That's why I needed a *real* man."

My breathing became shallow and the blood swooshed through my ears. I barely heard Caleb as he yelled at them to leave and never come back. I ran out of the room and all the way to my office, slamming the door shut behind me.

I paced the floor of my office. My hands yanked roughly at my hair as I struggled to breathe. I was having trouble processing the fact that my wife had been sneaking around behind my back for the entire last year of our marriage, all while I had been completely oblivious. I had been such a fool.

Juliana's words cut through me like a knife, wounding me, just as she had intended. I had always wondered what I had done wrong and now I knew. It wasn't about what job title I held or how much money I brought home; it was *me*. I simply wasn't good enough.

The door creaked open and Caleb stuck his head in before coming in and closing the door behind him. "Gio." He began slowly walking towards me with his arms stretched out, but I backed away and held my hands out in front of me.

He looked as if he was going to cry as I continued to back away from him and folded my arms across my chest, in a protective manner. I was afraid if I let go, all of the emotions I was trying to hold onto would spill out of me, landing on the floor in a gooey mess and there would be nothing left of me to put back together. I sucked in shallow breaths as I felt the walls closing in on me.

"Talk to me, Giovanni, please?" he pleaded.

I forced myself to take a deep breath and I felt a calming numbness take over my body. "What you saw out there, is why I've sworn off relationships. They cause nothing but misery and heartache and I've had enough of both to last me a lifetime. I don't need or want that any more, it's just not worth the pain." My voice was low with resignation.

"Please, Gio…"

"Did you hear me?" I shouted, getting right in his face. "It's not worth it! You're not worth it!"

Caleb shrank back away from me as if I had slapped him and I should have felt horrible at the stricken look I had placed on his beautiful face or the tears welling up in his eyes, but I couldn't feel anything except an overwhelming numbness and I welcomed it. It was better than the sharp, stabbing pain I had felt from Juliana's vicious words. I turned my back on him and listened as he walked out, the door closing behind him sounded like a gunshot.

I left my office a while later, noting Caleb's absence in the kitchen and ignored Marco and Lauren's sad looks as I headed out the back door.

CHAPTER
Sixteen

Caleb

I STUMBLED INTO MY APARTMENT, UNABLE TO REMEMBER ANY OF the drive home and locked the door behind me with shaky hands. I stumbled down the hallway to my bathroom and turned the shower on as hot as I could stand it. My body had felt cold since I left Giovanni's office. I gasped as just the thought of his name burned through me like a hot coal.

I stripped down and climbed into the shower, shivering as the heated water trickled over my trembling body. I stood there, replaying the scene at the restaurant in my mind and wondering what I could have done differently. I felt my legs give out beneath me and I sank to the floor of the shower as I remembered Giovanni's words to me. "*It's not worth it, you're not worth it.*" I had lost the only man I had ever loved and there was nothing I could do about it. My body slumped as a pain like I had never thought possible ran through me, and the tears I had fought back since leaving the restaurant washed over me like a tsunami that I was powerless to stop. I let it pull me under.

I woke as someone shook me relentlessly and slapped at my face rather hard.

"Stop!" I moaned and barely recognized the sound of my gravelly voice as I swatted at whoever was there, trying to ward off their continued assault.

"Caleb, wake up!" I heard a voice pleading and blinked my eyes, trying to clear my vision. Finally, Carter's face became clear to me. I stared up at him as he hovered over me, but I couldn't understand why he looked so panicked, or why tears streaked down his cheeks.

"Whazz wrong?"

"Oh, thank God," Carter sobbed, leaning his head against my shoulder. "Come with me, come on, that's a good boy." He spoke in soothing tones as he lifted me up to my feet. *Why had I been on my kitchen floor?*

"Whazz goin' on?" I slurred. I swayed on my feet and Carter caught me under my arms and walked me towards the bathroom.

"That's what I want to know," Carter fumed at me. "I've been trying to get ahold of you all day, but you weren't answering your phone. I called down to Romero's and they said they haven't heard from you for *two days!* Then I got here and had to use my key to get in since you wouldn't answer the door, only to find you passed out on the kitchen floor with two empty bottles of vodka lying next to you. What the ever loving fuck, Caleb? I swear, I thought you were dead when I saw you. You aged me about ten years today." He finished his rant as he pulled me into the shower, fully clothed and then followed me in.

The terrible events of my last night at the restaurant came rushing back and I began to cry as the water ran over me. Carter wrapped his arms around me, pulling me close and rubbing a soothing hand in circles over my back. "It'll be okay, everything will be okay." He chanted over and over like a mantra while I sobbed.

I don't know how long we stayed like that, but eventually Carter climbed out of the shower so I could strip down and wash, only after assuring him that I wasn't going to fall. When I was finished, I stepped out of the shower and grabbed a towel off the rack. I moved robotically as I dried off and then grabbed my toothbrush out of its holder. I squirted some toothpaste on it and then looked in the mirror.

Tears filled my eyes as I saw the faded mark on my neck and remembered that last day with Giovanni as he held me pressed against the wall, sucking on my neck passionately. I reached up and rubbed my fingers gently along the love bite. I had been so happy, feeling like I had finally broken through his walls and could reach him. *Had I just imagined the emotions, the tenderness I saw in his eyes as we made love that last morning?* I just felt cold and lonely, an empty shell of who I had been. I swiped at the tears that dripped down my face when Carter knocked at the door.

"You okay, Caleb?" he asked, his voice sounding muffled by the door.

I cleared my throat. "I'm fine, I'll be right out."

I came out of the bathroom and found a worried Carter propped up against the headboard of my bed with a quart of our favorite mint chocolate chip ice cream and two spoons in his hand. He smiled at me gently. "I laid some pajamas out for you." He gestured to the end of the bed.

"Thanks." I gave him a half attempt at a smile and quickly slid into my pajamas and climbed into bed.

I sat there with my brother, my best friend, and laid my head on his shoulder as he handed me a spoon. "You want to talk about it?"

"Not really," I whispered, but before I knew it the words were pouring out of me. I brokenly told Carter everything, even the parts he already knew, starting with how Giovanni and I had met and how he made me feel, all the way through the horrible scene with Juliana at the restaurant. "So that's it, he's done with me. He said I wasn't worth the risk to his heart."

"Oh, Caleb, I'm so sorry. I know how much you love him."

I was so grateful to have my brother there. Many people saw my twin as a player, a jokester, someone who never took life seriously, but I knew him better than anyone else on the planet. I knew that while he loved to have fun, he also felt things deeply which is what made him such an amazing musician. I also knew that if he loved someone, he would go through hell for them. "Thanks for being here, Carter," I whispered.

"I'll always be here when you need me, you know that." And I did know. "How are you going to manage working with him now?" He looked at me carefully.

"I'm not." I heard the sadness in my voice.

"What do you mean? You love that job and you've worked your ass off to get an opportunity like that."

"Well, I doubt it matters now. Giovanni was worried about working with me after the first night we slept together. I'm sure he feels very justified in letting me go after all that's happened. Not to mention, I haven't called or shown up to work for the last two days. Maybe I should just go back to Europe." My heart clenched at the thought of leaving again, but I just didn't see how I could live in the same city as Giovanni and not be a part of his life.

Carter opened his mouth to argue, but seeing the tears filling my eyes, he closed it and helped me slide under the covers. He stayed with me as I cried, until sleep finally took me.

I woke to sunlight streaming through my window and a headache that made my eyes water. I stumbled my way into the bathroom and found some aspirin, leaning my open mouth under the sink faucet to wash it down. I didn't bother to shower or shave before heading into the kitchen. There was no sign of Carter so I assumed he had left already.

I quickly made a cup of coffee and was just about to take a sip when I heard my phone ringing. I couldn't remember where I had left it and was surprised there was still any battery life left. I finally located it in the pockets of the work pants that I had been wearing that night, but the call had ended by the time I got to it. The caller ID showed it had been Mom and I had four other missed calls and three voicemails from her, each sounding more worried than the last. Knowing that if I didn't call her back she would just show up at my apartment, I hurried to call her. As I waited for her to answer someone knocked on my door. I looked through the peephole and slumped my shoulders, sighing loudly, and ended the call.

"There you are!" My mom swept passed me and into my apartment. "Do you have any idea how worried I've been? Why aren't you answering your phone?" She looked at me in exasperation.

"I'm sorry, Mom, I didn't mean to worry you."

She studied me closely and I fought the urge to squirm under her scrutiny. "What's wrong? Something's wrong. Did you and Giovanni break up?" she asked, seeing things in that psychic way that only someone who's your parent is able to.

"Well, we'd have to have actually been together to break up, wouldn't we?" I said with a bitter laugh.

"Oh, sweetie, what happened?" She moved into the kitchen, throwing her jacket on one of the chairs and rummaged around in my cabinet until she found a mug. Pouring herself a cup of coffee, she grabbed some cookies from the cabinet and settled down at the kitchen table.

I sighed as I picked up my forgotten coffee off of the counter and slid into the chair across from her. "He just doesn't feel the same way about me that I do about him." I felt the wound around my heart rip open again as I was forced to rehash the most painful night of my life.

"Now, I know you're wrong about that. I spent quite a bit of time with that young man while we were at the cabin and I saw the way he acted around you, the way he looked at you. Honey, that man is crazy about you."

"You don't understand, Mom. His ex-wife showed up at the restaurant…"

"Oh, so this has to do with that bitch, Juliana?" Mom spit out, rolling her eyes.

My head whipped up in surprise. I had never heard my mom speak badly about anyone else, much less use a curse word. "How do you know about Juliana?"

"Giovanni told me what happened while we were cooking together." She either didn't see or chose to ignore the shocked look on my face. Giovanni was an extremely private man and the fact that he had chosen to tell my mom about one of the most painful events in his past, proved how comfortable he had felt with her.

"I could tell how guarded he had become over the years in order to protect himself and I have to admit, I was worried about him finding it hard to let you in."

"Yeah, I worried about the same thing," I whispered as tears filled my eyes. "I thought we had come so far, but then he saw Juliana and completely shut me out again. He doesn't want me anymore." I slumped in my chair miserably.

Mom got out of her chair and came around to drape herself over my shoulders. "Just because he's shut you out, doesn't mean his feelings for you went away. I know these things because I'm a mother and we know everything."

I chuckled as I leaned my head against hers. "Thanks, Mom."

"He's scared, sweetie, give him some time and he'll come around." She kissed my cheek and stood, ruffling my hair lovingly. "I've got to go, I'm having the family over for dinner tonight, that's why I was trying to get in touch with you." She held up her hand waving off my protest. "I just wanted to invite you, but I understand if you don't want to be around anyone right now. Take some time for yourself, but promise me you'll call one of us if you need anything. You have a whole family that loves you, kiddo." I smiled gratefully at her as she blew me a kiss and walked out.

I sat there for a few minutes, mulling over my mom's words. I wished it could be as simple as she said and that given a little bit of time, Giovanni would come back to me, but I just couldn't see that happening. Unfortunately, I was going to have to learn to live without the other half of my heart.

I took Mom up on her offer to stay home that night. I loved my family and knew they meant well, but I was too emotionally drained to talk about what had happened again. Instead, I pulled on a soft pair of sweats and a worn old t-shirt and sat on the couch with my fourth beer in my hand, listening to sad songs on the radio. I'm not sure anyone understood heartache like Adele. I took a long pull of beer as another song started. I knew I wouldn't be able to continue drinking my troubles away, but I figured I deserved one more night of wallowing before I would have to look into finding a new job. It broke my heart to think of never working with Marco again or seeing Lauren's happy smile, but the thought of facing Giovanni and seeing nothing but indifference on his face caused a stabbing pain up under my ribcage.

I rubbed at the pain in my chest absentmindedly as I took another drink. I set my drink down when I heard my phone ringing from its charger in the other room. I walked in there slowly, expecting it to be Carter checking up on me and was surprised when the screen showed it was Lauren.

Illogical fear rushed through me as I pictured her calling to say something bad had happened to Giovanni and I swiped the screen quickly, answering her call. "Lauren? Is everything all right?"

"I could ask you the same thing," she snapped. "How dare you walk out without even a phone call to let us know you're alive."

"You know why I had to leave." I wandered back into the living room and settled into the couch, pulling a blanket over my lap to ward off the constant chill that seemed to have set up residence in my body ever since that night.

I heard her sigh and when she spoke again her voice was gentler. "I know how shitty everything turned out that night, and I know you're both hurting…"

"Both of us?" I interrupted snidely. "No Lauren, *I'm* hurting, *I'm* the one who put his heart on the line only to get it stomped on. *I'm* the one who's sitting at home drinking, while *he's* probably out at the clubs banging every guy he can find." My voice cut off and a sob tore from my chest at the painful images my words had conjured up.

"Is that what you really think? Let me tell you something, Caleb, I have never seen G happier than he's been since you started working at the restaurant and I have never seen him more devastated than when he left here that night. He finally got the answers he'd been craving for three years as to why Juliana left, only to find out that she had betrayed him in the worst way. Not to mention how she, and that asshat she was with, cut him down and tried to make him feel small. He's scared and he's hurt and when that happens, sometimes we lash out at those closest to us. In this case, that would be you. You are very important to him, Caleb. Not that he hasn't made it miserable for the rest of us to work with him. He's closed himself off in his office every night since and just comes out long enough to bark orders at us, then stomps back in and slams his door. That's why I took tonight off, I had to get out of there or lose my mind." She ended her dramatic rant with a chuckle.

"Thank you, Lauren." I whispered around the lump in my throat.

"I didn't say all that just to make you feel better, I said it because it's the truth. Now, I have something else to say and you better listen." I found myself sitting up straighter at her firm tone. "We're a family at Romero's and that includes you too. Just because we get upset with one person, doesn't mean we get to walk away from everyone else, you understand what I'm saying?"

"Yes, ma'am." I felt a small smile tugging at my lips as I answered her. She'd make one hell of a mother someday.

"Good, now one other thing. I was calling to make sure you were still coming to my wedding, and I'm sure," she added dramatically. "After the talk we just had about being family and not walking away from each other, you wouldn't plan on not showing up for the biggest day of my life. Right?"

I felt a laugh bubble up from my throat. "I wouldn't dream of it, I'll be there."

"Yay, thank you, Caleb!" I heard her kissing me through the phone. "Oh, one more thing. For God's sake, turn off Adele, that woman is so depressing," she ordered before hanging up.

I looked at the phone in my hand as her words ran through my head. While I should have been angry that Giovanni had hurt me, it hurt me more to know that he was in pain. Lauren was right though, she was my friend and I should be there to celebrate her happy day. So, I would go to the wedding to support Lauren, but it just might kill me to see Giovanni again.

CHAPTER
Seventeen

Giovanni

Aᴀfter I spewed my hateful words at Caleb, wounding the gentle man who deserved none of my wrath, I stormed out of Romero's and let the door slam behind me. I climbed into my car and sat there, unmoving, as my head spun. How could things have changed so fast in such a short amount of time? When I had woken up that morning, I had felt happy and for the first time in a long time, I was full of hope. After hurting Caleb, I felt nothing but pain and a bone chilling loneliness.

I had almost convinced myself that I would never see Juliana again and I had gotten to a point where the clawing need to find out why she had left was almost completely gone. I had come so close to throwing caution to the wind and opening myself up to a relationship with Caleb, but seeing Juliana again reminded me of all the reasons

I needed to protect my heart. I still had no idea what I had done to push my wife into the arms of another man, but obviously I wasn't giving her something she needed, so what made me think things would be any different with Caleb? Eventually I would fail him too and he'd leave me for some other man. I had barely survived Juliana leaving, losing a wonderful man like Caleb would surely kill me.

I rubbed at the ache in my chest as I pictured the devastated look on Caleb's face when I told him he wasn't worth it. I heard the lie as it left my mouth, but I was so caught up in my own pain that I was powerless to stop it. The truth was, *I* wasn't worth it. Caleb was a wonderful man and he deserved someone who wasn't broken, someone who knew how to be in a relationship without fucking everything up.

I swiped angrily at the tears streaming down my face and started my car. I needed to get out of there before a well-meaning Lauren or Marco decided to come out and check on me. I knew they had heard everything and I couldn't face the disappointed look in their eyes again tonight. I just wanted to go home, curl up in my bed, and shut out the rest of the world.

I had just put Roxie in reverse when my phone rang. Swiping at it blindly, I answered.

"Giovanni, are you okay, man? You don't sound good."

"Micah?" I choked out. My throat closed up around a knot of emotion at the sound of my best friend's voice. I suddenly didn't want to be alone tonight.

"Where are you at, buddy? I'll come get you." It amazed me that he could tell what I needed, by just hearing my voice.

"I'm in the parking lot at Romero's," I managed to choke out.

"You hang tight, I'll be right there." Micah hung up the phone and I turned the car off. I sat there in the dark, watching as the rain that had been a drizzle soon became a downpour, drowning out the sounds of my sobs in the otherwise quiet car. Everything in me hurt and I wanted to numb the pain.

When Micah pulled up next to me about five minutes later, I

sprinted to his Jeep, quickly folding myself into the passenger seat. He looked at me with concern as I shivered next to him. "Can we go somewhere to get a drink?" I knew he had to have a million questions, but after seeing the pain in my eyes, he simply nodded and pulled out of the parking lot. A few minutes later, Micah parked in the lot of a rundown looking bar and locked his Jeep as we climbed out. The rain had stopped, leaving the blacktop of the parking lot inky and slick from the oils on its surface.

We walked into the bar and Micah told me to go take a seat while he got us some drinks. I found an empty table towards the back of the dark bar and sat down. I had never been here before and I looked around, noticing the antique beer advertising signs hanging on the walls. An old time juke box that was belting out an Eagles classic stood near a small, makeshift dance floor where several couples were swaying together. I assumed it was a gay bar because I had yet to see a woman as I glanced around the room.

My eyes snagged on a man across the room from me. He wore a pair of tight blue jeans and a black t-shirt that was stretched thin across his massive chest. It was hard to tell how tall he was because he was leaning back along the edge of a pool table with a cue stick in one hand and a bottle of beer in the other. He stared at me as he brought the beer to his lips and took a long pull from it. My cock twitched in my pants at the sight of his Adam's apple bobbing in his throat as he swallowed and I pictured how good those lips would look wrapped around my dick.

My heart squeezed painfully as an image of Caleb's sweet face popped into my mind unbidden, but I brushed it off as I reminded myself that it was for the best if I just stuck with random hook ups. I couldn't afford to have emotional attachments in my life. The man smiled at me seductively just as Micah walked over to our table and sat down.

"They're bringing the drinks right over." I nodded at him, but avoided his gaze as he sat there staring at me. Even as kids, Micah had always won every staring contest we had. He had more patience than anyone I knew and could sit patiently until his opponent caved. He knew if he waited long enough, I would eventually tell him what was wrong when I was ready. Tonight he only had to wait until the waiter brought over a tray with two shot glasses, a bowl of lime wedges, a salt shaker, and a bottle of tequila. I quirked my eyebrow at him questioningly.

Micah smirked at me and shrugged his shoulders. "You sounded like you needed something a little stronger than beer tonight."

"Good call. Thanks for coming to get me." My voice sounded scratchy from crying and I quickly did a shot of tequila and then another, wanting to numb the pain that threatened to overwhelm me once again.

"Always," Micah answered simply as he did his own shot before setting the glass down gently on the table and folded his arms across his chest, waiting for me to talk.

"I saw Juliana." I quickly downed another shot and let the warmth of the tequila spread through my body.

Micah's usually unshakable demeanor vanished as his eyes grew wide with shock. "What? Where? Did you talk to her?"

I kicked back my fourth shot of tequila, not bothering with the lime or salt and enjoyed the burn from the drink as it slid down my throat. I set my glass back down and slouched back in my chair before telling him what had happened. Micah's jaw clenched and he made his hands into fists when he heard the pain in my voice as I told him about the year-long affair she had been having with Miles, during our marriage.

"Damn, I'm sorry I missed that." Micah got a gleeful look on his face when I told him how Caleb was kicking them out when I left the room. "Who knew that little guy was such a spitfire?" Pain burned through my chest as I pictured how I'd hurt Caleb. Micah quickly quit laughing when he noticed my pinched expression. "Why do you still look so upset if Juliana just proved what an evil bitch she is and the guy you're crazy about stood up for you? And why isn't Caleb here with you? What am I missing?"

"Because, we ended it. *I* ended it," I corrected.

Looking annoyed, Micah frowned at me. "Talk."

"I've known since the day Juliana left me that I should never be in a relationship ever again. I spent years wondering what I did wrong to make her leave with no explanation and now I know. I wasn't good enough. She needed someone better." I ended the last bit on a slur and was grateful that the alcohol had numbed the burning pain in my chest.

I glanced over at Micah and if I didn't know that he would gladly kill anyone who hurt me, I would have been afraid of the fierce scowl on his face as he glared back at me. "Is that all you got out of that shit? Because what I heard was that the woman you married finally showed what a miserable, cheating bitch she always was and that she never deserved your faithfulness. You're lucky she left when she did and you haven't had to stay married to her for the last three years. Besides that, you're the best man I know. Much better than she deserved." I poured another drink, but Micah put his hand over mine to stop me before I could drink it. "What happened with Caleb?" he asked gently.

"I told him I didn't want to be in a relationship and that it wasn't worth the pain. I told him *he* wasn't worth it," I whispered, shame evident in my voice.

"G,..." Micah shook his head.

"You don't understand, Caleb is the type of guy who was made for relationships, he's honest and faithful and so damn kind and loving. He should find someone who can love him back as fiercely as he loves them." I pleaded with Micah to understand.

"And what about you? What do you deserve?"

"I deserve some fun." I stood and quickly drank down another shot before sauntering over to the sexy man at the pool table, ignoring Micah's pleas for me to not do something I would regret.

"I was wondering if you were ever going to come over here," the man drawled, setting his cue stick down and leaning back against the pool table.

I smirked at him. "I just needed to talk to my friend first."

"And what do you need now?" He arched his brow at me flirtatiously as he tilted his beer bottle to his lips.

I watched as he licked a drop of beer from his bottom lip seductively before I took the bottle from his hand. I held his gaze as I took a drink then set the bottle down on the edge of the pool table. I reached for his hand and walked backwards, stumbling just a bit from the effects of the alcohol as I led him to the dance floor. "Right now, I need to dance with you."

"What's your name, sexy?" he asked.

"No names," I whispered. A cold chill swept through my body at the memory of the last time I said those words to a man.

He smiled at me and I pulled him close as a slow, seductive song came on. He leaned in to nuzzle my neck and I felt my body stiffen at the unfamiliar feel of his scratchy five o'clock shadow as it rubbed against my jawline. He didn't seem to notice because he reached around and grabbed my ass roughly, pulling me close enough to press his erection against my now flaccid cock.

I breathed in his strong, woodsy cologne and it smelled all wrong to my muddled mind. I craved the smell of citrus and sunshine. The alcohol churned in my stomach and I broke out in a sudden sweat.

He leaned in to kiss me, but I turned my head away before his lips could touch my own. "What's up with you, man?" He glared at me, a frown marring his handsome face.

"I'm sorry, this was a mistake." I turned to walk away from him, but he grabbed my arm. I stumbled a bit as I pulled away from him and I felt the tequila burning my throat as it threatened to come back up.

I suddenly felt a firm body pressing up against my back and my eyes widened in surprise. "Okay, baby, you had your fun getting me all worked up. I liked watching you with this hot, sexy piece of man-flesh, but now I want you to take me home and work me over." My eyes widened in shock at Micah as he spoke in a very uncharacter-istically campy voice, his hands running over my chest. "I'm sorry, sweetie." He wiggled his fingers playfully at the other man. "We didn't mean to tease, but you have to light those fires somehow after twelve years together. I'm sure you understand." I stifled a laugh as Micah batted his eye lashes at the man, who rolled his eyes and muttered something about cock teases before walking away.

"Thanks, man," I said around a laugh as the room began to spin around me.

"It's part of my job description." Micah took my hand, leading me through the bar and out the front door.

"Job description?"

Micah put his arm around my shoulder and turned me when I went the wrong direction. "Jeep's over here, buddy, come on."

"What job description?" My words swirled and I blinked heavily, trying to clear the foggy feeling in my brain.

"As your best friend, my job is to always, without fail, be on your side of any argument, that isn't with me of course," Micah answered with a smirk. "I'm also required to show up with a shovel when you need a body buried, and most importantly when you've had way too much to drink, like tonight, it's my job to keep you from doing some-thing I know you would seriously regret the next morning."

We reached his Jeep and he leaned my body against it as he dug in his pocket for his keys. He unlocked it quickly and grabbed my arm to help me into the car. "That's the most beautiful thing I've ever heard." I swooped him into a sloppy hug.

"Okay, buddy, easy now." Micah chuckled as he settled me into the Jeep and went around to climb into the driver's seat. I fumbled with my seat belt and he reached over to buckle me up.

"Micah," I said around a yawn. "I miss Caleb."

"I know you do, buddy, I know you do," he murmured right before I passed out.

I woke the next morning with my head pounding like a bass drum. I groaned in misery as I cracked an eye open but squeezed it shut when the light from my window threatened to burn my retinas. I threw my arm over my eyes to block the sun's rays and lay there for a moment, breathing through clenched teeth as my stomach roiled.

I could only remember bits and pieces of last night. I remembered Micah taking me to a bar and me dancing with a hot guy. "Oh God," I groaned as I searched my memory for what I may have done with the man. A sudden flash of memory showed Micah pulling me away from the man and... acting like we were a couple? *Was that right?* I sighed with relief when I remembered getting into Micah's Jeep. I owed him for taking care of me last night. Everything after that was a complete blur.

When my stomach had quit roiling enough, and I thought it was safe to get out of bed to search for some aspirin, I sat up very slowly and smiled. On my bedside table, I found a glass of water, two aspirin, and a note from Micah that said, "Here's Juliana's current address. Please, go talk to her and get the closure you need so you can move on. I just want to see you happy, you deserve it. If you do this, I won't even make you come over and scrub out the vomit from the front seat of my Jeep." I wrinkled my nose in disgust as I realized I owed Micah for much more than I originally thought.

I swallowed the aspirin gratefully and enjoyed the feel of the cool water as it slid down my parched throat. Gingerly, I made my way to the bathroom where I brushed my teeth and took a long hot shower. Memories of the times I had shared this shower with Caleb crept into my head, unasked, and I let the water rush over my body, washing my tears down the drain. I missed him so much.

I climbed out of the shower and stood in front of the mirror, staring at my reflection. A frown formed on my face as I looked at my usually bright, blue eyes, which now looked dull and held a deep sadness. Maybe Micah was right and I should talk to Juliana. I had waited a long time to get answers from her and Micah had provided the opportunity to get them. I needed this thing with Juliana to be over and done with, for my own sanity. I had already wasted too many years on that woman and it needed to end. Feeling determined, I quickly got dressed, not bothering to shave the scruff on my face, grabbed my keys, and headed out the door.

I parked my car and stood on the sidewalk for a moment, tilting my head back to peer at the giant high rise building in front of me. It was an all glass building with modern architectural slopes and columns and appeared to be at least forty stories high. It looked like Juliana was finally living in the lap of luxury, like she had always wanted. Sunlight streamed through the windows of the vestibule as I walked in and it felt stuffy and overly warm.

"May I help you, sir?" the brunette woman at the front desk asked me. She was twenty-something, thin, and her hair was pulled into a bun so tight it looked painful. Her lips, painted a bright red, pulled back in what I assumed was supposed to be a smile and I caught a glimpse of red lipstick smudged across her perfectly white teeth.

"Yes please, I'm looking for Juliana Romero...um, sorry, I suppose it's Juliana Jacobs now."

I felt my face flush as the woman gave me a hard look. "Is she expecting you?"

I didn't care for her haughty attitude, but I held my tongue since she was my only way in to see Juliana. "No, ma'am, I just decided to drop by."

"I.D please," she huffed, obviously feeling put upon by my mere presence. I handed over my license with a thin smile and watched as she picked up the phone, her entire attitude changing into something much more pleasant as the call went through. "Good afternoon, Mrs. Jacobs. I'm so sorry to bother you, but there's a gentleman here to see you." She listened for a few seconds and glanced down at my license before continuing. "It's a Mr. Giovanni Romero. Yes, ma'am, I understand, thank you very much." I wasn't surprised when her pleasant phone voice disappeared as she spoke to me once again. "The elevators are down the hall and to your right, she's on the thirty-sixth floor, suite 23B." She turned her back on me dismissively before I could say a word.

I rode the elevator up the long flight and wondered to myself how long Juliana had lived here. Had she and Miles recently moved back or had they been right here in the same city as me this whole time?

I stepped out of the elevator and quickly found suite 23B. I stood there for a moment, staring at her door and took a few calming breaths to steady my racing heart before finally knocking. The door swung open and Juliana stood in front of me looking nervous. She wore a red silk button up shirt and a black pencil skirt that showed off her trim waist and long legs. "Would you like to come in?" she asked politely. It seemed so strange to me that this woman, who I once knew so intimately and had planned on spending the rest of my life with, was now nothing more than a stranger to me.

I nodded wordlessly and followed her through a foyer and into a spacious living room. The furniture was very modern, with bright colors and bold designs. Her red stilettos made a clicking noise as she walked across the marble floors to grab a glass of water from a table made out of chrome and glass. "Can I get you something to drink?"

"No, thank you. Is Miles here?" I asked as she gestured for me to sit.

"No, he's at work still." She took the chair across from me and perched on the edge of it, her back perfectly straight.

I took a deep breath and looked down at my clasped hands as I gathered my thoughts. "I need some answers, Juliana."

"I know you do," she whispered as her shoulders sagged in resignation.

"I'm not even sure where to start…"

"I'm so sorry…" we each spoke at the same time.

"Just tell me why, what did I do wrong? Was I not a good enough husband to you?" I whispered.

"Oh, Giovanni, no!" Julianna moved over to sit next to me on the couch and placed her hand over mine, but I quickly recoiled. Just the thought of her touching me made my stomach roil. She looked like I had slapped her, but continued speaking. "It was nothing like that, you were an amazing husband, so kind and attentive. I never should have said those horrible things to you at your restaurant and I regretted them immediately. It's no excuse, but I was so surprised to see you there that I sort of attacked you before you could attack me. The difference is, you would have had every right to attack me, I've treated you so badly."

"Yes, you have!" I shouted. It was her turn to recoil as she heard the venom in my voice. I felt a small measure of satisfaction at finally being able to release some of the anger I had felt for her over the past three years, but I reigned it in, still wanting answers to the questions that had plagued me. "If I was such a great husband then what happened? Why did you have an affair with Miles?"

"You remember what my childhood was like, right? My father was an abusive asshole who couldn't keep a job because he couldn't control his alcoholism. He was nothing but a big joke in our town. My mother was never around because she always had three jobs to try to make ends meet, but we still ended up losing our home and had to move in with my aunt." I nodded, because I had heard the story before. "I promised myself that when I was an adult I would never live like that again. I would always have money so that I would never go through the humiliation of losing my home again. I would have an important job and a place in society so I would never be a joke to anyone. Then, I went to college and the very first week I met you." A small smile graced her lips as she spoke softly. "You were this gorgeous, funny, really sweet guy and I fell in love with you so fast that I barely knew what had happened. For a while, I was able to forget what my childhood had been like and I just enjoyed being in love for the first time in my life. It's important that you know that I really did love you."

There had been a time when those words would have thrilled me, given me hope; instead I felt cold indifference. I sat in stony silence as she continued.

"After a while my old fears started to creep in, especially when you talked about your dreams of owning your own restaurant. I knew you could make a decent living that way, but it would never be a prestigious job. I wanted you to have a career that commanded respect, so I nagged you until you switched to law. I watched you come home from the law office looking more and more unhappy each night and I knew it was all my fault. I loved you, but I was making you miserable because of my own insecurities and you would have given up all of your own dreams for me because you were the most generous, loving man."

"We always talked about having children, did you ever really want that?" I pleaded with my eyes for her to tell me the truth.

She looked at me with a sad smile. "I tried, Giovanni, I really tried. I never wanted kids because I was afraid of being the same kind of parent that I had grown up with, but you wanted them so badly and I figured you were already giving up so much for me that I should give you something."

"We're talking about children, Juliana, not a new tie. Jesus!" I spit out in frustration. It felt like our whole marriage had been a lie. "When did you start fucking your best friend?" I asked coldly.

I strained to hear her answer as she spoke quietly while staring at the floor. "Miles and I worked together at the design firm and we had a lot in common. He honestly was *just* my best friend for a long time. Then he started moving up the ladder and promised me he'd take me with him, and he did. We started collaborating on projects and were soon getting noticed for our design ideas and received several promotions. I was suddenly making really great money, people in our industry respected us, and I was able to travel to places I had only dreamed of before. I finally had the kind of life I promised myself I would have and Miles was a big part of that. One night we were working late and we kissed. The rest just kind of happened." Her eyes pleaded with me to understand, but I could never understand how anyone could betray someone they were supposed to love so horribly.

I laid my head in my hands and ran my fingers through my hair in frustration as I sifted through everything she had told me. "And so you just took off and never looked back. I wasn't even worth saying goodbye to?" My voice shook with my growing anger.

"You were definitely worth it, Giovanni, I just couldn't face the pain I knew I was putting you through. You were a much better man than I deserved, everything that went wrong in our marriage was because of me and I'm sorry for that. I'm so sorry I hurt you."

I levelled my gaze on her, seeing things clearly for the first time since she walked out of my life. "I would have given you everything, Juliana. Your happiness meant more to me than my own, that's why I walked away from my dreams and pursued a career in law instead. It's why I bought you a fancy house and let you decorate it any way you wanted, regardless of my personal tastes. Even after all of that, I wasn't what you wanted. I have spent the last three years torturing myself, trying to figure out what I had done to drive you away. But now, I realize that this was never about *me*, it was always about *you*. Yes, you had a terrible childhood, but you know what, Juliana? *Get over it*! A lot of people have rough childhoods. You should see what some of the kids at the center I volunteer at have gone through, but they don't use it as an excuse to destroy other people. You are an incredibly selfish woman and you almost destroyed me. I built walls around me to protect myself from ever being hurt again, the way you had hurt me. Because of those walls, I pushed away the one person who means the most to me. I lashed out at him because of the hurtful things you had said to me, but I'm not giving you that kind of power any more. You no longer hold *any* power over me because I don't give two fucks about you anymore." I walked towards the door and opened it. I turned back to see her stricken face. "I'm glad I finally got to see you again, because in doing so, you've set me free. Goodbye, Juliana." Without waiting for a response, I shut the door behind me. A feeling of complete calmness and peace washed over me and a wide smile spread over my face.

I left her building, climbed into my car and sat there, replaying our conversation in my mind.

After Juliana filed for divorce, I had been devastated and full of questions. I had lived with those questions for the last three years, using them as an excuse to keep anyone from getting close enough to hurt me. I had tried so hard to give her everything she wanted and to be who she wanted me to be and when she filed for divorce anyway, I had convinced myself that Juliana left because of some flaw she had found in me as a person, that I wasn't a good enough husband to her. Now I realized that the flaw lay within Juliana herself.

She came to me, damaged from a terrible childhood and carried those scars around with her like a cloak. She needed money and prestige to feel secure in her life and I wanted a family and my own restaurant. Simply put, we were two people who wanted different things out of life and therefore should have never gotten married. Looking back with clear eyes, I could see that as hard as I tried to change so that I could become what Juliana needed, I was only losing myself. I could honestly say that I wasn't happy back then. I leaned my head back on my seat and let the truth settle over me.

Three years ago Juliana had left me so suddenly and with no explanation that I was left with self-doubt and bitterness. I had quickly sold the house so that I could start the restaurant and threw myself into my business, telling myself that I didn't need or want anyone in my life…and then Caleb came along.

I started the car and drove to work feeling lighter than I had in a long time. I had gotten the closure I needed from Juliana and finally felt like I could finally let the past go and move on. As I pulled into Romero's and parked Roxie, I felt nerves stirring in my stomach at the prospect of seeing Caleb for the first time since that night. I felt horrible that I had lashed out at him, hurting him so badly. I knew I had probably ruined everything between us beyond repair, but I needed to apologize to him as quickly as possible.

I stepped into the back door and noticed Marco was alone in the kitchen. Checking the time on my watch I noted that it was way past time for Caleb to have started his shift. Marco smiled at me sadly as I moved to the dining area to check and see if Caleb was in there. Lauren saw me pop my head around the corner and shook her head at me. "No word from him, G, sorry."

Anger and self-loathing surged through me. Caleb had always been patient and loving to me and had come to my rescue when I was being attacked by Juliana and Miles. He had welcomed me into his family and opened his heart to me, always being completely honest with me about how he felt. All he wanted was to be allowed to love me, even when I insisted I couldn't love him back; and how did I treat him? I made him feel like garbage and threw his love away, like it meant nothing to me. To top it off, now he obviously didn't feel comfortable coming in to do the job I knew he loved because he'd have to see me.

I broke out in a cold sweat as I wondered if he was already out looking for another job. *What if I never saw him again? What if I had lost the one person that had broken through my walls and made me feel alive again?* As I stomped back to my office and slammed the door behind me, I knew one thing for sure, if I had lost Caleb forever, I had no one to blame but myself.

I spent the next morning with Micah, helping him move furniture into his new apartment. It was the least I could do after vomiting in his Jeep. When we were finally finished, I was exhausted and covered in sweat. I went home and took a long shower, letting the hot water soothe my sore muscles.

An hour later, I arrived at work and went into my office. There was a message on my desk from Lauren saying that she wasn't coming in because she was taking a mental health break. I felt horrible knowing that my bad mood was more than likely the reason she was staying away. She was already under enough pressure with the wedding coming up and I had just added to her stress. I'd have to buy her an extra big wedding present; *perhaps a car or a new house would get me back in her good graces.*

I worked for about an hour on things that couldn't wait and then pushed away from my desk. As much as I would love to hide in my office for another night, with Lauren gone I needed to go out and help. Being around the customers and helping out in the kitchen used to be my favorite parts of the job, but it just didn't hold the same appeal, now that Caleb wasn't here. I let out a long sigh and squared my shoulders, mentally preparing myself for having to fake happiness for the next several hours.

I was making my way through the hallway when I heard a large crash in the kitchen. I hurried in to see if everything was all right, but when I stepped through the doorway I stopped in my tracks.

"Damn, sorry," I heard him mutter and my breath caught in my throat as Caleb stood from where he was cleaning up the bowl full of diced vegetables he had obviously dropped on the floor.

"Are you feeling all right, Caleb? You're acting all nervous and twitchy tonight," Marco asked with concern.

Caleb glanced up and caught me looking at him and quickly spun away from me. Okay, so he obviously wasn't ready to talk to me, but I couldn't help the feeling of hope that swelled in me as I realized that he apparently hadn't quit yet. Maybe it wasn't too late to turn things around.

He looked good, I didn't see any of the dark circles under his eyes or the haunted look that I knew could be seen on my own face. Although Marco was right, he did seem nervous which was understandable; after all, so was I.

Not wanting to make him feel uncomfortable, I moved into the dining area and helped get things set up in there. It was another very busy night and we soon had a full dining room. I wandered around speaking to the patrons and was surprised to find many tables had been waiting a long time for their meals. I went to see what the hold-up was and was amazed by what was happening in my kitchen. Instead of the synchronized precision with which Marco and Caleb usually performed, the room was in complete chaos and resembled a scene from a disaster movie.

Marco's face was red as he rushed around stirring sauces and dicing vegetables, mumbling something under his breath, which I was probably lucky I couldn't hear. Meanwhile, Caleb was standing near the stove with what looked like marinara sauce dripping from his hair as he tried to flip something that was searing in a pan. As I stared wide eyed, the wrist of Caleb's white chef's coat got too close to the stove top and quickly caught fire.

"Caleb!" I screamed as I ran across the room, grabbing him and pulled him over to the sink where I held his arm under running water until the fire was out. Luckily the skin of his arm was unharmed.

We stood there staring at each other for a few long moments and I noticed Caleb looked scared and... a bit guilty? My heart continued to race with adrenaline and I took a few deep calming breaths as I watched him closely. My eyes narrowed and I growled in his ear, "My office, now!" I saw him gulp and his eyes widened slightly before his shoulders slumped and he turned to follow me out of the room.

Before I made it out of the kitchen, Marco rushed over and whispered in my ear. "Boss, you've gotta fix this, I think you broke him." Instead of answering, I simply nodded my head once and led Caleb to my office.

I shut the door and indicated that he should sit. As I moved around to take my seat behind my desk, Caleb let his apology tumble from his mouth. "Boss, I'm sorry. I don't know what's wrong with me, I think I ate some bad fish and it made me kind of woozy so that's why I'm acting all crazy out there. I promise I'll be better in just a few days…hopefully…I'll let you know. Just please, don't fire me yet."

I leaned back in my chair and crossed my arms as I stared at him, unflinchingly for several minutes. He squirmed self-consciously in his seat. "Don't worry, I won't fire you, yet…Carter."

His eyes bugged out and his jaw dropped open. "How did you know?"

I couldn't stop the bark of laughter that escaped my mouth. "Are you serious? Should I list all the ways?"

"Yes, I think you should. Nobody has ever been able to tell us apart except Mom." He stared at me incredulously.

I smirked and raised the fingers of my hand as I counted out the list. "You don't move like Caleb, you don't smell like Caleb, Caleb never calls me Boss, and the tornado that just blew through my kitchen, leaving a wake of destruction, was most certainly not Caleb. He could move around that kitchen and create amazing dishes with his eyes closed."

He tilted his head at me as he studied my face. "Wow," he whispered. "You really love him don't you?"

Instead of answering his question I asked my own, quietly. "How is he?"

Carter pursed his lips, seeming to weigh his answer. "He's a mess. I've never seen him hurting so badly. I could feel his pain and it took my breath away." Seeing my questioning look he explained.

"Sometimes we can feel what the other is feeling, especially if it's a really strong emotion. I guess it's just one of those twin things." He shrugged his shoulder. "I can tell you now, he's never felt like this before. He loves you and his heart is breaking."

I winced at Carter's words, but appreciated his honesty. "I have no excuse for what I said to him. He's the most amazing man I've ever met and he didn't deserve the cruel way I treated him." I stared down at the floor, feeling too ashamed to meet his gaze.

"Then fix it before it's too late, please," Carter pleaded. "You're not the only one who stands to lose him."

"What are you talking about?"

"Caleb thinks maybe he'd be better off moving back to Europe. I can't lose my brother again, he's my best friend."

I rubbed at my chest, suddenly finding it very difficult to draw enough air into my lungs. The thought of never seeing Caleb again caused a searing pain to shoot through me. Even though I hadn't known Carter all that long, it was still shocking to see the usually playful, happy-go-lucky guy acting so distraught. "Do you think he'd listen to me if I tried to talk to him?" My voice sounded weak to my ears.

"What have you got to lose?"

Everything, I thought painfully. "So, why did you do all of this?" I gestured towards his sticky hair and destroyed uniform.

He chuckled slightly and looked a little embarrassed. "I was worried about him losing his job since he hasn't shown up in a few days and I figured, what the hell? I've pretended to be him lots of times before, how hard could it be to do his job?" I raised my eyebrows at him in amusement. "Yeah, yeah," he said laughing at himself. "I guess there's a reason why I live off of cold cereal. That cooking shit is *hard*!"

We both laughed as we finally found the humor in the situation. "You know, Caleb mentioned that you often look for odd jobs to supplement your income in between music gigs. I need a waiter if you're interested."

He looked at me in surprise. "Seriously?"

I nodded my head. "Yes, I am. Just promise me you won't ever step foot in my kitchen again. *Ever*."

"Sure, no problem," he answered through a laugh.

"All right, I better go help Marco scrape the lasagna off the ceiling," I teased.

We stood and headed towards the door, but just before he opened it he spun around to face me. "What does he smell like?"

"Pardon me?" I asked, wrinkling my forehead in confusion.

"You said I don't smell like Caleb, what exactly does he smell like?"

A blush heated my face. "Oranges and sunshine," I murmured quietly, avoiding eye contact.

An amused smirk teased his lips. "Good to know." I was man enough to admit that the mischievous gleam in his eye scared me just a little bit.

As I helped Marco clean up the kitchen and got dinner out to the customers, I sorted through ideas for how to win back the man I was in love with.

CHAPTER
Eighteen

Giovanni

I WOKE THE NEXT MORNING AND STRETCHED OUT IN MY BED. I had slept fitfully, tossing and turning most of the night. I still hadn't come up with how to approach Caleb or what I would say when I finally saw him, but I knew one thing for sure, I would do anything to get him back.

I missed everything about him. I missed his dimples, the sound of his laugh, the feel of his skin. Most of all, I missed how I felt when I was with him: like life was full of possibilities and maybe all of my dreams hadn't died the day Juliana left me. I had spent a lot of time thinking about my conversation with her and I finally felt like I could truly move on. The only problem was, the only man I wanted to move on with was thinking of moving all the way to Europe to get away from me. I had to find a way to convince him to give me another chance. I refused to entertain the thought of never holding him in my arms again.

At least I had a few days off of work to try and form a plan. I had shut down Romero's for Lauren's wedding so that all the staff could attend and the day after was Sunday which was a day the restaurant was typically closed anyway.

I checked the time and saw that I needed to get ready or I would be late for the wedding. I rolled out of bed and headed to the bathroom, where I quickly shaved all of the scruff off my face that I had neglected for the past few days. I brushed my teeth and then climbed into the shower, letting it rejuvenate me after my sleepless night and washed away the stress that lingered in my body.

After toweling off, I splashed on some cologne and got dressed. I checked my reflection in the full length mirror on the back of my closet door. The custom made black suit fit well and the bright blue shirt made my eyes look brighter. I looked through my ties and chose one that had purple and blue stripes which matched my shirt.

Smoothing down my tie, I walked out to the kitchen. I drank down a glass of orange juice as I sifted through the mail that had been piling up, throwing away the junk mail and making mental notes about the ones that needed attention soon. I checked the time on my watch and grabbed my keys, I didn't want to show up late.

It was a beautiful sunny spring day with blue skies and white puffy clouds. I opened the windows and the sunroof on Roxie and revved her engine, letting her answering growl rumble through my chest. I smiled as I left the city behind and enjoyed the thirty-minute drive down open roads, letting Roxie open up and run a bit wild on the way.

I checked my GPS and pulled up to the church about twenty minutes early. "Not bad, Roxie girl, not bad at all." I lovingly rubbed her dash before climbing out and locking her up.

I wandered around the spacious church, trying to find the sanctuary where the service would be held and found myself in a long hallway with several rooms which I assumed were used as children's Sunday school rooms, if the tiny tables and chairs were any indication.

I was walking past one room when I heard my name being called. I stopped and poked my head around the doorway, a broad grin slid across my face as I saw Lauren. "Wow, you are absolutely stunning," I said in awe. Her auburn hair was swept up in a beautiful twist and was covered by a veil that trailed down her back. Her long, white satin dress was cinched tight, showcasing her trim waist and had tiny pearls sewn into the bodice which perfectly matched the ones in her ears. Her big brown eyes twinkled with joy and a smile graced her lips as she swooped me up into a hug. "Careful now, I don't want to wrinkle you." I chuckled as I hugged her back, despite my words.

"I don't care," she laughed. "I'm so glad you're here to share this with me."

"I wouldn't have missed it for anything." We stepped apart still grinning at each other. "Are you absolutely sure about this?" I teased. "Because I brought Roxie, all you have to do is say the word and we'll head to the coast."

Lauren laughed and punched my arm playfully. "Thanks for the option, but there's nowhere else I want to be. I can't believe in just a little bit of time Gracie will finally be my wife. I have wanted this my whole life." Her eyes teared up as she finished, overcome with emotion.

"I'm so happy for you. You deserve this and I know you and Gracie will have a wonderful life together." I was surprised to find I truly meant my words. I no longer felt the bitterness that I used to when someone mentioned marriage. We shared a genuine smile before her mom rushed into the room and began fussing over Lauren's makeup which had smeared with her tears. "I better go find a seat; enjoy every moment of today," I said with a small wave and then moved back out of the room.

I followed the sound of voices and soon located the large

sanctuary which was beautifully decorated with fresh flowers and white satin ribbons that adorned each pew. I stood at the back of the room for a few minutes, looking around, when my gaze landed on a man sitting by himself towards the back. His head was turned and he appeared lost in thought as he stared at the intricate stained glass windows that took up the entire left wall of the room. The sunlight streamed through them, casting sparkling colored patterns on everything it touched, including his brown hair, which I knew felt silky in my hands.

"Caleb," I whispered longingly. As if he had heard me, he suddenly turned his face and looked directly at me. His eyes widened in surprise and then I saw him swallow hard as pain washed over his features. I hated that I had put that look in his eyes and I took a step forward, my hand reaching out towards him, but he had already turned his head to face the front of the church and was biting down on his bottom lip as he tried to reign in his emotions.

I wanted nothing more than to carry him out of there and make love to him until every moment of pain that I had caused him was erased, but I knew it would never be that easy. I had hurt him badly and he deserved a genuine apology and explanation.

I watched as Marco walked over to Caleb and kindly asked if he'd like to sit with him and his wife. With a grateful nod, he stood and followed Marco, and I saw him introduce Caleb to his wife, Maria. Caleb smiled as they spoke and he slid into his seat at the end of the pew.

Taking a deep breath and squaring my shoulders against possible rejection, I walked over to them and looked down at Caleb. "Mind if I sit with you?" I asked, my voice sounding strained.

Caleb looked up, startled to see me there, but nodded his head slightly before sliding down the wooden bench to make room for me. I sat down and Marco gave me a nod and a toothy smile. I struggled to find something to say, but the organist began to play music and the wedding attendants began their trek down the aisle.

I watched as Gracie appeared from a door on the right, looking beautiful and proud in her police dress blues. Her father had died when Gracie was a teenager and so her police captain was filling in to give her away today. They made their way down the aisle and when they reached the end, the captain kissed her on the cheek before taking his seat. Gracie turned to face all of us, but her eyes were intently focused on the door to the left of the room, where Lauren stood with her father. The look the two women shared held so much devotion and promise that I looked away, feeling as if I was intruding on an intimate moment.

Lauren made her way to the front, where her father placed her hand in Gracie's. The service began and I tried to stay focused, but found it extremely difficult when my thigh ended up pressed against Caleb's in the tight confines of the pew. I could feel the warmth of his body through the thin material of my suit and my heart beat wildly. I wondered if our close contact was having any effect on him. I peered at him from the corner of my eye and found him sitting rigid in his seat, his hands clasped so tight his knuckles were white. I couldn't help but feel pleased that I still had an effect on him and a smile curved my lips.

I turned my attention back to the ceremony as Lauren and Gracie began exchanging vows. As they promised to love each other and stay devoted to each other until death took them, I heard Caleb sniffle beside me. I found it adorable that he got emotional at weddings. Without thinking, I reached over and laid my hand on his leg. He jumped slightly and glanced up at me with a startled look. I gave him a small smile and turned my attention back to the ceremony, but I left my hand where it was, taking it as a good sign when Caleb didn't push it away.

As soon as the ceremony ended, Caleb stood and hurried out of the sanctuary. I followed quickly behind and saw him duck into the restroom. I walked in and found him staring into the mirror, his hands gripping the edges of the sink in front of him. He saw me in the reflection of the mirror and whipped around to face me. I noticed the wariness in his eyes and longed to take it away. "Can we talk?" I asked him hopefully.

Many emotions warred over his features, but the strongest was pain and it cut through me like a knife. He shook his head slowly and tears filled his eyes. "I don't know if I can," he said, his voice shaking. "It hurts to even look at you right now." I winced at his words. "I'm sorry, I'm not trying to hurt you," he whispered and then ran out of the room.

I chuckled ruefully as I watched the door swing shut. Even after everything I had put him through, all the pain I had inflicted upon him, Caleb still worried about hurting *my* feelings with his honest words. I let out a low growl and then stepped to the sink and splashed water on my face. It was glaringly obvious that Caleb was a much better man than me and he deserved more than I could offer him, but I was feeling selfish and so I dried my face and headed out for round two.

I arrived at the banquet hall where the reception was being held and went inside, scanning the crowd for Caleb. I found him standing near a large round table with the other Romero's staff members. As I approached, I noticed that my name card had been placed right next to Caleb's and I made a mental note to give Lauren a hefty raise. I shook hands with my friends and hugged Maria, congratulating her on her new grandchild. She beamed and pulled out pictures to show me. I had already seen them all thanks to Marco, but gave the appropriate ooh's and ahh's, smiling at Marco as he gave me an appreciative wink.

Someone announced the arrival of the new couple and we all applauded as Lauren and Gracie swept into the room, wearing identical happy smiles. We took our seats as the waiters began serving dinner and I saw Caleb give a slight eye roll when he noticed the seating arrangement.

He ignored me throughout dinner, but the conversation with my friends remained lively. I barked out a laugh at Caleb's confused look when Marco teased him that he might want to be careful around the candle centerpiece on the table. I hadn't told Marco that it was actually Carter who had destroyed the kitchen, not Caleb.

Lauren and Gracie made their way around the reception hall as they visited with their loved ones and eventually stopped at our table. We all took turns congratulating them and telling them how beautiful the wedding had been. I watched as Lauren introduced Gracie to Caleb and then spoke to him quietly for a few minutes, her eyes occasionally darting to mine.

After the cake had been cut and toasts had been made, the wives enjoyed their first dance together as a married couple. Then the DJ invited everyone out onto the dance floor. I had just finished speaking to Marco when Caleb stood and began to make his excuses to leave early.

I jumped up from my seat, nearly knocking my chair over in the process and Caleb looked at me in astonishment as I grabbed his arm. "Please, dance with me?" He started to protest so I quickly cut him off. "Just one dance, please, Caleb," I implored him with my eyes.

He clenched his jaw and glanced around the room, but reluctantly gave me a single nod. I held his arm as we made our way to the dance floor, afraid that if I let go he would bolt for the nearest exit.

Luck was with me as "Who I Am With You" by Chris Young began playing. I had always loved that song and thought it appropriately described how I felt when I was around Caleb. I pulled him near and felt him trembling as I placed my hand in his and slid my other hand around his slim waist, pulling him up against my body. We both groaned as our bodies made contact. I let the music carry me away as I held him close, reveling in the feel of my arms wrapped around him. I wasn't sure I would ever get the chance to be this close to him again and I took the opportunity to breathe him in. His fresh, clean smell filled my senses and brought tears to my eyes as I felt what could only be described as homesickness.

He stiffened in my arms as I leaned down putting my mouth to his ear. "I've missed you so much."

He started to back away, but I held tight, not letting him go. "What do you want from me, Giovanni?"

My heart flipped as I heard my name tumble from his mouth and I fought the urge to lean down and suck on his plump bottom lip. Instead, I looked him directly in the eye. "I am so sorry I hurt you, Caleb," I answered huskily. "There are some things I really need to talk to you about. Will you please come with me so we can talk?" I couldn't breathe as I stood there waiting for him to make a decision that could ultimately break me if he said no.

"Okay," he answered simply and I felt my knees go weak with relief.

We told our friends goodbye and walked beside each other, out to the parking lot. "I'll follow you," Caleb said.

He turned to go to his car, but I stopped him. "Thank you, Caleb, for listening to me."

He looked at me for several seconds before saying anything. "Well, it has to be done I suppose." His shoulders slumped in resignation as he turned to walk away.

I watched him as he climbed into his car and started it before turning to my own. I kept an eye on Caleb's car the entire drive back to the city. Half of me was convinced he would change his mind and go on home and I prayed the whole way that that wouldn't happen.

I pulled into the parking garage at my condo and Caleb pulled into the spot next to mine. He got out, locked his car, and followed me into the building. We rode the elevator silently to my floor and entered my condo. "Would you like a drink?" I tossed my keys on the table by the door and walked into the kitchen.

"I could use a beer if you've got any."

I pulled out two beers and handed one to him. We walked into the living room and he sat on the edge of the couch. Things had always been so playful and easy between us and I hated how awkward we had become around each other. I loved Caleb and wanted to be with him more than anything, but I also missed him being my friend.

"You said you wanted to talk," he prompted me as he rolled the beer bottle between his hands.

"Yes, I do, but I'm feeling nervous, sorry."

He released a low sigh. "You don't have to do this, Giovanni. I already know what you wanted to talk to me about and I understand. It's not your fault, okay?" The look he gave me was sincere, but I was confused by his words.

"What do you think I want to talk about?"

He gave me a small smile. "You warned me from the very beginning that you didn't want to get close, didn't want a relationship. It's not your fault that I fell for you and tried to make more out of it than it was. Then I got my feelings hurt and blew off my job. I appreciate that you brought me somewhere private to fire me, but there's…"

"You think I brought you back here to fire you?" I asked incredulously.

"Didn't you?" Caleb looked at me in confusion.

"Hell no! That's not at all what I wanted to talk to you about," I said emphatically, sitting next to him on the couch.

"What is it then?"

I studied the label on my beer bottle for a moment trying to organize my thoughts. "You're right, I never intended to be in a relationship with you or anyone else, ever again. I was afraid of being hurt again after Juliana left me, so I held everyone at arm's length. Then we became friends and you introduced me to your family and the time I spent with you left me feeling freer and happier than I had in a long time. I was constantly amazed at how sweet and honest you were." Caleb was listening to me intently and I reached over and picked up his hands, cradling them between mine. "Things began to change and no matter how hard I tried to fight it, I started to develop feelings for you. You reached inside and grabbed my heart, Caleb, and I started to believe that maybe we could have something more."

I reached up and stroked his cheek gently with my fingertips and he leaned into my touch. "Then Juliana showed up and once again, I was left feeling like she had ended our marriage because of some flaw in me. Maybe I hadn't been a good enough husband to her, maybe I hadn't loved her well enough, maybe *I* just wasn't good enough. I took all those feelings of worthlessness and I projected them onto you and for that I am so, so sorry. I never should have said the things I said to you because it was a lie." Tears rolled down both of our faces, but his eyes were filled with hope. "Caleb, you are the best man I have ever met and I am completely, ridiculously, head over heels in love with you." A sob broke from his chest as he began to cry harder. "I want a relationship with you, I want to take a chance with you because, Caleb, you *are* worth it, you are worth everything to me, sweetheart."

His face showed his hesitation and my stomach roiled at the real possibility that I may have messed up too badly for him to give me another chance. "Did you… were you…"

I watched as he bit his lip. "Was I what?"

He glanced up at me nervously. "Were you with anyone else?"

I knew if we had any chance at a future, I would need to be completely honest with him. "There was a guy…" I saw Caleb flinch and he looked at the floor. I reached for him and lifted his chin so I could see his eyes. "Let me finish, I went out for a drink with Micah and there was a guy there. For a brief moment, I thought maybe I could use him to help me get over you."

"I understand," he said dejectedly.

I smiled gently at him. "No, you don't. I danced with him, *just danced* and that was enough to prove to me that I didn't want anyone else. He felt all wrong in my arms and he was very handsy." Caleb's eyes narrowed at that. "Luckily, Micah saw that I was trying to get away from the guy and came to my rescue." I chuckled at the memory.

"Remind me to thank Micah next time I see him. So, nothing happened then?"

"I haven't been with anyone else since the night I met you, Caleb. I haven't wanted to be." He sighed in relief. I cradled his face in both of my hands and rested my forehead on his. "Please, tell me I'm not too late, Caleb."

"You're not too late, I've waited my whole life for you." I felt the smile on his lips as I slanted my mouth over his. We kissed until we had to come up for air. "Make love to me, Gio."

I smiled when I heard him use my name that was reserved only for him. Without a word, I picked him up from the couch and carried him into my bedroom. I laid him down gently on my bed and straddled his body. "I am the luckiest man in the world." I gazed at him lovingly as I slowly unbuttoned his shirt.

He sat up and reached a hand behind my neck as he pulled me down for a long, languid kiss. "I'm the lucky one. I have always known what an amazing man you are, with so much love to give. I'm just glad you're finally starting to realize it too."

I kissed him again, letting my tongue sweep in and explore his sweet mouth. "Thank you for giving me another chance because I really don't know how I would have gone on without you."

"You'll never have to find out, baby. I'm exactly where I want to be."

I worked his shirt free of his wrists and threw it over my shoulder then began unbuttoning my own. Caleb laid back on the bed, propping himself up on a pillow so he could watch me intently. I tossed my shirt behind me, letting it join Caleb's on the floor. Then lifted up on my knees and popped the button of my pants. He licked his lips seductively, his emerald green eyes heavy with lust.

I lowered my zipper slowly and was surprised when Caleb slithered his body down the bed until I was straddling his head. He reached up and pulled my pants and briefs down below my ass in one fluid motion, letting my thick cock spring free of its confinement. I quickly kicked free of my pants and straddled his head again. Caleb leaned up and captured my cock in his mouth, swallowing it until it hit the back of his throat.

I let out a shout at the wet heat that engulfed my aching shaft. I groaned at the sight of his glistening lips, stretched wide around my cock. He looked up at me with hooded eyes and hollowed his cheeks, increasing the suction. I reached down, cradling his head in my hands so he wouldn't strain his neck and began thrusting into his hungry mouth. He moaned and I felt the vibration travel through his body and up my shaft, making me break out into a sweat as I tried desperately to stave off my orgasm.

I rocked back and forth for several minutes, fucking his mouth, and Caleb took everything I gave him; all while making happy mewling noises around my dick. Fire built in my spine and I knew I should stop him soon, but it felt so damn good it was impossible.

Caleb suddenly reached up and slid a wet finger between my ass cheeks, searchingly. My body stilled as I fought for control, but when he slid that slick finger gently into my hole, I knew the fight was over. I threw my head back as I rocked myself on him. My sac drew up tightly against my body and I screamed Caleb's name as I came down his throat in hot, thick spurts. In my sex induced haze I registered the sound of licking and slurping and peered down at my lover as he cleaned my cock. He ran his tongue around the rim of foreskin as he captured every drop of my cum, not bothering to hide his pleased smile.

Still feeling a bit numb, I dropped down to lie on my stomach beside Caleb on the bed. "I think you just killed me," I mumbled into the pillow.

He pulled my socks off and then apparently removed the rest of his clothing because I soon felt his smooth, warm skin glide along mine as he laid on top of my back and began gifting me with warm, tender kisses along the back of my neck and shoulders. He leaned up to whisper in my ear, "I can't kill you yet, I still have a lot of plans for this incredible body."

His words made me shiver and I felt my cock surprisingly begin to fill out again. We lay there for a few quiet moments, just breathing together and when I felt him fully relax above me, I surprised him by flipping our bodies until I was above him, balancing my weight with my forearms. He laughed out loud and I smiled down at him, happily. *How could I have ever thought of letting this man go?* I needed him like I needed my next breath. I leaned down and licked at his dimples with the tip of my tongue, then sucked his bottom lip into my mouth. I swept my tongue into his mouth and he opened up to me, allowing his tongue to mate with mine. He licked his tongue across my teeth and explored every crevice of my mouth as his hands gripped my shoulders in desperation.

I tilted my head and licked the fine sheen of sweat at the base of his throat and began nibbling along his collarbone. I felt him stiffen slightly under me and I pulled back to search his face. "What's wrong?"

Caleb bit his lip. "It's nothing."

"If I've done something wrong, I want to know, baby. Please, tell me."

Caleb looked down shyly until I lifted his chin with my fingers so I could look in his eyes. "It's just that the last time you left a mark on my neck, was right before…" He looked at me apologetically. "And it hurt every time I looked at it because it reminded me of you, then it started to fade and that broke my heart."

I looked at him seriously, my words sincere. "I promise you that this time is different. This time, when I mark you, it's to show the world that you are mine. This time when it starts to fade, I'll be here to mark you all over again because you will always be mine. I'm never letting you go again."

"Please, Gio, make me yours." He tilted his chin up, exposing his smooth, soft neck to me and I bent my head down to suckle his neck gently and then more firmly before pulling back to admire my handiwork. I smiled in satisfaction at the red mark left on his creamy skin.

"Mine." I growled possessively. Caleb sighed in relief and smiled at me happily.

"And who do I belong to, Caleb?" I asked teasingly.

"Oh, that's easy, you've always been mine, it just took you a while to figure it out." He laughed hysterically as I grabbed him and began tickling his ribs mercilessly. His laughter quickly faded as I settled my body over top of his. We stared at each other seriously. "This won't be easy, Caleb. I've spent a lot of time trying to keep people at arm's length and I'm still scared to death of being hurt, but I want this. I want *you*."

Caleb stroked his fingers lovingly down my cheek. "I will never, ever hurt you." I could see the promise in his eyes.

"I believe you," I answered before sealing my mouth to his. I held myself up on my arms and heard him gasp as I ground my hips into his, our dripping cocks sliding against each other. We both looked down to watch where we were joined as I swayed my hips back and forth slowly.

I reached over and grabbed a condom and lube from the bedside table. Kneeling between his legs, I dropped the condom beside him and clicked the bottle of lube open. Caleb squirmed on the bed in anticipation and I winked at him. "Don't worry, I'm going to take care of you, sweetheart."

I poured the lube onto my fingers and rubbed them together to warm it before reaching between us to circle his hole with the tip of one finger. Caleb grabbed onto his legs, behind his knees, and pulled them up to his chest; offering himself up to me. He let out a whimper as I slid my finger inside his tight hole. I added a second finger, twisting them so that they rubbed along his sensitive nerve endings and stretching him so he could take my thick cock.

I added more lube to my fingers and then slid three fingers inside him. I held still until he nodded his head and then curved my fingers to rub against his prostate. "Fuck!" he yelled as his body surged up off the bed.

"Shh, sweetheart, it's all right. I've got you," I whispered soothingly to him. Caleb began riding my fingers and I sat back on my heels as I watched my fingers disappear inside his hot hole, stretching it wide. The sight of him using me to pleasure himself was so fucking sexy that I had to reach down and squeeze the base of my cock before I erupted.

"I need you now, Gio." The desperation in his eyes had me removing my fingers and sliding the condom down my thick shaft, quickly slicking my length with lube. I grasped his ankles and gently placed them over my shoulders.

"I love you so much," I whispered before sliding into him slowly. Fighting my natural urge to thrust, I waited as he panted through gritted teeth, trying to relax the muscles that kept me from fully entering his body.

"I'm good," he nodded at me.

I leaned over his body and dipped my head down to lick the drip of sweat that rolled down his temple. I wanted to drink every bit of him in until his body was my own. I kissed him as I slid the rest of the way inside of him. The heat from his body felt feverish to my sensitive cock and I felt his tight walls squeeze me, drawing me into his waiting depth. I wanted to live inside the warm, welcoming safety of him.

Caleb rocked his body up against mine and I took it as a cue to pick up the pace. I knelt up on the bed again and thrust hard several times before pulling out. When he started to protest, I slid back in swiftly, making him gasp. I did that a few times, sliding out slowly and thrusting back in hard, enjoying the sight of my thick cock entering his quivering hole.

"So fucking perfect," I murmured before adjusting my angle so that each thrust pegged his prostate.

His eyes rolled up in his head and he began mumbling nonsensically. I felt my orgasm quickly approaching, but fought it, wanting us to come together. He reached for his cock, but I swatted his hand away and took it in my own firm grip. His eyes fluttered closed as I used my thumb to spread the pre-cum from his weeping cock over the head of his dick.

"Keep your eyes open, sweetheart. I want you to see what you do to me." His eyes popped open and his gaze locked with mine.

"I love you, Gio." His words filled my heart and I leaned down to kiss him before kneeling over him again.

I squeezed his cock as my hand glided up and down, twisting my wrist at the tip in the way I knew would drive him crazy. My hips swiveled as I thrust into him fast and hard. As we both neared the end, we kept our eyes locked on each other, each of us murmuring low words of love. Caleb gave a shout and threw his head back with the force of his orgasm and I watched him, knowing this was the most spectacular thing I had ever seen.

I felt the familiar fire race through my veins and my cock grew impossibly large, right before I tipped over the edge and my orgasm tore through my body. "Caleb!" I screamed as my muscles clenched and the veins in my neck threatened to explode. I hung there suspended over him for what seemed like hours, my eyes never leaving his as I rode out my powerful orgasm. I needed that connection to him to tether me to the earth or I would surely fly away.

Finally, my orgasm subsided and I dropped limply on top of him. I lay there shaking as the aftershocks of that mind blowing orgasm continued to ripple through my body. "I need to move. I know I must be crushing you."

"Don't you dare move," Caleb threatened as he wrapped his legs and arms around me, cradling me in his warmth. He whispered his love in my ear as his hands traced soothing circles on my back.

We lay there until I had to remove the condom. I lifted gently, suffering the loss of his warmth as I pulled out of his body and quickly tied the condom and tossed it in the trash can. I went to the bathroom and ran a washcloth under warm water before returning to Caleb.

He lay still on my bed, watching me as I cleaned him. "Please tell me this was all real. Tell me you aren't going to leave me again."

I tossed the washcloth onto the floor and lay next to him, covering us with the blanket. I looked him in the eyes as I spoke so he could see how serious I was. "I'm not going anywhere, Caleb. I want you to be a part of my life, every day. I want to hear your laughter in my ears and see your sexy dimples when you smile. I want us to share our dreams and our fantasies. I want to know all of your secrets that you won't tell anyone else. I want a real relationship with you."

He smiled at me sweetly. "I love you, Gio. All I've ever wanted was to be yours."

I pulled him close, spooning him and wrapping my arms securely around him. "I love you too, sweetheart." I'm not sure he heard me though because he was already snoring softly.

I woke the next morning to a thunderstorm raging outside. Caleb was still sleeping soundly so I quietly made my way to the kitchen and turned on the news as I made us a breakfast of omelets, toast, and coffee. I smiled as the weatherman reported heavy storms throughout the entire day.

I was still smiling as I made my way into the bedroom, carrying a tray with our food. Caleb was propped up on a pillow and smiled when he saw me. "Good morning. What has you smiling so much?"

"You mean besides the gorgeous, naked man in my bed?"

He chuckled and sat up straighter as I laid the tray between us on the bed and sat next to him. "Yeah, besides that. This looks delicious by the way." He picked up a piece of toast and began nibbling on it.

"Yes, it does," I said leering up and down his body and causing him to laugh happily. "I'm smiling because the weatherman said that it's supposed to storm all day."

He gave me a confused look so I explained further. "The restaurant's closed today so we're both off work and with the storms, it's too nasty to go outside. Sounds like the perfect day to stay *inside*." I waggled my eyebrows at him suggestively.

"Well, sir, whatever will we do to pass the time?" he said in a southern accent.

"I have a few ideas," I said looking very serious.

"Oh, really? Like what?"

"It's probably best if I show you." I set the tray on the bedside table and climbed over his body. "But if you can still walk tomorrow, I've done something wrong."

CHAPTER
Nineteen

Caleb

I FINISHED PULLING ON MY BOXER BRIEFS AND MADE MY WAY INTO the kitchen. I stopped in the doorway and leaned against the frame, enjoying the view. Giovanni stood with his back to me, wearing nothing but a pair of black sweats that hung low on his hips. I took my time drinking him in, from his tousled hair, across his wide shoulders, down the curve of his spine, to the gentle swell of his perfect ass. My eyes continued down his muscular thighs to his sexy bare feet. I sighed, still finding it hard to believe that he was all mine. Out of all the men in the world, by some miracle he had chosen *me*.

"Ahem." My head jerked up at the sound of Giovanni clearing his throat and I blushed when I saw him smirking at me over his shoulder. I'd been caught red handed. Oh well, he might as well get used to lots and lots of ogling if he was going to wander around the house looking so damn sexy all the time.

"Good morning." I made my way over to the table and gingerly sat down on the seat, wincing as my abused ass hit the chair.

He chuckled. "Sore, sweetheart?" He came over carrying a plate of toast and a glass of orange juice and sat down.

I gave him a mock glare. "You don't have to sound so smug, you know."

"I am actually quite smug about our sexlympics and you should be as well. I'm pretty sure I lost a layer of skin off of my dick from all the friction yesterday…and last night…and again this morning." He smiled wickedly as he leaned towards me and fed me a bite of toast.

I laughed. "They should make sex a category in the Olympics. I'm sure we'd take the gold medal."

"The way we do it, it's definitely an athletic sport. I wonder who we would need to contact to make that suggestion?" he mused. He stood and went over to the cabinet, returning quickly with two aspirin to ease my pain. I looked at him lovingly as he slipped them in my mouth then handed me the glass of orange juice.

"Thank you. You'd win with that thing you do with your hips, oh my gawd, and your mouth, dayum, boy!" I said in a southern accent, fanning my face dramatically.

"And you, with how bendy you are. Who knew my boyfriend could even get in that position, much less hold it for that long? I'm getting hard just thinking about it."

I felt my heart trip at the word boyfriend. I hadn't had a boyfriend since high school and I loved having that claim on Giovanni. *He is mine.* I smiled at the thought. "I had so much fun yesterday. We should spend every day we have off that way. Although I'm really not sure how I'm going to work all day when I can barely walk," I said teasingly.

"I did warn you, didn't I?" He fed me another bite of toast and his eyes filled with lust when a bit of jelly maybe, perhaps, probably, okay *most definitely* on purpose landed on my bottom lip. I slowly slid my tongue out to capture it, but he bent in swiftly and licked it from my lip before I could.

We both groaned at the contact. "Do you think this insatiable need to have each other will fade over time?"

"Not a chance," he growled. I sighed as his tongue swept into my mouth. He tasted like oranges, strawberry jelly, and Giovanni: three of my favorite flavors.

After a quick shower together, where we agreed just to wash each other because we really were quite sore, we got dressed and headed out the door. It was still storming as we drove to my apartment to drop off my car and I ran quickly to jump into Giovanni's Mustang so I wouldn't get soaked.

A large clap of thunder sounded as we pulled into the parking lot at Romero's and we raced inside where it was dry. Marco was in the kitchen when we walked in and he glanced up from a recipe, a wide smile making his eyes crinkle at the edges. "So, can I assume you two finally got your heads out of your asses and are back together, where you belong?"

"No, why would you think that?" Giovanni deadpanned. Marco's smile slid from his face and he started to apologize.

"Don't tease him," I scolded Gio then slid my arms around his waist and rested my head on his shoulder.

"Oh, you!" Marco shook his finger at Giovanni in a reprimand, making him laugh.

"Yes, Marco, I finally wised up and Caleb was very forgiving. I'm a lucky man." I smiled at Giovanni as he gazed down at me lovingly. I felt warm all over when he looked at me like that.

"Glad to hear it, now maybe you won't destroy the kitchen, son."

"Umm, Marco…" I started to explain just as Carter walked into the kitchen.

Marco's expression was comical as he glanced back and forth between us. "I'd like you to meet my twin brother, Carter, otherwise known as the tornado that ripped through your kitchen," I teased.

"Hey, I wasn't that bad," he protested.

"Carter, you were wearing marinara sauce like a hat," Giovanni said incredulously.

Everyone laughed as Carter blushed, staring down at his feet. I took pity on him and threw my arm over his shoulder. "Seriously though, thank you for being willing to do anything to help me. And I don't just mean with my job, but everything. I was really hurting and I don't know what I would have done if you hadn't shown up."

Giovanni wore a very serious expression as he stepped forward, thrusting his hand out towards my brother. "Thanks for helping me get my head on straight too."

Carter shook his hand and smiled happily. "I'm just glad you guys worked everything out. You both deserve to be happy." I hugged him tightly and heard him sniffing my neck. I leaned back to look at him, but he was smiling mischievously at Giovanni. "Well, what do you know, he *does* smell like sunshine."

I looked back and forth between my boyfriend and my brother in confusion. Giovanni's eyes widened and he began pushing Carter out into the dining area. "Didn't I tell you not to step foot in my kitchen ever again? Get out, you trouble maker!" I heard Carter cackling from the other room and turned my questioning gaze back to Gio. "Nothing, just forget you heard that," he mumbled as he walked towards his office. I was almost positive he was blushing as he left. I turned to Marco and we both shrugged our shoulders and began getting everything ready for the dinner rush.

Several hours later, Marco was on a break and I had just put the finishing touches on a plate of eggplant parmesan when the lights flickered and then cut out completely. I heard a lot of noise, like the sound of chairs scraping on hardwood and then people yelling. I used the light from the emergency exits to find my way around the long counter and towards the swinging door that led to the dining room. I needed to help calm everyone down and assure them that the lights would be back on soon.

I stepped into the dining room and immediately smelled smoke. My eyes darted around as the smoke quickly began filling the room. People were running around frantically, bumping into things and knocking others over. "Everyone calm down," I shouted, but no one seemed to hear me.

I glanced up at the emergency lights and noticed that they looked very hazy as the smoke began to thicken around me, I coughed as it entered my lungs. I needed to hurry and get everyone out as quickly as possible. I grabbed a woman's hand as she brushed past me. "Grab someone's hand, I work here and I can lead you outside." She grabbed the hand of a man near her and we added others, making a human chain as we slowly made our way through the crowd of people. I got them to the door and then went back in for more. It seemed that most of the people had made their way out, but I could hear some crying. The smoke was so thick now that I could barely breathe. I covered my mouth with my sleeve, using it to filter the air and my eyes began to tear as the smoke burned them.

I stared in horror as the entire back wall of the restaurant became engulfed in flames. I stood frozen as fire washed over the ceiling above me like a wave. I might have found it beautiful if terror wasn't surging through me. The intense heat from the fire made my skin feel like it was melting.

The roaring of the fire was so loud that I barely heard my name being called. Suddenly a body landed on me hard, tackling me to the ground, just as a part of the ceiling caved in where I had been standing only seconds before. I blinked my eyes as I tried desperately to see and was just able to make out Giovanni leaning over me, a wild look in his eyes. "We've got to get out of here," he shouted as he yanked me up and dragged me towards the door.

Four firemen were making their way inside as we reached the door, their movements heavy and slow under the weight of their thick uniforms and fire equipment. "You guys get outside where it's safe, while we check for anyone else in the building."

We stumbled through the front door and I choked on the fresh air as it hit my lungs. Giovanni was next to me, bent over with his hands on his knees as he coughed violently. When his wracking coughs had subsided he stood and grabbed me in a fierce embrace. "Oh God, sweetheart, I couldn't find you, I was so afraid of losing you. I love you so much." He began peppering my face with kisses before landing on my lips and stealing the breath from me.

"Gio, your restaurant," I sobbed as my body continued to shake, I couldn't push back my feelings of panic and dread.

"Nothing else matters as long as everyone made it out safely." His hands dove into my hair and he leaned his forehead against mine. Tears streaked through the soot on his face and I wrapped my arms around him, desperate to feel close to him, to reassure myself that he was alive and safe with me.

Marco rushed over to where we were standing, a look of grief and horror etched on his face.

An EMT approached us and ushered us over to a waiting ambulance where she began checking us for injuries. She finished with Giovanni and turned to me, but a sharp stabbing pain hit behind my eyes and my head felt like it had exploded. I grabbed my head and fell to the ground, screaming from the pain. An intense heat travelled down my arm and I thought I was going to be sick. I felt Giovanni's hands on me as he pleaded for me to tell him what was wrong, but I couldn't speak as panic surged through my body.

I lifted my head, my eyes searching wildly until they landed on a group of firemen standing near one of the fire trucks. I leapt to my feet, scrambling to get to them and grabbed one by his thick jacket. "Please, my brother's in there. He's hurt and you need to go get him," I begged.

The fireman stepped back and looked down at me, speaking in a calm manner. "Sir, we just got the all clear. They didn't find anyone else in the building. Your brother is probably wandering around out here looking for you."

Marco spoke up and his words turned my blood to ice. "I saw him right before I headed outside for my break. He was headed downstairs to the cellar to get more wine."

"You don't understand," I pleaded, my voice breaking with emotion. "He's in there. I know he is, I'm his twin and I feel it. He's hurt."

I felt Giovanni's reassuring presence behind me. "I'd listen to him; they can sense what the other is feeling. If he says that his brother is in trouble, then he is." The group of men shared looks between themselves, silently communicating how crazy they thought we were.

"I'll go take a look. If he's in there, I'll find him." I stared up at the tall, blond fireman who had stepped forward.

I almost wept, my body sagged in relief as the fireman spoke into the radio attached to his shoulder. "Captain, it's Marshall, we've got reports of someone down in a wine cellar. Do I have permission to check it out, sir?" I held my breath as I waited what seemed like a lifetime for the captain's response.

Finally, his radio crackled to life. "Go ahead, but proceed with caution, the building is very unstable. I'm sending Gomez in with you for back up."

"Okay, what's your brother's name? It'll help if I can call out to him," the fireman explained kindly.

"Carter, his name's Carter. Thank you."

"You can thank me when I bring him out." He zipped his jacket, making sure his oxygen tank was secure before lowering his mask and helmet then disappeared into the blazing heat of the restaurant.

My knees turned to jelly and Giovanni caught me as I fell. He slowly lowered me to the ground and wrapped his arms around me from behind as we waited for a miracle.

What felt like hours later, I looked up to see a tall figure stumbling out of the building. He was carrying a bundle of some sort and I shot to my feet, running towards him. He dropped to his knees on the pavement, kneeling over the bundle that lay on the ground as he gasped for air. He bent his head and his helmet rolled off, revealing his sweat drenched hair and the back of his dirt streaked neck.

As I reached him, I realized he was bent over Carter and he was performing CPR on his lifeless body. I dropped to my knees beside him, sobbing uncontrollably as I felt my brother slipping away from me. I fisted my hair and let out a guttural scream as Giovanni held me tight and rocked me. I finally registered his words as he chanted in my ear. "He's alive, he's alive, he's alive."

I tore my eyes to my brother and saw his eyes still closed, blood running down his face, his clothes singed and torn along his right arm, but I cried out in joy when I saw his chest begin moving up and down, ever so slightly.

"We need a medic, this man needs to get to a hospital," the fireman shouted and two EMTs rushed over and started checking Carter's vitals.

"Sir, you need to move out the way, we need to work on your brother." I couldn't move. I couldn't feel my legs at all as my mind and body tried to shut down to protect itself.

"Where will you take him?" I heard Giovanni ask. I never heard their response because I lost focus just as Giovanni swooped me up into his strong, protective arms and carried me. I felt myself floating and wanted to stay safe in his warm embrace forever.

I came out of my daze and found myself beside Giovanni in his car as he raced through the streets, his phone to his ear speaking quietly with someone. "Thank you, Landon, we'll see you there." He glanced over at me when I shifted in my seat. "Landon's letting the rest of the family know what happened and they'll meet us at the hospital."

"Thank you, Gio," I whispered. "You can just drop me off. I know you have a million things to take care of at the restaurant." I tried not to let my anxiety show at the thought of being apart from him, for even a minute.

He snapped his head towards me, his face looking angrier than I'd ever seen. "I'm not fucking leaving you, Caleb. There is nothing more important than being there for you and our family right now," he shouted.

"Okay," I whispered as I reached for his hand, threading my fingers with his. I couldn't help the tears that flowed down my cheeks.

"I'm sorry I yelled, sweetheart, please don't cry." He brought our cupped hands up and wiped the tears from my face.

"It's not that. You called them *our* family." I gave him a quivering smile.

"Well yeah, they are, right?" he asked sounding unsure.

"Yes, they most definitely are." I kissed our joined hands and said a silent prayer for Carter as well as a thank you to God for bringing Giovanni into my life.

We parked the car and quickly ran to the front desk of the emergency room. A nurse smiled politely at me, probably used to seeing people rushing in looking half crazed. "Can I help you?"

"I'm looking for my brother, Carter Greene. He's being brought in by ambulance. He was in a fire." The words rushed out of my mouth and I hoped she was able to understand me.

"Give me just a second and I'll see if he's arrived yet," she said kindly and began clicking the keys of her computer. "It looks like he's here and the doctor is with him. Why don't you have a seat while the doctor evaluates him and someone will come get you as soon as they know something."

I started to object, but Giovanni wrapped his arm around my shoulder. "Thank you, we'll just wait over here." He led me to a row of uncomfortable looking plastic chairs and I sank down in one, exhausted, placing my elbows on my knees and my head in my hands. Giovanni sat next to me and rubbed little circles on my back in a soothing gesture.

We sat like that for several long minutes each lost in our own thoughts until we heard my dad's frantic voice, asking for Carter. I jumped from my chair. "Dad, Mom!" They turned at the sound of my voice and raced towards me. Dad hugged me and shook Giovanni's hand while Mom grabbed me in a bone crushing hug and began to sob.

"Do you know how Carter is?" Dad asked.

"We don't know anything yet; the doctor is with him now." I explained.

"I am so sorry Mr. and Mrs. Greene..." Giovanni started to say.

"What in the world are you sorry for, son?" Dad asked.

Giovanni looked grim as he met my parents' eyes. "Well, the fire was at my restaurant..."

"Unless you purposefully started that fire, which I know you very well didn't, then you have nothing to be sorry about. From what Landon told me, you not only made sure Caleb got out safely, you also convinced that fireman to listen to Caleb's instinct that Carter was trapped. We have you to thank for helping both of our boys, so you just stop this I'm sorry business," Mom scolded, scooping Gio up in a big hug. Suddenly, she jerked back. "Oh, no! Your restaurant, was it completely destroyed?"

"My friend Marco is taking care of everything so I could be here. We'll find out more later, but it seems that everyone else got out safely. What matters now is Carter."

The rest of my family arrived just as a doctor came out. All eyes flew to him as he spoke. "I'm looking for the family of Carter Greene?"

"That's us." Dad stood with his back straight, bracing for bad news and Mom clutched his hand. We all held our breath as we waited for him to continue.

The doctor motioned for us to sit and took the seat next to my mom. "My name is Dr. White and I'm taking care of Carter. Carter has a severe concussion and we'll be monitoring him for any swelling in his brain. He's also suffered from smoke inhalation, so we're giving him pure oxygen. My biggest concern is his arm. It's my understanding from the EMT's report that Carter was trapped by a collapsed beam that fell on his arm. The beam appears to have caused some nerve damage, but I'm not sure how severe. It's very important that we do surgery right away to prevent permanent damage, which may alter his ability to use his hand." He waited patiently letting us absorb his words.

We all glanced at each other and I knew we were thinking the same thing: if he couldn't use his hand, how would he play his music? Music was Carter's whole world and it would destroy him if that were taken from him.

"Do whatever you need to do, doctor. Please, help our son."

The doctor nodded and stood. "A nurse will keep you updated periodically on Carter's status. I'll take good care of him."

He shook my dad's hand and quickly walked through the door to where Carter lay beyond. My head ached, but I wasn't sure if it was from stress or my connection to my twin. I sat back down in my seat and put my head in my hands. Giovanni stood behind me, rubbing my shoulders and threading his fingers through my hair. He gently massaged my scalp, relieving the tension in my shoulders. I reached behind me and grabbed his wrist, pulling it towards my lips, and kissing the palm of his hand tenderly. I was so grateful to have him with me.

Emma and Mark walked down to the cafeteria to get coffee for everyone and the rest of us sat, alternating between talking quietly and praying.

Three long hours later, Dr. White emerged looking weary and more than a little rumpled. We gathered around him and listened intently as he told us about Carter. "The surgery went very well and the blood flow to his right arm is strong, but only time and physical therapy will tell if he regains the full function of that hand. I want to keep him overnight to watch for any problems due to his concussion and we'll reevaluate him tomorrow. Do you have any questions?"

"When can we see him?" Michelle asked.

"He's still under heavy anesthesia from surgery so he probably won't know you're there, but you can take turns going in to see him. No more than two people at a time though, please."

We all took turns thanking him and hugging each other in relief. Carter had a lot of work ahead of him, but we were just thankful he was alive.

My parents went in first and I turned to look at Giovanni. His hair was a tangled mess, his face streaked with dirt and his white shirt was mostly black from the smoke with several rips in it. He had never looked more beautiful to me. He caught my stare and smiled at me. We wrapped our arms around each other and I snuggled against him laying my head on his chest as he kissed the top of my head.

When it was our turn to go in and see Carter, I took Giovanni's hand, pulling him along with me. My brother looked so fragile lying in the hospital bed, hooked to multiple machines. His arm was heavily bandaged and his forehead looked swollen and bruised. I took his hand and was comforted to feel its warmth in my own. Tears filled my eyes as I thought of how close I'd come to losing the other half of me. I smoothed the hair off of his forehead and kissed him there. "I love you, Carter," I whispered as tears streaked down my cheeks. Giovanni took my hand and held me close to his side as we left the hospital.

By the time we got back to Giovanni's place, I could barely keep my eyes open. "Come on, sweetheart, we need to get cleaned up before we go to bed." He led me into the bathroom where he turned on the shower and stripped his clothes off, then turned to where I sat slumped against the sink and began carefully undressing me. I took his hand as we climbed into the shower and he held me close as the hot water washed the terrible day down the drain.

I choked on a sob as I slid my hands around his neck. "God, Gio, I'm so sorry. I've been so caught up in what was happening with Carter that I haven't even really thought about everything that you've lost tonight."

"Shh, it's okay. The restaurant can be rebuilt and everything in it replaced. People are what matters when something like this happens and I'm just so glad no one lost their lives tonight."

I felt him shaking and looked up into his eyes which were filled with tears. "What is it, baby?"

"I came out of my office and heard everyone screaming, the smoke was so thick and I heard the fire roaring all around me. I was so afraid that I was going to lose you. I just got you back and now I was going to lose you."

I pulled him closer, cradling his body with my own. "I'm right here, baby. We're both safe and everything's going to be all right." I reached for the shampoo and poured some in my hand. I gently washed his hair, massaging his scalp as he had done for me at the hospital. His crying stopped and I felt his shoulders relax as I silently washed the rest of his body. When I had rinsed him, he picked up the shampoo and returned the favor by washing me. As the last of the suds washed away, he bent his head to kiss me slowly, sweetly.

When the water cooled, we quickly dried off and brushed our teeth. Finally, we climbed between the sheets and Gio curled his body around my back. He kissed the delicate skin behind my ear and we both drifted off to sleep.

I woke with a start the next morning as the nightmare I had been having slowly receded from my memory. I reached for Gio but came up empty; his side of the bed cold. I brushed my teeth quickly and pulled on a pair of sweats before padding out to the living room to find him.

He stood in front of the floor to ceiling windows with his back to me, wearing sleep pants and a soft blue t-shirt and holding his cell phone to his ear. He turned when he heard me approaching and my steps faltered when I saw the amount of love in his eyes. He held his hand out to me and pulled me in close to his body as I heard him say, "Yeah, I'll do that. Thank you very much, Frank." He ended the call and tossed his phone to the couch then bent down to give me a lingering kiss.

"Who were you talking to?" I sounded breathless from our kiss.

"Frank Carpese, my insurance agent. The fire inspector completed his investigation and found that lightening had struck the roof during the storm, causing the fire. Since it wasn't any negligence on my part, everything will be covered by my insurance. We can start rebuilding right away."

"Oh, thank God!" I pulled him down for another kiss, which soon became heated. I broke the kiss reluctantly after several minutes. "I need to get to the hospital, I want to see Carter."

"Okay, I'll drive you, but later I need to be with you. It feels like forever since I was buried deep inside of you."

I groaned at the raspy quality of his voice. "Carter can wait a little bit longer."

Giovanni chuckled, causing his chest to vibrate against my own deliciously. "Nope, we'll go to the hospital first because when I finally get you alone again, I don't want any interruptions for the rest of the night."

He swatted my ass as he walked past me towards the bedroom and I might have swooned just a little bit.

We saw Dr. White as we walked towards Carter's room. The grim look on his face immediately had my heart plummeting. "Dr. White, is everything all right with Carter?"

"Yes, he'll be fine," he assured me quickly. "I spoke with him a bit ago about the possibility that he may not regain the full function of his hand. It's good that you're here now, he's very upset."

I watched him walk down the hallway. "What am I supposed to say to him?" I asked Giovanni. "Music is Carter's life."

"I think he's probably pretty scared and a bit angry. Just remind him that he's not going to go through any of this alone. He has all of us to support him and love him."

I nodded my head. "Thank you, Gio. I don't know what I'd do without you. I love you."

"I love you too, baby. I'll give you two sometime alone and I'll go get us some coffee."

He kissed me and I turned just in time to see someone who looked familiar coming out of Carter's room. As he approached I recognized him as the fireman that had saved Carter. "Excuse me," I said as he brushed past me, his mouth set in a firm line. He looked up, startled. "My name is Caleb. I just wanted to thank you for saving my brother's life last night. I can never repay you for what you did."

He shook my outstretched hand. "You're welcome, but I was just doing my job." He glanced towards Carter's door and a frown appeared on his face. "I'm sorry, I've got to go." I followed him with my eyes, confused by his brisk behavior, but then turned to go see my brother.

"Knock knock." I peeked my head in the door before walking in. I saw a bouquet of flowers scattered on the floor by the door and stooped to pick them up.

Carter glared at me before turning his head back to look out the window. "What do you want?" I was surprised at his gruff attitude, which was very out of character for him, but I figured he had the right to be angry right then.

"I just wanted to see you. You gave us all quite a scare last night and I just needed to see for myself that you were all right." I laid the flowers on the table by his bed then sat in the chair and reached for his hand, but he flinched away from me before I could touch him.

"Well I'm not all right, am I?" he bit out angrily. "My hand may not work right, which means I won't be able to play my music anymore." Tears filled his eyes and my heart broke for him. I could feel the fear and sadness that coursed through his body.

I climbed into the bed with him, careful not to jostle him and held his hand in mine. "Carter, it's the doctor's job to tell you every possible outcome, but he doesn't know you like I know you. If there is one tiny fraction of a chance that physical therapy will fix your hand, then there is no one in the world who will work harder in therapy to achieve that goal. You live and breathe music and I know you won't stop until you're back in top form. You can do this."

He laid his head on my shoulder and sighed. "You really think so?" I had never heard his voice sound so small and I wished I could fight his battles for him.

"I know so. You're the other half of me after all and my half is pretty darn awesome, so yours can't be all that bad."

We laughed as he picked up the pillow at his side and whacked me in the face with it. "So, are you going to tell me about the yummy fireman that left here, looking like someone shot his dog?" I teased. "I'm assuming those flowers are from him."

"I don't want to talk about it," Carter shot back grumpily.

"Okay, I won't bug you…"

"Thanks," he mumbled.

"While you're in the hospital," I finished, quickly jumping from the bed with a laugh before he could hit me again.

CHAPTER
Twenty

Giovanni

I WALKED THROUGH THE FRONT DOOR OF ROMERO'S CARRYING A box of items for my office and breathed in the smell of fresh paint. It had been a long four months, but the contractor I had hired to do the rebuild assured me that he just had to do some finishing touches and we should be able to reopen up next week. I looked around, pleased with his work. We had decided to decorate the interior as close to the original as possible, with just a few minor upgrades here and there. The customers had always enjoyed the familiarity of the place, so I didn't want to make any drastic changes. I inspected the work being done in the kitchen and knew that Caleb would be happy with the finished product, since he had designed the space, adding his own personal touches.

We were excited to get back to work at the restaurant, but we had enjoyed having so much time to ourselves, really getting to know everything about each other. We learned each other's likes and dislikes and we found that we really had a lot in common. We each loved to surf and agreed that we would always choose lying around on a beach over a sightseeing vacation any day. We both obviously loved cooking and had spent many nights working together to create some new dishes for the restaurant. We learned what habits the other had that got on our nerves, but most of all we discovered just how much fun we had together and how much we loved each other. Caleb had taught me that I had many things to offer in our relationship and that he valued me. I knew that I could trust him, in all things, completely and with no hesitation. He was my best friend and the love of my life.

We had also taken advantage of the time off to volunteer more at Agape House. Marco had gone with us on one of our volunteer days and fell in love with the kids there. He quickly signed up to help and spent many nights giving the kids boxing and basic self-defense lessons, using the skills he had learned from his street fighting days, as well as in the military. His wife, Maria, came in three days a week to read stories to the younger children and teach the older children gardening skills.

I loved spending time with the kids and had grown particularly close to a twelve-year-old boy named Nathan, who had been living on the streets for over six months before finding Agape House. His mother was dead and his father had recently remarried and decided he had no room in his life for a gay son, so he kicked him out with just the clothes on his back. Nathan had survived by eating out of dumpsters and selling his body for money. It broke my heart that any parent could be so cold and heartless to their own child and I was even more grateful for the loving, open-minded parents that Caleb and I had been blessed with. Fortunately, Nathan would soon be adopted by a sweet couple who had been told about him through their church, which helped Agape House as an outreach program. Nathan was one of the lucky ones. For every child with a story like his, there were hundreds more that would never get a happy ending and probably wouldn't live to see adulthood.

I heard voices in my office and headed that way. Lauren was seated at my desk, laughing at something Kristopher had said. Kristopher was an art student at the University of Chicago and I had hired him to paint a new mural in my office. This time I wanted to feature more of the important places in my life, so he was painting the small village of Manarola in honor of my parents, but he was also including a painting of Romero's and the Greene family cabin in Tennessee.

I set the box down on the edge of my desk and admired Kristopher's work. His artistic flair and attention to detail made him an artistic genius in my eyes. I told him so and he thanked me quietly, a blush blooming across his young cheeks.

"Quit being so modest. You're a brilliant artist and the whole world will soon know it," Lauren insisted as she got up from my desk and came around to give me a big hug. "How's everything with you and Caleb?"

The smile on my face probably said it all, but I answered her anyway. "Better than I ever thought possible."

"I'm so happy for you guys. Caleb's a great guy and he's just perfect for you."

"I think so too. Now, let's get some work done so I can get back to him." I smiled at her to let her know I was joking, but she laughed at my obvious eagerness to get home to my boyfriend.

We worked for several hours, ordering supplies, making up fliers announcing our grand reopening, and creating the staff schedule. Kristopher had finished the mural and left shortly after I arrived and it was quiet so I assumed the construction crew had all left for the evening.

Lauren yawned and stretched her arms out over her head. "I better get going, I promised Gracie I'd be home in time to go to the movies."

"Have fun and give Gracie my love."

Lauren grabbed her purse and went to the door. She winked at me and said, "No, but I'll give her *my* love." I laughed as she shut the door behind her.

I finished a few things and then closed out my computer. I picked up the box I had left on my desk and started unpacking the items inside. I had brought a few small plants to set around the space and the *kiss the cook* mug Caleb had bought me. I pulled out the framed picture of my parents and set it on my desk and then added a picture of the Greene family, who treated me as one of their own. Finally, I pulled out a picture of me and Caleb, smiling as I looked at it.

We had joined Caleb's family at their cabin to celebrate the Fourth of July weekend. We had enjoyed hiking and swimming throughout the day and cookouts each night. On the Fourth, we all gathered on the large back deck and enjoyed the fireworks being displayed in the town below. I had stretched out on a chaise lounge and Caleb had climbed between my legs, resting his back on my chest. He had turned to say something to me and we were both smiling happily, when Kathy had snapped our picture. She framed the picture and gave it to me a few days later and it was easily my favorite. I stared down at our happy expressions, our love for each other clear on our faces, and I sighed happily. I placed the picture carefully on my desk and grabbed my keys. It was time to get home to the live version of my man.

I walked in and tossed my keys in the bowl on the table by the door. I kicked off my shoes and sifted through the mail as I walked into the living room. Caleb was sitting on the couch folding a pile of our laundry and he smiled when he saw me. I sat next to him and gave him a quick kiss. "Hey, baby, how is the restaurant coming along?"

"Dust off your chef's hat, sweetheart, we will be back up and running next week."

I laughed as Caleb tossed aside the jeans he had been folding and climbed over me to straddle my lap. "That's fantastic!" He threaded his fingers through my hair and pulled me closer until he could claim my mouth and just like a switch being flipped, I suddenly had to have him.

I eased my fingers under the waistband of his sweats and gripped his firm ass cheeks in both hands, groaning into his mouth when I found he had no underwear on. I sucked on his tongue and slid a finger through his crack in search of his puckered hole.

The sound of a buzzer going off made us jump and Caleb leaned his head on my shoulder with a groan of frustration. "Dinner's ready."

"You've got to be kidding me. Let me turn it off and then get back to turning you on," I teased.

Caleb smiled at me impishly. "All you have to do is walk in the room and you turn me on."

"A new car? Is that what you want? Because if you keep saying sweet things like that, I'll get you anything you want." I smiled at him.

"You're the only thing I want. Oh, and the roast I made for dinner because I'm starving!"

"Sounds good." I followed him out of the living room. "Let me go change really quick and I'll be right back to help you."

I quickly changed into a comfortable pair of sweats and a soft cotton t-shirt. Hoping to get lucky later, I followed Caleb's idea and went commando. I went back to the kitchen and smiled as I saw Caleb moving around my kitchen like he had always been there. I wanted him with me all the time and even though he hadn't officially moved in yet, he spent more time at my place than he did his own. I loved sharing my space with Caleb, finding little pieces of him left behind when he wasn't there, like we were intertwining our lives one t-shirt at a time.

Caleb stirred a brown gravy and glanced at me over his shoulder. I saw something flash in his eyes, but it was gone before I could figure it out. "Will you pour the drinks, please?" He turned back to the stove and I looked at him for a moment trying to figure out why he was acting strangely.

I poured the drinks while Caleb carried the plates over to the table and I brought the glasses over to join him. "This is delicious," I said as the tender meat melted on my tongue. "Tell me about your day."

He began speaking, but I noticed he wasn't really eating. "I went to see Carter today. He's nearly got full use of his hand again. I'm so proud of how hard he's worked to get back to where he was before the fire. I knew he could do it." Caleb's face beamed with pride and I covered his hand with mine.

"That is really great, now he can get back to his music."

I ate a few more bites as Caleb pushed his food around on his plate. Finally, he laid his fork down and grabbed the napkin that was in his lap, twisting it around in his hands as if he were nervous. "Are you okay?" I tilted my head and studied him with concern.

"I made you a haircut appointment," he blurted out instead of answering my question.

"Okaaay, thank you." I was even more confused by his behavior now. He had seemed fine when I got home.

"Excuse me, I'll be right back." He jumped up from his chair and sprinted out of the room.

"Sweetheart, are you all right?" I called out, wondering if he was getting sick.

"I'll be right there. Go ahead and eat," he shouted from somewhere in the condo.

I pushed my plate away from me, too concerned to eat until I knew that he was all right. He came back a minute later and sat in his chair stiffly. I could see his pulse racing at the soft spot on his neck that I loved to kiss. His eyes were wide as he looked at me.

"What's going on, Caleb? You're starting to worry me."

I watched as he gulped down a drink of water with a shaking

hand and then took a deep breath. He reached for my hands and I placed them willingly in his. Touching me seemed to calm him because when he spoke, his voice was calm and clear. "I've been making myself crazy trying to figure out how to do this." I looked at him in confusion but didn't interrupt him. I needed to know what had been bothering him so I could help fix it. "I considered all the possibilities: skywriter, singing telegram, putting it in your food."

My eyes widened and my heart began to beat wildly as I finally understood what was happening. I sucked in a quiet gasp as he continued. "Then you came home tonight and it just clicked, this is it, this is how I want to do this. We don't need grand gestures or outrageous proposals. I want what we had tonight. Having dinner together and talking about our day and making haircut appointments, I want a life with you, Gio." The tears I had been holding back spilled over and flowed freely down my cheeks as he lowered himself to the floor, knelt in front of me, and pulled a ring out of his pocket. "Will you spend a lifetime fighting over the remote with me and arguing about whose turn it is to take out the trash? Will you be a father to my children and spend your days off training for the sexlympics with me?" I let out a loud laugh at that. "Giovanni Michello Romero, will you marry me?"

I slid out of my chair, kneeling on the floor with him. Emotions threatened to choke me, but I managed to get my answer out. "God, yes, baby. I can't wait to spend the rest of my life with you."

He reached for my hand and slid the silver band on my finger. We looked at each other and I pulled him close, our mouths fusing together in a burst of passion. I felt like I would die if I didn't get inside of him right away. "I love you, Caleb." I pulled his shirt over his head and leaned him back gently with my arms until his back lay on the kitchen floor.

"I can't believe you're mine." I kissed his chin and began nibbling along his jaw and down his neck, stopping to suck on the tender spot at the base of his throat. He arched his hips up into mine, searching for friction.

"And you're mine, my fiancé," he gasped.

I leaned up on my knees and trailed my hand down his smooth, firm chest. My fingers traced a circle around his navel and I dipped my head down to swirl my tongue inside, making him writhe under me. I sat back up and gripped the waistband of his sweats with my fists. Yanking hard I removed them swiftly from his body and his cock stood proud, a tiny drop of moisture clinging to the tip.

"And what does my fiancé want?" I whispered seductively.

"I want you to fuck me, hard." A tremor rocked my body at the lust in his eyes and the low growl of his voice. I would spend the rest of my life giving this man anything and everything he asked for.

I quickly removed my clothes and bent down to kiss him. I reached up to the table and felt with my fingers for the glass from my ice water. Dipping my fingers in, I pulled out an ice cube and brought it to his lips. I traced a wet line down his neck and over his chest, swirling it around his nipple until it stood at a stiff peak and then I bent down to cover it with my mouth. I teased his nipple with my tongue and pulled gently on it with my teeth, making him hiss.

I continued to trail the ice down his stomach and let it drip into his navel, so I could lap the water from him. I popped the ice into my mouth and swirled it around, getting my tongue icy cold. I bent my head and sucked his stiff cock in deep, not stopping until it hit the back of my throat. He jolted at the cold, but the heat from his shaft warmed my mouth quickly and I sucked my cheeks in, adding pressure around his cock.

I moved down, laving his balls until they glistened with my saliva and took turns sucking them in and swirling them with my tongue. I placed my hands at the back of his knees and looked up the length of his body. His half lidded eyes had turned a dark hunter green and he watched my every move, licking his lips in anticipation. I lifted his legs so that they rested over my shoulders and buried my face between his firm cheeks, licking a line up the length of his crease. He cried out as I pointed my tongue and speared his hole, wiggling my tongue until I gained entry. I continued fucking him with my tongue until he was jabbering mindlessly.

I swiped the bottle of olive oil from the counter and quickly wet my fingers, swiftly sliding two into him. He gasped at the intrusion, but was soon riding my fingers as he relaxed under me. I leaned down and swiped my tongue around his stretched hole, my fingers still buried deep inside him and he whimpered in pleasure. I added a third finger and watched closely as he sucked me in, then I twisted my hand stretching him farther.

"Please, Gio, I need you inside me."

I hurriedly knelt over him and slicked my swollen cock with the olive oil, not caring when it spilled on the floor beside me. We had decided a month before to get tested and had both come back negative. I wanted to be as close to Caleb as possible and I was so glad to not have anything between us any more, even a thin layer of latex. I wanted to crawl inside of him and live there forever, our bodies never parting.

I covered his body with my own and lined my weeping cock up with his hole. "Are you ready?" I whispered.

"Fuck me, Giovanni." I felt his breath ghost across my lips and kissed him as I slowly slid my rigid cock into his tight, wet heat. He relaxed and we both gasped as the rounded head of my shaft popped through his ring of muscle. Caleb lifted his hips and swiveled his ass onto my cock.

I rose above him and grabbed his ankles with my hands. I raised his legs above him, spreading them wide so that I could easily watch as I slid into him, hard. I repeated this several times until I felt my head swimming from the pleasure. His body slid on the slick surface of the floor, so I laid over him and slid my hands under him until they cupped his shoulders. Holding him tightly, I thrusted against him, adjusting my angle to hit his gland.

"Oh God, Gio. I'm close, I'm so close!" Caleb reached between us and began yanking on his dick with a jerky, uneven pace.

"I'm right there with you, baby. You tell me when you're ready and we'll fly together." I clenched my jaw as I fought my impending orgasm. I wanted us to share this moment.

I shifted my hips, pegging his prostate over and over and bent my head to suck on the tendon in his neck. Caleb raked his nails down my back and I prayed he'd leave his mark on me. His body went rigid under me and he screamed, his hand flying fast over his cock as ribbons of white cum painted his chest. His walls squeezed me in their tight grasp and I was suddenly flying with him, shouting his name as I came hard; my cum spilling inside of him and leaking out around my cock as I continued thrusting into him.

When our spasms had subsided, we lay on the floor, our arms and legs tangled together, trying to catch our breath. "That was amazing, baby."

"It was okay, but it was missing something." I bit the inside of my cheek as I struggled to look serious as his eyes shot up to mine.

"What was missing?"

"Chocolate sauce."

Caleb's eyes widened as a smile spread across his face. "I'm marrying such a smart man." I laughed as he climbed up to straddle my body.

An hour later, we sat on the kitchen floor, our backs against the wall. We were both gasping for air after another amazing round of sex. My tired eyes took in the mess around us. Chocolate sauce dripped from the counter, making a puddle on the floor, cherries lay spilled across the room, and there was whipped cream dripping from the ceiling. I chuckled.

"What's so funny?" Caleb asked.

"I just realized that this is what the kitchen at Romero's looked like when Carter decided to cook there." Caleb barked out a laugh and laid his head on my shoulder. I rubbed my hand absentmindedly up and down his leg. "We're getting married," I said in wonder.

"I'm going to live my life making you as happy as you've made me," Caleb whispered.

"You already have." I rubbed my lips over his. "We should probably clean up."

Caleb looked around the room, tilting his head in concentration. "Hmm, I don't even remember using carrots."

"That's because you weren't the one using them."

CHAPTER
Twenty-One

Caleb

"I THINK WE LIKED THE CANDLE CENTERPIECES BETTER THAN the plain flowers, didn't you?" My mom, Giovanni, and I had met with Kip, the wedding coordinator, the day before and needed to let him know our final decisions for some of the wedding reception details. Both the wedding and reception would take place at our family's cabin in Tennessee, with only our closest friends and family in attendance.

"Okay I'll let Kip know. Did you get the DJ all lined up?" Mom asked.

"Yep, all taken care of, he'll be at the cabin around noon on Saturday to start setting up all of his equipment." I finished loading the dishwasher with the last of our dinner dishes and wetting a sponge, wiped down the stove top, scrubbing at some of the stickier spills. "Giovanni and I plan on heading out on Friday afternoon, as soon as we can get away from work. What time is everyone else getting there?"

"Your dad and I are going to the cabin on Wednesday. I want to have plenty of time to get all of the rooms fresh and clean and make sure everything is set up. The flowers are all being delivered Friday morning and the caterers will be there around Thursday afternoon to see what their work space will be like."

I finished cleaning and washed my hands. "I can't thank you enough for all of your help, Mom. There's no way I could have done all of this without you. I wouldn't have even known where to start."

I heard her tinkling laugh. "Oh sweetie, you would have figured it out just fine, but it has been my pleasure. Your father and I are just so happy for you. We couldn't have chosen a finer man for you to marry if we had hand picked him ourselves."

"Yeah, he's pretty wonderful." I sighed dreamily as I pictured Giovanni in my mind.

Mom laughed. "You sound like a man in love." I agreed and told her I'd talk to her later.

As I hung up, I glanced at the clock on the stove. We had a couple of hours before we needed to leave for our combined bachelor party and I smiled to myself as I thought of how I'd like to spend that time. I wandered through the condo, wondering where he had disappeared to when dinner was over.

I peeked into the living room, but didn't find him there. I smiled as I saw the pictures of my family intermingled with Giovanni's pictures on the mantle. Just another way we were joining our lives together. I had officially ended my lease and moved in with him last week. We still had a few boxes to unpack, but so far we had managed to meld our two lives into one fairly easily. My brightly colored throw pillows mixed well with his masculine furniture and I felt a small thrill every time I opened our closet door and saw my clothes hanging there with his. I knew those were small things, probably insignificant to most people, but to me they were little promises of how we chose to be part of each other's lives in every way.

I decided to check his office next. He had spent several hours in there earlier during the day and I had heard him on the phone with someone, but I wasn't sure who with because he had kept the door shut. I had found that a little odd because he never shut the door to his office at home, but I shrugged it off because I knew he had a lot of details to take care of at Romero's before we left town for the wedding.

When I didn't find him in the office either, I moved on towards the bedroom. "Gio?" I called as I rounded the corner and entered our room. I stopped dead in my tracks, my mouth watering at the sight of a very naked Giovanni, stretched out on our bed.

He was laying on his back with one arm tucked under his head and the other hand wrapped around his engorged cock, tugging on it lazily. He smiled at me seductively. "I was wondering how long it would take for you to join me." He glanced over at the clock on the bedside table. "We have some time to kill before we need to get ready, is there anything you can think of for us to do with that time?" I stared at him stupidly. All of my blood had moved south, filling my cock, and I was no longer able to string together the words needed to answer him.

His smile got wider watching the effect he was having on me as I continued to stare at him, unmoving. "Okay, I guess I'll just do this on my own then," he teased and I watched, mesmerized as he took the hand from behind his head and used it to reach between his legs, cupping his heavy sac and pulling it gently. He groaned and started thrusting his hips as he began fucking his palm and I finally woke up out of my lust filled daze. "Stop! Don't you dare move your hand one more time until I get over there." A growl rumbled through my chest as I began ripping my clothes off. "You're an evil man, Giovanni Romero." He chuckled and I gave him a mock glare.

"I got what I wanted though, didn't I?"

"Oh, yeah? And what's that?" I pulled my pants and boxer briefs down in one fluid motion, my hands shook in my rush to get to him.

"You, naked."

I quickly moved to the bed and climbed my way up his body, nipping and licking as I went. He groaned as I moved passed his stiff erection without touching it and I looked up at him, winking. "Paybacks are a bitch, aren't they?"

He narrowed his eyes at me but then let them roll back in his head as I pulled a nipple into my mouth and began sucking it hard. I puckered my lips and blew a cooling breath over the abused peak to soothe it, then licked my way up his throat, loving the slightly salty taste of his skin.

My lips grazed his and he opened up, granting me entry. I licked into his mouth, caressing his tongue with mine and licking along the roof of his mouth. His hands smoothed over my back and along my ribs as we continued to explore each other's mouths.

When the need for air became too much, I pulled back, both of us were panting. "How can I love you more with every passing day?" Wonder was evident in his voice.

"I feel the same way, baby. I can't wait to be married to you."

He pulled me in for another kiss and soon we were frantically rolling our hips, pressing our cocks together, and groaning at the delicious friction we created.

"Move up here, sweetheart, I want to taste your cock."

I sat up and looked in his eyes. "I've got a better idea." I turned around on the bed and swung my leg over his body to straddle him, this time facing opposite directions. I looked at him over my shoulder with a smile. "Now, I can suck you too."

I heard him chuckle. "I'm marrying a brilliant man."

I heard his gasp as I licked the large crown of his dick. The taste of pre-cum bursting on my tongue. I grasped the base of his cock in my fist and circled my tongue around his foreskin, tugging it gently between my teeth, in the way I knew would make him crazy with need. I was rewarded with a loud groan and he bucked his hips. I took him into my mouth and grunted as I felt a wet heat engulf the head of my cock.

Giovanni wrapped his arms tightly around my back, immobilizing me. My head swirled at the intense dual sensation of his mouth on my cock at the same time his thick shaft slid down my throat. He hollowed his cheeks, which caused the pressure on my cock to build and I let him slip from my mouth for a few seconds as I leaned my head against his thigh, riding a wave of pleasure.

I sucked him in again and felt the thick veins of his shaft as it slid over my tongue, the broad head hitting the back of my throat. I slid my mouth to his tip again and licked at the pre-cum threatening to drip. I drank it up, loving the taste of him and craving more.

The only sounds in the room were the wet slurping sounds of us pleasuring each other and it was that sexy sound that had my orgasm drawing my balls up close to my body and spilling my seed down his waiting throat. I could feel a tightening around my cock as he swallowed over and over, drinking me in.

I continued sucking him as I rode out my orgasm and my lips stretched as his cock grew impossibly bigger, right before streams of cum began pulsing over my tongue and down my throat. I took everything he gave me, wanting every last drop of him. I licked the last of his cum from his cock, making sure to clean him completely, then I got up and turned to face him.

I could see the love in his eyes and knew mine reflected the same. We shared a long slow kiss, moaning at the combined flavors of our cum. I felt his smile against my lips. "How much trouble do you think we'd be in if we just stayed here tonight and did that all over again?"

I laughed. "As tempting as that is, I know my brothers and if we don't show up for our party, they'll just show up here and there's no way I want to be in that position when they come banging on our door."

Giovanni sighed. "Yeah, you're right. Micah would drag us out of here too."

I glanced over my shoulder, checking the time on the clock. "We better get a shower and get ready."

Giving him one last kiss on his chest, I started to scoot to the side of the bed, but he stopped me when he wrapped his fingers around my wrist. "I want to talk to you about something first." He slid up the bed, leaning his back on the headboard. I sat back down next to him as he reached into the table drawer beside him and pulled out a manila folder. "I've been on the phone most of the day with my lawyer, having some papers drawn up."

I stilled as I noticed the serious look on his face. "What kind of papers?"

He looked at the folder in his hands and then back up at me. I waited patiently as he took a deep breath, giving him time to organize his thoughts. "You know how hard it was for me to open myself up to the possibility of being in a relationship again, but then I found someone worth having a relationship with and now I can't live without him." I reached for his hand and gave him a gentle squeeze as he continued. "I want to share every single part of my life with you, for the rest of my life. That's why I had my lawyer draw up the papers to have you added as a full partner at Romero's."

I blinked several times as tears filled my eyes. "Are you sure, Gio? Romero's means everything to you."

"You mean more than anything else in the world to me and I want you to be my partner, both in business and in life." He smiled as he brushed the tears from my cheeks.

My heart felt like it would burst from my chest as it expanded with my love for this man. "Thank you," I whispered as I wound my arms around his neck and pulled him in for a kiss. "You are the most generous man and it would be an honor to be your partner, in all ways."

He kissed me back and then opened the file. "All you have to do is sign and Romero's will be yours too." I signed the papers and then he let out a loud whoop of joy and I laughed at his obvious delight.

"Come on, let's go take a shower. I want to soap up until I'm slick and then slide deep inside of you." He tugged on my hand and I jumped off the bed, following happily. It was our bachelor party, we were allowed to be late if we wanted to, and right that moment, there was nothing I wanted more.

We stepped out of our condo an hour later and Giovanni raised a hand to flag down a taxi. We had agreed that it would be best to take a taxi so that we could each enjoy the evening and drink if we wanted to, without having to worry about driving home. Also, as Giovanni had pointed out, we could make out the whole way there and back if someone else drove us.

We climbed into the taxi and Gio rattled off the address that Micah had texted him. "So, Carter and Landon didn't give you any hints where the party is?"

"Nope, they kept as quiet as Micah apparently. Do you think we should be scared?"

"With this group of guys planning our bachelor party, hell yes!" We laughed as we held hands and looked out at the lights of the city. I laid my head on his shoulder and let out a happy sigh.

"Happy, sweetheart?"

"Yes! I was just thinking that I can't imagine life getting any better. I'm getting ready to marry my best friend, who happens to be the sexiest man in the world. I have my dream job, my brother is recovering and getting his life back, and we're going out for a fun night with friends and family." I looked up into his eyes and smiled wide.

He smiled back and bent his head to place gentle kisses on each of my dimples. "But it will get better, sweetheart. We have a whole lifetime of memories to make. Our wedding, first Christmas together, children..."

My heart squeezed as I looked into his eyes. "Our children," I said dreamily, picturing Giovanni holding a little boy or girl.

"Eventually yes, but I want some time with just the two of us first before we jump into parenthood. That way I can do things like this, whenever I feel like it."

He put one arm around my shoulder as his other hand cupped my groin. I watched his hand as he applied gentle pressure to my cock, making it spring to attention. I moved my gaze to his and found him looking down at me with heat in his eyes.

"Waiting would be good," I whispered as he leaned down and sucked my bottom lip into his mouth.

We made out for the rest of the ride until the driver announced that we had reached our destination. I quickly fixed my disheveled clothes as Giovanni paid our fare. We climbed out and stood in shock in front of a gay strip club.

"This should be interesting," I said with a chuckle.

"Your poor dad is coming here tonight isn't he?" he said with a wince.

"Yeah, but he deserves it for all the TMI we've had to endure about him and Mom. Paybacks."

"You are all about the paybacks, aren't you?"

I pulled him in close to me and waggled my eyebrows at him. "Don't you forget it."

He threw his head back with a loud laugh. "That's okay, I happen to like your paybacks."

We walked into the strip club holding hands and scanned the room for our group. It was very dark, except for the spotlight on the stage where a man was twisting his oil-slicked body around a pole. *How in the world did he hang on with all that oil all over him?*

I chuckled at my own musing just as someone yelled from across the room. "It's about damn time you boys showed up!" I turned my head to find Carter, winding his way through the crowded room, making his way over to us. "Hey, guys, welcome to your bachelor party!" He spread his arms wide like a model on a game show, presenting a prize.

"Thanks, man." Giovanni smiled as Carter engulfed him in a tight hug. It was clear from his somewhat glazed eyes and behavior that he had already started the party without us. I laughed as he reached down and squeezed Giovanni's ass. Gio sprang back and his eyes grew to the size of saucers. "You're right, he does have a fantastic ass."

I laughed harder when I saw Giovanni blush, but then brushed Carter's hand off, which had still been lingering on his ass. "Yes, but that fantastic ass is all mine, so keep your hands off!" Giovanni moved over to stand behind me, like he needed protection from my brother. I blew him a kiss over my shoulder. "Where is everyone else?"

"Come on, I'll lead you over there." Carter was still laughing as he wrapped an arm around my waist and I grabbed Giovanni's hand as Carter led us through the crowd to the back corner of the room, which had been sectioned off for the party.

Several of the staff members from Romero's were there and we shook hands with them as we walked into our section. My brothers-in-law, Jason and Mark, were seated at a table, watching the stripper on the stage and appeared to be playing some sort of drinking game, based on how many times the stripper grabbed his own junk and wiggled it at them. Whoever got the wiggle had to drink. I loved how the two very straight men never batted an eye at the fact that they had three very gay brothers-in-law. Of course, knowing how protective my sisters were, if Mark or Jason had any issues with us being gay, they wouldn't have lasted long enough to marry into our family. They greeted us with warm handshakes and friendly slaps on the back.

"So who's winning?" Giovanni asked them.

They looked at each other in question. "I have no idea, but I don't care. I plan on getting just drunk enough and then going home and making your sister scream my name."

Carter and I groaned at the same time. "Dude, just stop!" Carter backed away, holding his hands up in front of him while Mark and Jason laughed hysterically.

I spotted Dad in the corner, deep in conversation with three men, who based on their attire, I assumed worked as strippers at the club. We wandered over to say hello and Dad jumped up from his seat, gave us each hugs, then gestured towards the three men he had been talking to. "Boys, this is Tony, Keith, and Josh. They work here and I was just talking to them about how important it is to practice safe sex."

I'm sure my eyebrows were in my hairline and Giovanni covered a laugh with a fake cough into his hand. "And how is that going, Dad?" I asked as my eyes slid over the three men.

"Your dad's awesome, man," the guy who I think was Keith, said. "He's given us a lot to think about." The other two men nodded their heads with sincerity.

The one named Josh spoke up next. "Yeah, I've always just had random hook ups with guys I met in the clubs, but the way your dad described the relationship you two have, I want that in my life."

While I was a bit uncomfortable with Dad discussing my relationship with strangers, it warmed my heart to know that he saw my relationship with Giovanni as something to strive for. I felt proud that our devotion to each other was apparent to the people around us.

"No random hook up can ever compare to being with someone you love and trust." I was surprised when I heard Giovanni join the conversation, but when I looked over my shoulder into his eyes, I found him staring down at me. His eyes held such intensity and I suddenly found it hard to breathe around the lump in my throat. I reached back and squeezed his hand, and he leaned down brushing his lips over mine.

I heard one of the men sigh. "You're right, Rick," he said clapping his hand on my dad's shoulder. "I've been selling myself short. I deserve to have someone love me."

My dad spoke up. "I believe everyone has someone out there who is meant just for them. Be patient and you'll find him. Just promise me you'll use condoms until then." I shivered as I heard his stern Dad voice that he had used at various times on all of his children as we were growing up. "Once you find *the one,* you can feel free to ride him bare cock or whatever you guys call it."

"Oh, God!" I groaned in embarrassment and grabbed a laughing Giovanni by the hand, pulling him over to an empty table and plunking my forehead down on it. "That was so embarrassing," I groaned against the table.

He rubbed his hand over the back of my neck and let his fingers fan soothingly through my hair. "It's actually quite wonderful to have such a supportive and caring father."

I raised my head and nodded. "It is, and I know I'm very lucky to have a dad like him. I just wish he didn't have to be quite so vocal about it." Giovanni chuckled again and kissed the top of my head.

"What do you want to drink, sweetheart? Oh, wait, here we go."

I swiveled my head around to see what he was looking at behind me and saw Micah weaving his way through the tables with a tray full of shot glasses. He set the tray down carefully on our table and offered a wide smile. Micah was already a sexy man, with his tightly defined muscles and tattoos peeking out from the sleeve of his black t-shirt, but when he smiled, his face turned into something remarkable. If I wasn't already head over heels in love with Gio, I might have pursued Micah. I smiled as I watched Giovanni stand and hug the man he considered his brother and thought to myself, for the hundredth time, how lucky I was that they had never developed feelings for each other beyond friendship. From everything Giovanni had told me about Micah, he was an incredible friend and an amazing man in general. I couldn't wait to get to know this man that was so dear to the man I loved.

Micah stepped out of his hug with Giovanni and turned to shake my hand. "Congratulations, Caleb, you've found a wonderful man to share your life with." I looked in his eyes and saw nothing but honesty and happiness for his friend.

"Thank you and I have to agree." I smiled up at Gio who insisted that he was the lucky one.

We sat down and Giovanni and Micah shared some funny stories from their childhood with me as we drank down our shots. Carter soon joined us and announced that we needed more shots if we were going to catch up with everyone else at the party. "Of course that wouldn't have been a problem, if you weren't a half hour late to your own party. What exactly were you two boys up to that made you so late?" he asked as he playfully waggled his eye brows at us.

"Come on, trouble, let's go get some more shots." Giovanni said to Carter, trying to change the subject.

"Oh, are you going to tell me the juicy details on the way?" Carter rubbed his hands together eagerly. I heard Gio laugh loudly as they walked away.

I was still laughing when I turned to see Micah staring at me with a serious expression that sent a cold chill down my spine. I could suddenly see him as he must have been as a Navy SEAL: focused and intense. He leaned forward, placing his forearms on his knees and he looked directly in my eyes. I suddenly felt like prey, caught in the cross hairs of a hunter.

"I like you, Caleb, I really do and from everything G has told me, you're a great guy, but my loyalty lies with him. That man has been my best friend and my brother for as long as I can remember. He and his family saved me, first from my father and then from myself. He is the kindest, sweetest, most loving man I've ever known and there isn't one damn thing he could ask for that I wouldn't do. I know he got his heart torn to shreds by that bitch, Juliana. I was far away serving as a SEAL at the time so I couldn't be here, like I would have liked to be, but I called as often as possible and I honestly wasn't sure he'd ever recover. He did though, and that is in large part because of you. So, I thank you for that, but I also have to warn you that my service to the Navy is over now. I'm here to stay and if you hurt him in any way, if you run off and break his heart, I will be here to hunt you down and you will pray that I never find you."

I stared at him for several long moments. He was a scarily intense guy when he wanted to be and I didn't doubt that he meant every word he had just said to me. I probably should have been offended by his threat, but instead I found myself grateful to him. He looked stunned as I threw my arms around him and hugged him tightly. "Thank you for being an amazing friend to Gio. He deserves only the best and I can tell you are." I sat back, looking at his shocked expression. "I give you my word that I will never, ever, hurt him, but if I ever do, I want you to hold up your end of the deal. Because I would want to be punished for ever causing him pain."

Micah studied my eyes for a long time, looking for any falseness in my words. Seeing none, he reached his hand towards me. He shook my hand, smiled, and nodded his head as his shoulders relax. "All right then, welcome to the family."

I smiled at him and breathed a sigh of relief that I had passed his inspection. Finally, Giovanni and Carter returned with another tray of drinks just as Landon walked up to our table.

"Hey, guys, sorry I'm late. I got stuck at work." He walked around giving us each hugs until he stopped at Micah. I saw Landon's eyes widen and his Adam's apple bobbed as he swallowed hard. I flicked my gaze to Micah and saw him smirk as he ran his eyes slowly up and down my older brother.

I cleared my throat and they both looked at me like they were surprised to see someone else at the table. "Micah, this is my brother Landon. Landon, this is Gio's best friend, Micah." They shook hands and I didn't miss the fact that they held on a little longer than necessary. I looked over at Gio, who was watching them with an arched eyebrow. He turned to look at me with a knowing smile and a shrug.

Landon pulled a chair over to our table and joined us in drinking a shot just as I heard Carter's voice reverberating around the room. I swiveled in my chair to find my brother standing on the stage, holding a microphone. My face turned a bright red as he introduced Giovanni and myself and made us stand up. There were several cat-calls and one man yelled that he wanted to see us use the pole together. Gio squeezed my hand as Carter continued.

"We're here to celebrate the upcoming marriage of these two lovebirds. For the rest of their lives they will only sleep with each other. Giovanni, you're lucky my brother has the same fantastic ass I have, since it's the only one you'll be looking at from now on." Everyone laughed as Carter turned and shook his ass at the crowd and he received several loud whistles and crude comments himself. "Anyway, I felt like it was my responsibility, as one of your best men, to make sure that you don't start your marriage with any regrets. So I want you two to sit back, relax, and enjoy the lap dances I bought for you." Gio and I looked at each other in surprise then turned to see Carter wink at us with a devious smile.

"I'm going to kill your brother," Giovanni hissed as he plastered a fake smile on his face.

"Not if I get to him first."

The crowd went crazy, clapping and whistling as two men came over to us. Their muscles were slicked with oil and they had a gener-ous coating of glitter over their chests and down their washboard abs. They wore extremely tiny shorts that barely covered the giant bulges protruding in front of them. The one in the red shorts began twerk-ing his ass in front of Giovanni's face, while the one in blue sauntered over to me and placed his arms on each side of my chair, so I was caged in.

My eyes widened and I leaned back as far as I could in my chair as he stood in front of me, wiggling his junk in my face to the beat of the pulsating stripper music. I turned my head away, but the guy was suddenly gone and Giovanni stood in front of me. "Sorry, we may not be married yet, but I'm still the only one allowed to give him a lap dance."

My jaw hit the floor as Giovanni straddled my lap and began swiveling his hips in a slow seductive imitation of sex. The smell of his clean sweat, mingled with his spicy cologne, filled my senses making my head spin. I reached for him instinctively, gripping his hips, and urging him closer. He held onto the back of my chair and leaned down to rub his lips with mine, but when I tried to capture his lips, he pulled his head back teasingly. I growled out my frustration as he let his cock graze mine, only to stand and turn so that he was straddling me backwards.

I ran my hands up and down his flat stomach as he simulated a reverse cowboy. The crowd cheered wildly as the music ended and Gio stood and looked at me with a naughty smirk. He leaned down and spoke into my ear so only I could hear.

"No one else is allowed to touch what is mine, ever." I shivered at the possessiveness of his words. I loved that I belonged to him and he belonged to me.

"Nice dance," Mark teased as he, Jason, and Dad brought their chairs over to sit with us. I discreetly pulled a napkin onto my lap, but Giovanni saw and winked at me with a smug smile on his face. His smile spread and his blue eyes twinkled in amusement as I mouthed the word *paybacks*.

Next we opened presents, which were mostly gag gifts, and Carter laughed heartily when we opened his gift to us; he had given us matching shirts with bright yellow smiley faces on the front. Knowing they represented the smiley face condom he gave me a long time ago, I gave him a mock glare, but then we each pulled the shirts on over our heads and thanked everyone for their gifts.

A few hours later, Dad walked up to where we were sitting. "Have you boys seen Landon? I wanted to tell him goodnight, but I can't find him anywhere."

I glanced around the room. "No, I haven't seen him since we

opened gifts. He must have gone home early."

"I guess Micah left too. I don't see him anywhere," Giovanni said.

"Well, if you hear from your brother, tell him to call me so I know he got home safely."

Dad told us goodnight and then helped Mark and Jason out to the car to take them each home. Giovanni and I sat holding hands and talking to Carter as we watched a particularly flexible man hang upside down on the pole. He used his strong abdominal muscles to pull himself up until his head was bent over his groin. His legs wrapped around the pole to hold himself steady as he began to bob his head up and down as if he were sucking his own cock. I swallowed as I felt myself becoming aroused and I quickly glanced over at Giovanni, to find him staring at me with lust darkening his blue eyes.

"I knew a guy that could do that." Carter gestured to the stage. "Fucking hot to watch, especially when he came. Swallowed the whole load."

"How many of these strippers are you going home with tonight?" I asked him, only half teasing.

"None." His voice held a note of finality and I saw something flicker in his eyes, but it was gone before I could figure out its meaning. "I'm just focusing on my physical therapy and my music."

"Caleb told me you're almost back to your full potential. I'm impressed with how hard you've fought to come back from your injuries."

Carter smiled at Giovanni's praise. "Thanks, G, I appreciate that."

I covered my mouth as a yawn suddenly swept through me and I glanced at my watch, surprised at how late it was.

"I'm taking you home to bed," Giovanni said in a voice that allowed no argument. "Thank you for the party, we had fun." He thrust his hand out to Carter, who stood and hugged him instead.

"You're welcome. Thanks for being good sports with all of my teasing. It's all meant in fun."

"Oh, we know, but don't think for a second we won't get even."

Even though his tone was light, there was no mistaking the threat in Giovanni's words.

"Looking forward to it." Carter sounded excited as he walked away.

"I need to use the bathroom really quick before we go."

"I'll go with you, you're just drunk enough and I don't want you to stumble upon a glory hole or something." I laughed at Gio's teasing, but was grateful for his strong arm around my waist as I stood and the room spun. "Easy, sweetheart, I've got you." I heard him chuckle and when the room finally held still, I was able to start walking towards the bathrooms.

"How come you're so steady when you drank just as much as I did?" I grumbled at him.

"I'm bigger than you, it takes more to affect me."

I reached over and grabbed his cock through his jeans, thrilling at the gasp that escaped his mouth as I touched him. "Yeah, baby, you are bigger."

CHAPTER
Twenty-Two

Caleb

I FINISHED ADDING THE INGREDIENTS TO A SIMMERING POT OF marinara sauce, which would be used later that evening and looked over at Marco and Curtis. "Anything else I can help with?"

"No, Boss, go get the other boss man and get out of here," Marco chuckled as he pointed me towards Giovanni's office.

"I will, I just feel bad leaving you to take care of everything."

"I'm not alone any more. That's why you hired Curtis here and he's a big help."

"You're right." We had made the decision to hire another chef who could be used in a rotation to help out when either Marco or myself needed a night off. Curtis had come highly recommended by his instructor at the culinary school he had recently graduated from and had impressed me already with his capabilities in the kitchen. I knew the restaurant was in good hands while we were away, but after suffering the devastating loss the fire had caused, I couldn't help the protectiveness I felt for the place. For the time being, Romero's was our only child and the legacy we would eventually leave our real children.

"Caleb!" Marco barked in a gruff voice when he caught me lingering in the doorway.

"Okay, okay." I held my hands up in surrender and started walking towards Gio's office. When I walked in, he and Lauren were having basically the same conversation.

"You hired me to be your second in command, so let me command your ass right out of here." Lauren stood in front of Giovanni's desk, with her hands placed firmly on her hips in a no nonsense manner. She turned as she heard me enter. "Oh good, maybe you can talk some sense into him. He's worried about leaving, but he's being ridiculous. I know how to run this place with my eyes closed."

I stepped around her and walked over to Giovanni. The firm set to his mouth relaxed and his eyes gentled when he saw me. "She's right, you know. Marco just had the same talk with me. We've got very capable people that can run this place in our absence and we need to let them."

"Thank you," Lauren said haughtily as she stuck her tongue out at Giovanni, before quickly darting out of the room when he growled at her.

"But, sweetheart…" He started before I cut him off.

I straddled his lap and kissed him thoroughly until I was sure he was no longer thinking about work but was instead focused solely on me. He chuckled against my lips and I felt the rumble between our chests.

"How do you distract me so easily?" He smiled at me and his blue eyes shone with love.

"It's a gift," I answered cheekily. "Now, what do you say we get out of here and go get married?"

He placed his hands on either side of my face and gazed at me adoringly. "There's nothing I want more."

After a quick drive home to grab the bags that we had packed the night before, we slammed the trunk and climbed into the car, smiling excitedly at each other. We passed the long drive to the cabin by playing car games. For each state license plate we saw, we earned a sexual favor of our choice; which could be redeemed at the recipients choosing. By the time we pulled into the long driveway that led to my family's cabin it was dark, we were starving, and I was leading with twelve states to Giovanni's nine. I considered us both winners though if it meant spending more time in each other's arms, naked.

We said hello to my parents and Mom insisted on making us something to eat while we put our bags away and cleaned up.

Giovanni cornered me in the bathroom, caging me between his body and the sink. "Do we really have to stay in separate rooms tonight?" His pout was adorable and I pulled his bottom lip into my mouth, sucking on it. When I let go he continued pleading his case. "I'm a grown man, I can be in a room with you and keep my hands to myself."

I glanced down pointedly at his hands that were roaming over my ass and laughed. "Sure you can, baby," I said sarcastically. "Look, it's tradition and just think of how much better it will be the next time we have sex, if we had to go without tonight."

"Honey, if our sex gets any better they'll have to display it in a museum somewhere." I laughed delightedly at his words, but I had to agree. I couldn't imagine it getting any better between us. "Okay," he finally conceded. "If this makes you happy, I'll do it. Just be warned that whatever I do to you tomorrow night, I'll have to do twice to make up for lost time."

I shivered at the promise in his words. "Deal."

My parents were sitting at the kitchen table enjoying a cup of tea. Mom jumped up when she saw us walk in. "You boys sit down and rest while I get your food dished up. I had some soup left over from our dinner that I've heated up and I made you some cold cut sandwiches."

"Thanks, Mom, it sounds great. I'll get our drinks." Mom looked at Giovanni and tears filled her eyes as her lips lifted in a small smile. He grabbed two glasses out of the cabinet and turned in time to see her reaction. "What's wrong?" He set the glasses down on the counter and took her hands in his, glancing at me nervously.

"I'm fine, sweetie, it's just that that's the first time you've called me Mom." Giovanni blushed and looked at his feet. She put her head under his to catch his gaze and laid a gentle hand on his cheek. "It's about time." Mom moved over to the stove and began ladling the soup into bowls and Gio picked up the glasses and walked to the refrigerator, but not before I caught the happy smile spreading over his face.

We spent nearly an hour going over details that needed attention in the morning, before Dad took Mom's hand and pulled her from her chair. "Kathy, if you don't get some sleep soon, you'll be too tired to enjoy tomorrow. Let's go to bed, my love." We took turns kissing Mom's cheek and when they had left the room, we started cleaning up our dishes.

When there was nothing left to clean, I heard him sigh loudly. "I guess I better head to bed…alone." He sighed again dramatically and I couldn't contain my laughter any more.

"Oh, you poor baby." I slid my arms around his waist and nuzzled my face against his chest, inhaling his familiar scent. I leaned up to kiss him and whispered into his ear. "Goodnight, my love." Gio groaned, but I heard him whisper that he loved me as I walked away.

I quickly brushed my teeth and turned off the light before removing my clothes and climbing into bed. The bed seemed too big and the sheets too cold without Giovanni there to hold me. I plumped my pillow, trying to get comfortable, but it wasn't the same as leaning my head against my lover's firm chest or having his heartbeat lull me to sleep.

After tossing and turning for what seemed like hours, I picked up my phone that had been charging on the table next to the bed and opened it, smiling at the picture of us that was my wallpaper. I had taken it on a lazy Sunday morning. Giovanni had been sleeping on his stomach and I woke before him. I had crawled over his body and lay on top of him and began kissing his ear. I had snapped a selfie of us just as he opened his eyes and in the picture, he wore a beautiful expression of sleepy, happy, bed-warmed man. I smiled at the intimate scene and quickly typed out a text.

You still up?

Depends on what you mean by up, because if you're referring to the stiff rod in my underwear that my sexy fiancé sent me to bed with, then yes, I am most definitely up.

I snorted out a laugh as I read his response. **Why haven't you taken care of that problem already?**

Because I promised my fiancé that I would wait until tomorrow and because my hand could never feel as good as his sweet body wrapped tightly around my cock.

I moaned as my cock filled with blood. Texting might have been a bad idea.

(Shiver) He sounds like a very lucky guy. What's special about tomorrow?

I'm the lucky one, and tomorrow is only going to be the best day of my entire existence. Tomorrow, I will marry my very best friend and the love of my life. Tomorrow, I will become whole.

God, I love you so much, baby.

I love you too, sweetheart.

I laid my phone on the table with a happy sigh. I just had to get through tonight and then I would never sleep away from my man again.

I woke with a start the next morning to someone leaping on my bed. I peeked a groggy eye out from beneath the blanket I was burrowed under, to find Carter jumping up and down on my bed. He grinned like a fool as he sang "Going to the Chapel" at the top of his lungs. I couldn't help but smile at his enthusiasm and I felt warmth flood my veins as I realized this was truly my wedding day. It seemed like I had been waiting all of my life for Giovanni Romero and finally, by the end of the day, he would be my husband.

"Quit jumping on the bed, you're going to break something!" Carter laughed as I did my best impersonation of Mom's scolding voice.

Carter made one more jump and landed next to me with a thud, causing me to bounce in the air. Carter's face was red and he was breathing hard from the exertion as we both laughed at our childish fun.

I sat up in the bed, scooting up to lean beside him against the headboard. He took my hand and twined our fingers together. His fingers were callused from long hours spent playing his guitar and I smiled because I was so glad he was able to play again.

He looked over at me with a matching smile. "I wanted just a few minutes alone with you before all of the wedding craziness starts."

"What's up, Bubby?" His eyes grew soft at the use of our childhood name for each other and he swallowed hard, fighting back emotion. I felt my eyes getting misty in response.

"First of all, I wanted to tell you how happy I am for you."

I squeezed his hand in mine. "Thank you, I appreciate that, Carter."

"I also wanted to say that I know you are marrying an amazing guy and you're starting a new life together, that I'm sure will be filled with lots of love and exciting adventures. Just promise me that you'll never forget that I'm here for you, day or night, and that there is nothing I wouldn't do for you, ever. I love you more than you could ever know."

Tears rolled down my face at my brother's affectionate words. "I do know how much you love me, because I feel the same about you. I've been very blessed to have all of my siblings, but I will always treasure the bond you and I share. The same goes for me too, even though I'm getting married, if you ever need anything I'll be right there. The only difference now is that if you need something, Giovanni will show up with me because he loves you too."

Carter smiled at me. "Yeah, I guess it's true that I'm not losing a brother today, but gaining a new one."

"Absolutely."

"Oh, I almost forgot, I have something for you. I got you a special condom for tonight, it's cake flavored," Carter teased as he pretended to pull a condom out of his wallet. Something resembling a business card fell out of his wallet and landed on the comforter.

Carter dove for it, but I picked it up before he could reach for it. I glanced at the card and then over at my brother who was blushing more than I had ever seen before.

"What's this?"

"It's nothing," he mumbled as he grabbed for the card again, but I held it out away from his reach.

"It doesn't look like nothing." I looked at the small "Thinking of You" card that looked like it belonged in a flower arrangement. I flipped it over to see *Hope you're feeling better. Ryan.* He had included his phone number and a smiley face. "Is this Fireman Ryan?" I cocked my head as I looked at Carter, who was staring at his lap and twisting the comforter in his hand nervously. He had always been a prankster, the life of every party, so it was strange to see him acting shy and unsure of himself.

He tilted his head back against the headboard and stared at the ceiling. "Yes, it's from the fireman. It was in the flowers he brought to the hospital. It's no big deal, I haven't even seen him since that day."

"Carter, you get phone numbers from guys all the time. If it's no big deal, why are you carrying this card around in your wallet?"

He looked like he was struggling to figure out what to say, but he finally blurted out, "I fucked everything up."

"What do you mean?"

"I don't know. I mean I don't even know the guy. Seriously, I don't even know his full name, but for some reason I can't get him out of my mind. Unfortunately, when he showed up at the hospital, I had just found out I may never be able to play again and I was in a shitty mood and had a crashing headache and I kind of took it out on him. Now there's no way he will ever want to see me again. I fucked it all up." Carter looked miserable as he stared at his hands.

"I don't know him either, but it seems like he was thinking about you too or he wouldn't have brought you flowers and given you his phone number. I'm sure he doesn't do that for everyone he rescues."

"Yeah, but that was all before I was so nasty to him. I'm sure he doesn't ever want to talk to me again after the horrible way I treated him. I know I wouldn't if I had been treated like that."

"Was it really that bad?"

Carter looked at me with sorrowful eyes. "The worst."

I took his hand and gave it a comforting squeeze. "Well, here's what I know about it. At the fire, I could feel your pain and I knew you were in trouble. I found a group of about ten firemen and I begged them to go search for you, but they just kept saying that the area had been given the all clear signal and that you were probably just outside somewhere. Then Ryan stepped forward and said he would go look for you. He's the only one who was willing to listen to my intuition and thank God he did, or you probably wouldn't be here right now." My heart squeezed tightly at the painful thought. "Even if he's upset about how you acted at the hospital, he at least deserves a phone call from you thanking him for saving your life."

Carter nodded his head. "You're absolutely right. Now I just have to work up the nerve to call him." He smirked at me. "Enough about me, this is your big day and even though we're adults, Mom may ground me if I don't get out there and help."

"I'm going to get a shower." I climbed out of bed as Carter walked to the door. "Hey, Carter?"

"Yeah?"

"Promise me you'll call him."

Carter looked down at the doorknob in his hand. "I'll try," he said quietly before slipping out the door.

I stood in front of the full length mirror, trying to get my tie to lay right. Giovanni and I had decided to wear matching black suits with white button down shirts. The only difference would be our ties. His was a brilliant sky blue to match his eyes while mine was an emerald green color.

I turned at the sound of a knock on the door and my parents walked in. My mom squealed when she saw me all dressed up. "Look how handsome you are, baby!" She cupped my face in her hands and gave me a quick peck on the cheek.

"Thanks, Mom." I smiled at her and waited for her to look away before quickly wiping any lipstick off of my cheek and glancing in the mirror to make sure I had gotten it all.

She removed something from a box on the bed and carried it over to me. "We got one of these for each of you. Giovanni looks extremely handsome I have to say." She pinned a white rose boutonniere to my lapel and smoothed my tie into place.

"He would look handsome in a burlap sack." My parents glanced at each other and smirked back at me.

"Yep, our son has got it bad," Dad said with a chuckle.

"Guilty. So, any last words of advice from you two?" They looked at each other and it made me happy to see the adoration they still had for each other after all their years together.

"Always treat every moment like it was your last with him," Mom replied.

"Remember that he is your very best friend and always treat him with the respect that that title deserves." Dad smiled at Mom and then me. "Oh, and your partner is always right."

I chuckled as Mom swatted his arm playfully. "I can see I've taught you well." She turned to me with a smile. "Are you ready? It's almost time."

"Yes, I am." I had never felt more sure of anything.

"Okay, we're going to take our seats then. We love you."

I kissed them both and then they shut the door behind them. I looked at my watch, noting that I had two minutes until I should head out. My heart raced wildly, not with nerves, but in anticipation. As special as this day was, I just wanted to get to the part where I was declared Giovanni's husband.

I took a deep breath and opened the door. I walked down the hallway and smiled when I neared the end and saw my man waiting with his back to me. As if he sensed my presence, he turned and I allowed myself a moment to drink him in. He was always sexy, but the way he looked in his suit was absolute perfection.

His broad shoulders filled out the suit jacket perfectly and the wide expanse of his chest was showcased in the crisp, white shirt. His blue eyes looked even brighter next to the blue of his tie and his thick black hair had one loose wave that brushed over his forehead, refusing to be tamed.

"You are breathtaking." His deep voice shook a little as he looked at me with the same expression of awe that I felt when I looked at him.

I quickly stepped forward and leaned up on my toes to kiss him. "Last night was so hard. I will never spend another night away from you again," I swore to him.

"I'm going to hold you to that because last night nearly killed me," Giovanni admitted as he leaned his forehead on mine.

After a few moments he leaned back and helped me smooth my hair while I fixed his tie. "Any cold feet?" I asked him jokingly.

He looked at me very seriously. "Not even a little bit."

I smiled at him. "Let's do this then."

He held the door open for me and we stepped onto the deck and looked out over the expansive back yard, each of us taking the time to commit this moment to memory. The lush green grass and color-ful flower gardens had been beautifully landscaped and a long, white aisle runner was laid out down the middle of the rows of white chairs that held everyone who was important in our lives. At the end of the aisle, where we would recite our vows, was a small table with a single candle that had been lit to represent Giovanni's parents' presence at the wedding. It had been my mom's idea and I knew it had meant a lot to him that she would think to include them that way.

He reached for my hand and I nodded to him, then we began making our way down the steps. When the traditional wedding song started playing, we slowly walked hand in hand down the aisle. We reached the end and everyone took their seats. Standing with me was Carter and Landon. Giovanni had Micah and Marco as his best men. We faced each other as Pastor Reif started the ceremony.

I didn't hear anything as I was suddenly overwhelmed with the realization that this incredible man had really chosen *me* to spend the rest of his life with. It was very humbling to know that someone could love you so much, that they never wanted to be apart from you again.

Everything I envisioned for our future flitted through my mind like a movie playing. I could picture us laughing, crying, making love. I saw snowball fights and long drives in the country. I imagined children and Christmas trees, cooking together, and even death. It truly was the beginning of the rest of our life together and there was no one I would rather take this journey with, than the man standing before me.

I suddenly heard everyone chuckling and Gio squeezed my fingers. "Sweetheart, it's time to say our vows."

"Sorry," I murmured as I felt my face flush.

Pastor Reif nodded for me to go on. I cleared my throat, trying to dislodge the ball of emotions that threatened to choke me. I looked in Giovanni's eyes and felt a calmness settle over me.

"Giovanni, I have spent my whole life praying for someone I could trust. Someone I could love, who would love me back. Someone who I could laugh with and cry with and dream with. Someone who I could share a life with and grow old with. God heard my prayers because he sent me you and you are all of those things. You are everything. So, I stand here today before God and all of our friends and family and I vow to always love only you. I vow to take care of you, and cherish you, and to stand by your side forever. I will never falter, I will never stray, and I will *never* leave you. I am yours and you are mine, from this day forward."

Tears streamed down Giovanni's face as I said my vows and his hands shook in mine. He used one hand to wipe his eyes before speaking.

"Caleb, when I met you, I was just a shell of a man. I was going through the motions of life and no longer understood what it meant to love and trust anyone. I was drowning in my misery and rejected the idea of getting close to anyone and leaving myself vulnerable. Then you walked into my life and it was like I had woken up from a deep sleep, like I could suddenly breathe again. Even though I fought it, you made me remember what it was like to laugh, to live, and to love again. You showed me that it was okay to trust again and that I was worthy of love. You are the best man I have ever known and I am humbled that you would choose to spend the rest of your life with me. So, I stand before God and our friends and family and I vow to spend the rest of my life trying to be the kind of man you deserve. I vow to spend every day making you as happy as you have made me and doing my best to make your dreams come true. I will always love only you, with absolutely everything that I have and all that I am. I am yours and you are mine, from this day forward."

I smiled at him through my tears. Pastor Reif walked us through the exchange of rings and then I was wrapped in the strong arms of my husband as he kissed me until my head spun.

Everyone began clapping and we turned to face our friends and family who were either crying or smiling. Pastor Reif spoke up. "It is my pleasure to present to you, Mr. and Mr. Romero." I felt a thrill rush through me at hearing myself being called Mr. Romero for the first time. We had decided I would take his last name, since it was the name of our restaurant, and I couldn't be happier for the whole world to know that I belonged to him.

Darkness had fallen by the time the photographer had finished taking a multitude of pictures and we were released to enjoy our reception. The party was being held in the side yard of the property, along the stream. The white lights hung throughout the large white tent, along with the candles that served as table centerpieces, brought an intimate and romantic feeling to the occasion.

After we ate a quick dinner, Gio held my hand as we made our way around the room visiting with our guests. As we sat at a table talking with Lauren and her wife, Gracie, Micah walked up and apologized, saying that he had been called away on a work related emergency. He hugged each of us before sprinting off. On the other side of the tent I noticed Landon's eyes following Micah. His shoulders slump and he turned and walked away when he saw Micah disappear. I made a mental note to check on my brother later and find out what was going on.

We enjoyed all of the traditions of a wedding, including feeding each other cake and my toes curled as he licked the icing off of my fingers. He smiled deviously at me, knowing the affect his mouth was having on me. I promised myself that I would pay him back in the best possible way once I got him alone.

Marco and Landon took turns toasting us and then Carter stood in front of the microphone holding his guitar. "I want to offer my own congratulations to the new couple. I am lucky to get to call both of these men my brothers and I wish you both a lifetime of happiness. I love you guys. Now, if you'll all make room, I'd like to invite the happy grooms to enjoy their first dance as a married couple."

Giovanni took my hand and led me to the dance floor as Carter began strumming his guitar. He pulled me into his arms, placing one hand in mine and the other on the small of my back, urging my body closer until our chests pressed together. He smiled down at my up-turned face as Carter sang "Now and Forever" by Richard Marx. I closed my eyes as the song swirled around us and nothing else existed, but my husband and me.

EPILOGUE

Giovanni

I CHANGED MY CLOTHES AND CAREFULLY HUNG MY SUIT IN THE garment bag. I smiled as I felt Caleb's arms wind around my waist and his head rest on my back.

"Hey, sweetheart."

"Hi, baby," he whispered and I heard him breathe deeply. I loved when he breathed in my scent like I was becoming a part of him.

I turned in his arms and wrapped him in an embrace. "Are you ready to go, husband of mine?"

He sighed happily. "I love the sound of that…husband."

"I can't wait to get you alone." I bent my head and kissed him deeply, my tongue sliding in to taste his sweet mouth. A growl rolled up from my chest as I drank in his addicting flavor. I pushed my hips into his and captured his answering groan in my mouth. "I want to fuck my husband."

"Oh, God, let's go!" I barely had time to grab my bag because Caleb grabbed my hand and began pulling me out of the room and down the long hallway.

Mom and Dad Greene had rented a limo to take us to an unknown destination. All they would tell us was that it was a surprise. We walked out the front door and saw everyone lined up along the sidewalk. As we made our way through them, they tossed birdseed; letting it rain down over us. We turned and waved to our loved ones before ducking into the waiting limo.

We settled into the plush seat of the limo and I pulled Caleb close to me, fully intending to take advantage of the ride to wherever we were going. Before I had a chance to kiss my husband, the limo driver turned in his seat and held out a white envelope. I reached for it and he turned back around, sliding up the privacy glass. I raised my brows in question to Caleb, but he shrugged his shoulders. I slid the envelope open and pulled out the letter inside, reading it aloud.

Dear Caleb and Giovanni,

Congratulations on your wedding and on your future together. We could not be happier to have Giovanni as a member of our family. Because that's what you are, Giovanni, you are our son and brother and we love you.

We know that it was difficult for you, not having your parents here to celebrate your special day and we wanted you to feel like you were sharing this wonderful part of your new life with them.

Enclosed you will find two tickets to Manarola, Italy. Caleb told us that this place was very important to you because it was where your parents met and fell in love and that you've always wanted to visit it. Now you can.

Your bags are all packed and the restaurant is in good hands, so relax and enjoy your honeymoon. We love you both so much and wish you all the joy life has to offer.

Love always,
Your new family

I felt tears blur my vision as I finished reading the letter. Caleb pulled me towards him and I buried my face in the crook of his neck. He kissed the side of my face and nuzzled his cheek against mine soothingly.

"Are you okay?"

"I can't begin to describe how good it feels to be part of an actual family again. As much as I love the staff at Romero's, it's not the same as belonging to a group of people who will be with you through all of life's ups and downs." I looked up at Caleb's sweet smile. "You have brought more joy into my life than I ever imagined. Thank you for sharing your family with me, but most of all, thank you for thinking I was worth spending the rest of your life with."

The look in his eyes could only be described as complete adoration. "You are worth it, baby." I pulled him onto my lap with his legs straddling my own and held his firm, round ass in my hands. "You know, I bet we have quite a while until we get to the airport. Is there anything you'd like to do?" he asked coyly.

"I can think of a few things." I reached for the button of his jeans and swiftly popped it open. "I'm going to need more time than just this limo ride to do all the things I want to do to you though."

Caleb kissed me as he ground his hips against mine. "Well, you're in luck, because we just happen to have the rest of our lives."

The End

ACKNOWLEDGMENTS

It has been said that it takes a village to raise a child. Well, the same could be said for writing a book. Without the skills, support, creativity and patience of these people, this book would not have been possible.

First and foremost, a huge thank you to my family. My husband, who cheered me on, loved me through my crazies and talked me off the ledge on more than one occasion. When I first told you I was going to write a book, your response was to buy me a new computer so I'd have what I needed. You have been my best friend and the love of my life for more years than I can count and you have never failed to have my back. I love you baby. To my kids who talked me through my nerves, congratulated me on each milestone and when I said I was going to write, responded with "Yes! It's about time!" You two continually amaze me with the outstanding young man and woman you have become. It is my greatest pleasure to have the honor of being your mom.

A huge thank you to Aimee. Without your encouragement and at times handholding (LOL) I never would have even tried writing. I can never thank you enough for absolutely everything you have done to help me get to this point. You are one of my very best friends, my evil twin and my sister. I am constantly surprised by your strength and your bravery. I love you.

Thank you to Deena. You are the best friend anyone could ever ask for. You love and support me no matter what, both in work and in life. You keep me from taking life too seriously and help me find the brighter side of any situation. Over the years you've seen the good, the bad and the ugly parts of me and you're still here (what does that say about you? LOL). I love you.

Thank you to Kerry. I can't imagine a more supportive and loving sister than you. Through all of life's ups and downs, you have been there for me. You are my cheerleader, my confidante and my friend. I am so awed by who you are as a person. The world would be a much better place if everyone in it was as kind, compassionate and generous as you. I love you, sis.

Thank you to the following women for working so hard to make my book something I could really be proud of. Pam Ebeler of Undivided Editing, who offered amazing insights and suggestions as well as wading through my many written flaws. Jay Aheer of Simply Defined Art for the beautiful cover and teasers. You took my vision, brought it to life and I couldn't be happier with the results. Stacey Blake of Champagne Formats for your incredible work on the formatting and design of my book. Judy Zweifel of Judy's Proofreading for your painstaking work to clean up my punctuation deficiencies. Jodie Temple for offering great suggestions and for your encouragement. Thank you so much ladies for your kindness, guidance, patience and friendship as I learned my way through the twists and turns of producing a book. Your help was invaluable.

ABOUT THE AUTHOR

I am married to my high school sweetheart who let's face it, is a saint for putting up with me all of these years. Together we have been blessed with the chance to raise two amazing human beings and so far we haven't screwed it up; I'll let you know for sure later. I am a business owner and spend more time laughing than actually working most days. I love watching movies, cooking, going to the beach and spending time with my family and best friends. I am an obsessive reader who is a complete sucker for a good love story, but loves to feel a broad range of emotions throughout a book. I think real life is hard enough and so my books offer twists and turns, but always with a happy ending.

I love to hear from my readers. You can reach me at:

Twitter – www.twitter.com/annabellamicha1

Facebook – www.facebook.com/profile.php?id=100011438515157

Blog – annabellamichaels.blogspot.com